BENEATH
Kit Tinsley

To Becky
all the Best
Kit Tinsley

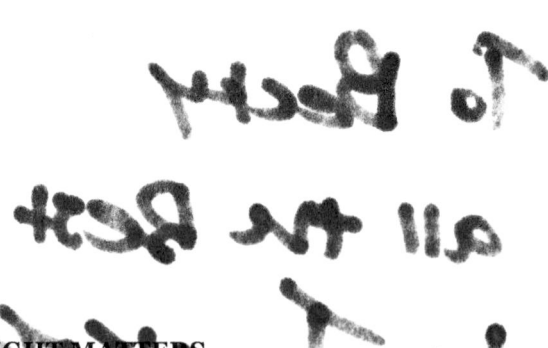

This book is dedicated to my
Mum and Dad
For everything you've ever done.

"The oldest and strongest emotion of mankind is fear, and the oldest and strongest kind of fear is fear of the unknown."
H.P. Lovecraft

CHAPTER ONE

This is the story of a house. Our dream house. A dream that turned into a nightmare, a nightmare from which I cannot wake up. Even now, months later, so far away from it, I am still trapped in that house. I know I will never escape. I don't expect you to believe the things I am about to tell you. I don't need you to believe. What I need is to tell my story, write this whole mess down before the madness takes me forever. I can feel it coming. The nightmares are visiting me when I'm awake now. Soon I will not be able to tell dreams from reality and memory from fantasy. To be honest, though, this is no bad thing, considering the reality I have endured. You can make your own decision about me, but please let me tell you how this happened.

My name is Dan Martin. I am thirty-five years old. I was a chemistry teacher. I was not the kind of man given to flights of fancy. I would always look for the rational explanation. Where do you turn, though, when no rational explanation can be found? This is the question that led me here. You see, everything I believed about the world and how it works was tested and then shaken to its core. I have seen things that no mortal should see and done things no man should ever have to do.

It all started with a dog, Mojo, our four–year-old Jack Russell. I am not blaming him for everything that happened to us. I am merely trying to piece things together for you as logically as I can, but perhaps I should go a little further back to the time Rachel and I first looked at the house. I guess that was really the day that changed everything for us all, even poor Mojo — the day I first set foot in 5 Blackfriars Crescent.

It was early in July, it had been a hot week and I had come straight from school. I hated the hot days, sweltering in a school lab in a shirt, tie and jacket. I was stuck in traffic trying to get through town, and the air conditioning was playing up. I was getting hotter and more frustrated by the minute. All I wanted to do at that moment was get home, have a refreshing cool shower, slip on some shorts and have a nice cold Grolsch on the patio as the sun began its descent. Of course, this couldn't happen yet as Rachel had gone and booked a viewing on a house in Glenley, a small village a few miles out of town. I was feeling quite annoyed about this; she'd called me at lunchtime to let me know. We had only talked about this once, just the night before, about maybe moving to a bigger house somewhere out of town. We had both agreed that we could afford it, and with our eldest daughter, Anna, about to turn fourteen, we wanted to get her away from the lifestyle that so many of the teens her age in town led. We didn't want her roaming the street drinking at all hours.

I thought, though, that it was something we would spend the next few months mulling over before really starting to look for somewhere. Rachel had obviously had different plans and had been looking on Rightmove the second I left for work. It was always her way. She would jump in and do things without discussing it with me properly. In the early days of our relationship I had found this annoying, like when we first got engaged and she booked the wedding venue without even consulting me. As time went on, though, it

8

was one of the things I loved most about her; it showed her determination and her strength of conviction. It was something I could never do. I always had to think about things, research them and weigh up the pros and cons before I could make a decision. Besides which, I soon realised that Rachel was right nine times out of ten.

She had told me it was a five bedroomed, three storey property that was well within our budget. I was always more in favour of getting older houses; they always seemed to have more character. The houses out at Glenley, however, were all new builds. They had built a vast estate after demolishing the old hospital that used to stand there. I wasn't sure what I was going to make of a new build; Rachel, though, had a soft spot for them. She said that they were always so clean and neutral that they made the perfect blank canvas for making them your own. I said that they were dull, sterile and characterless. Rachel had laughed and said that I always romanticised about old houses, never looking at the potential problems like bad plumbing, old wiring or maybe even ghosts. At that I had laughed. I am not laughing now.

As I sweated through the traffic on Darton's one-way system, my mobile began to ring. I took it out of my pocket and saw that it was Rachel. I answered it, despite still driving. I was crawling along so slowly I thought it would do no harm.

'Hello?' I answered, my tone a little harsher than I had intended.

'Wow!' she said. 'You sound cheery.'

'Sorry,' I said. 'Just stuck in traffic and sweating my bollocks off.'

She laughed; she had the most beautiful laugh. It was so loud and unashamed, and so full of life. It always brightened my spirits and I found myself smiling.

'It's not funny,' I said.

'Sorry, baby,' she said. 'Just wanted you to know I've taken the girls over to Mum's and I'm here at Glenley now. I'm parked outside the house. Oh Dan, it's beautiful.'

'We'll see,' I said.

'I think even you'll like it. It has a sort of old world vibe going on.'

'I should be there in about fifteen to twenty minutes. What time's the estate agent meeting us?'

'About fifteen minutes, but I'll wait for you to get here before going in,' she said.

'Okay, hun, I'll see you soon.'

Rachel said goodbye, and made some joke about me putting my foot down and then hung up. I slipped the phone back into my pocket and then went back to crawling slowly through the centre of town in a sweltering metal box.

I pulled up behind Rachel's Ford Focus exactly seventeen minutes later. She was stood on the doorstep of the house with a thin, balding man in a three-piece suit, who wore the same smug smile I had seen on every estate agent I had ever met.

Rachel was right, though, the house was beautiful. It was designed to look like one of those Georgian style town houses. It was huge. I was finding it hard to believe that the house was in our price range, let alone well within it as Rachel had said. As I got out of the car, I took off my tie and stuffed it into my trouser pocket. Rachel came running down the path and hugged me. She whispered in my ear, not able to contain her excitement.

'What do you think?' she said, then added, 'I love it.'

I hugged her back and then said, 'It looks nice, but I'm not going to say anymore than that until we've looked around it.'

She took my hand and nearly skipped back up to the front door. The estate agent looked even more weasel-like close up. He offered me his hand for a half-hearted shake and introduced himself as Alan.

'Well, let's get this show on the road,' he said as he unlocked the door. It opened up onto a large and well-lit hallway. A staircase went up on the left. Two doors were on the right wall and another was on the back wall. It was, as I had suspected it would be, decorated in magnolia, with biscuit coloured carpets and a glass chandelier light fitting.

I will not bore you with all the details that Alan told us of the house. Suffice to say it was large, well finished, and an absolute bargain. This was something he would reiterate constantly as we viewed the house.

On the ground floor, the two doors on the right of the hallway led to, respectively, a large lounge, and a dining room with French windows. Despite the two doors the rooms were semi-open plan, with the dining room accessible through an archway in the living room. The rooms were decorated and carpeted like the hallway, as too was the rest of the house.

The door on the back wall of the hallway led to the kitchen which was finished with all modern units and granite effect work surfaces. There was another door that led outside. The back garden was larger than I had expected. These houses were at the edge of the development and backed onto a field and then woodland.

Up the stairs, there was a spacious landing, leading to another staircase; four doors were on the landing. There were three bedrooms, two of which were double and one good-sized single, and a family bathroom.

On the second floor were two more double bedrooms, one with an en suite toilet and shower.

I had to admit it that, despite the bland and featureless decor, I could see the potential the place had. The space was unbelievable. We were falling over each other in our current three-bedroomed cottage in Darton. Here we could potentially go days without seeing each other. I looked at Rachel who was grinning wildly the more of the house we saw.

After he had finished the tour, Alan told us to take some time and look around on our own. He would wait for us downstairs and answer any questions we had. As he walked down the stairs, I looked out of the master bedroom's window; from this point you could see most of the estate. Blackfriars Crescent itself was a row of nine houses that curved around the rear of a large traffic island, which was decorated with concentric circles of different coloured flower beds. Number 5 was dead centre of the row. Looking out of the window it almost felt like the whole estate had been designed to lead to the house. This was, of course, a stupid notion. It was just a coincidence of the house, but it did make the house feel like it stood apart from all the others.

Rachel walked over to me and put her arms around my waist.

'Well?' was all she asked.

'Well," I said, 'I can see how you feel about it. Seriously, Rach, haven't you ever heard of a poker face?'

She slapped me gently and stood next to me looking out of the window.

'Wow. What a view,' she said. 'But really, what do you think of the house?'

'I love it,' I said, not even realising this myself until the words left my mouth.

Rachel turned to me smiling but looking a little shocked.

'Really?' she asked.

'Yes,' I replied. 'Despite it being a new build, and despite how boring the decor is, I really like it. There's so much space. So come on, how much do they want for it?'

'This is the great part, £180,000,' she said.

Now was my turn to look shocked. A house this size should have been at least half that price again, maybe more.

'We could almost get that for the cottage,' I said. 'Why are they letting it go so cheap?'

Rachel explained what Alan had told her on the phone. Dessevy, the company that had built the estate, had been hit quite badly by the recession and was desperate to sell of as much of the estate as they could, so they had dropped the prices hoping to attract people into the estate. It was working, too, Number 5 was the last house empty on Blackfriars Crescent and the rest of the estate was filling up quite rapidly.

'He said that houses like this will never come up this cheap again,' Rachel said in conclusion. 'If we're going to do this, we need to do it now.'

I said yes. That's how it happened. Within a month of our first conversation about moving out of town, we were moving into Number 5.

CHAPTER TWO

The girls took the idea of moving in different ways. Izzy, our youngest, was ecstatic that she was getting a bigger bedroom. I suppose that at six that is a great selling point. We had decided to let Izzy have the double room as she had so many toys to fit in. Anna would be comfortable in the single room; it was much bigger than her room in the cottage. She was less thrilled about moving. We had tears and tantrums the night we told her. We tried to explain to her that she would be staying at the same school; it was the one I taught at and was only going to be a few miles out of town. At fourteen, though, this seemed like we were taking her to the other side of the world. Rachel took her out shopping and bought her some new clothes and lunch in Pizza Hut. On the way home she took her to see the house. I don't know whether it was the mother-daughter time, the retail therapy, or just seeing the house, but when they got back that day Anna seemed happy to be moving.

On moving day we took the girls to Rachel's parents for the day. We had professional removal men doing most of the work, but decided it was best to get the girls out of the way. They would just be in everyone's way all day, and Anna would just end up bored and moody. Rachel was going to stay at the old place in Darton and I was going to wait at the new house and show the movers where to put things. I took Mojo with me. The house at Glenley had a much bigger garden for him to play in until the work was done.

When we arrived at the house the dog investigated it thoroughly, sniffing each room in turn downstairs, before running up to do the same in the rest of the house. I watched him disappear onto the first floor landing, his tail wagging in excitement so fast that he was doing that thing where his whole back end was swaying from side to side. I decided to let him explore the house for a while. The movers wouldn't arrive here for at least another hour.

I unloaded the few boxes I had in the car. These contained the essential things like a kettle, mugs, milk, tea-bags, coffee and sugar. The other box held some of my tools, which I would need to assemble some of the things we had taken apart and to put up pictures and things, not to mention wall mounting the television.

I left the box of tools in the dining room and took the other one into the kitchen. I unpacked it onto one of the work surfaces. There was no point in me putting anything away. Rachel would have to devise her system for how things were stored in the kitchen. She always did this. It was a fool-proof system that meant that she could lay her hands on any implement, ingredient or condiment instantly. The system also meant that no one else could ever find anything. There was no visible pattern to how she organised things, but it worked for her, and it was those quirks that made her the woman I loved. Perhaps it was connected to her impulsiveness, the way she would make decisions without planning. When she did this she was usually right. So maybe when she organised the kitchen she used the same instincts, putting things in the place that seemed most natural to her.

We had met at university in Leicester. I was studying biochemistry. My aim was to get a PhD and do valuable research work that would change the world, but plans change. Rachel was studying English literature. She had aspirations of becoming an author. Funny how things work out. It should have been her writing this story, not me. Believe me when I tell you it would have been better written. I read much of her work and it was beautiful. Her use of language in prose seemed to verge on poetic.

I was a scientist, obsessed with the rational. She was a writer, one who lived in the realm of the imagination. We complemented each other perfectly. We met in the Student Union bar. I was on a night out with some friends who were trying to get me to relax a little. I had spent the previous three weeks constantly studying, day and night, so their plan was to get me out and get me very drunk. It worked. I was barely able to stand as I crossed the room crowded with students. This led to me colliding with someone; I knocked her drink to the floor. She was more stable than I was and managed to stay on her feet. I, on the other hand, in my stupor, soon followed the glass to the floor. Rachel helped me to my feet. As I saw her face for the first time I felt myself sober up instantly. I avoided my friends for the rest of the evening and spent the whole night talking to Rachel. From that night on we were pretty much inseparable.

I had been born and raised in Shropshire. Rachel was from Lincolnshire. After we had graduated we spent the summer flitting between my mother's home in Shrewsbury and her parents' in Grantham. The plan was that the following year we would both return to Leicester and get our masters degrees. The following year I would start my PhD and Rachel would start work on her first novel. The year after that we would get married.

Fate, however, intended for us to marry far sooner. It also did not have me becoming a research biochemist in its plan either. A month before we were due to start our masters degrees we discovered that Rachel was pregnant with Anna. I changed from a masters course to a P.G.C.E and became a teacher. Rachel kept on writing short stories, but with a young daughter, never found the time or the energy to undertake a novel. She still makes a living out of writing. She does articles and short fiction for several of the women's magazines, but it's not the ground-breaking literary fiction she always dreamed of writing.

I was roused from my memory by Mojo running into the kitchen and not being able to stop easily on the polished wood floor. He looked like a floundering ice skater as he slid towards me. He got his balance, and looked up at me, his eyes bright. His tail was still wagging exuberantly.

'Like the house, boy?' I said.

He yapped in response then stood there panting with his tongue hanging out.

'A drink? That's a good idea, Mojo,' I said, stroking his head. I poured some water into the bowl I had brought for him. I set it on the floor and he set about lapping it up noisily. I made my self a coffee and then went out into the back garden for a smoke. Mojo finished his bowl of water and then followed me out into the back garden. It was three times the size of the garden we'd had in Darton. Mojo seemed to appreciate it, tearing around it in wide circles. I walked down the sandstone path that separated the two halves of the grassed lawn. At the end of the path was an area of bare earth that I supposed some people would have used as a vegetable patch or flower garden. I, however, was never big on gardening, so I would probably get around to putting down some grass seed there in the next few weeks.

I looked over the fence at the field behind the house. It was just wild land. Long grass and weeds stood just under waist height on me. I could see a few paths that had been trampled down. They led from the edge of the woods all the way to a play park at the end of the crescent.

I finished my cigarette and flicked the butt over the fence. As I turned back to the house, I spotted a man in the next garden looking at me. He smiled and waved. He started to walk to the fence. I did the same on my side.

'Hey there?' he said.

'Morning,' I replied.

'The name's Bill,' he said, extending a hand over the fence. 'Bill Jenson.'

I shook his hand. He had a strong grip. This was not surprising, though, really. Bill was a giant of a man. He stood a good five or six inches taller than me, and must have weighed at least twenty stone of mainly muscle. Despite his impressive size, though, he had a soft almost babyish face. He must have been in his late forties.

'Nice day for it?' he said. He was right too. It was another glorious July day. It seemed like every time I set foot in this house the sun would shine. It seemed like a good omen. How wrong I was.

'Yes, indeed,' I replied to Bill before introducing myself.

'Nice to meet you, Dan,' he said with a warm smile. 'So are you moving in today?'

I told him that I was, and that I was just waiting for the removal men to arrive.

'Big houses aren't they?' he said. 'Me and the wife rattle around here a little. Our daughter moved out last month and our son is away at university. He'll be back for the summer soon, though. You have a family?'

'Yeah. There's me and my wife, Rachel. Then we have two daughters; Anna, who's fourteen, and Izzy, who's six.'

Bill laughed and shook his head.

'I don't envy you having a fourteen-year-old. I remember what that was like.'

Now I laughed.

'She can be hard work at times, but on the whole she's a good kid.'

'You from around here?' Bill asked.

I told him that I was originally from Shropshire, but Rachel was from just down the road in Grantham. I explained that we'd moved to Darton just before Anna was born and that I'd got a job teaching at St Thomas'. Bill explained that he had been a policeman, a detective, but had retired early on medical grounds. He had angina and it had gotten so severe a few years ago that he could no longer work. Once he had retired and had less stress in his life, the attacks became less frequent and less severe. 'So you remember the hospital?' he asked. Something in his face changed. There was a hint of concern in his expression that had not been there before.

'Not really,' I said. 'I've driven past it a few times, but it had just closed down when we moved to the area, bit of a scandal right?'

Bill nodded slowly, not meeting my gaze. Instead he looked off to the field behind our houses. He dropped his voice low.

'Yes it was,' he said, his eyes never leaving the field. 'The hospital covered most of that field and this estate in its day. Most of the space was taken up by the main hospital and the nurses' residences. The hospital proper closed in the fifties. It wasn't practical to keep it running when there are big hospitals in Lincoln, Boston and even Grantham, but the one thing it had was its psychiatric wards. It was a hospital-sized building in its own right. It was a big Victorian building. It had been a workhouse. Then it was a veterans hospital during the war. Then it became the psychiatric hospital. They kept running until the late nineties, but they'd been downscaling it since the mid-eighties, since the whole Dr Richards incident.'

He paused and turned his head back to me, looking to see if there was any recognition in my face. There was a little. I had heard stories about the infamous Dr Richards. They were local folklore, stories told by all the schoolchildren around Halloween to freak each other out and test who had been brave enough to enter his hospital of horrors. I had always assumed that the stories had been exaggerated by years of retelling.

In the versions I heard, Richards was like a cross between Dr Frankenstein and a Nazi scientist, who had conducted foul experiments on his inmates, things that hinted at the occult, like he was some sort of Satan-worshipping psychopath.

'I've only heard the playground rumours,' I told Bill. 'The ones about illegal experiments and black magic.'

Bill nodded again and then turned his head back to look out on the field.

'Yes, I've heard those stories. The truth, though, was so much worse. I worked that case. I was there when they brought the bodies out, those they found at least. Richards had an exemplary record before he started work at Glenley Mental Hospital, but when he got here he changed. Something dark got inside him. He took to raping the female patients, even some of the children. Then he started pimping them out to others, making money off people who wanted to rape women and children and get away with it. Any of the patients who threatened to expose him were drugged up to the eyeballs, or worse. By the time it all came out it's suspected that he had killed at least twelve of them, maybe more. The youngest was only eight years old.'

As Bill finally turned back to me the horror must have been evident on my face.

'He was sentenced to life in prison,' he continued. 'He didn't serve much of his sentence before he killed himself though. He scrawled the word 'sorry' in giant letters over his cell wall in his own blood as he died.'

'Jesus,' I said. 'I thought the truth would be better than the rumours.'

Bill nodded.

'I know, it was awful,' he said. 'Once they closed the place down they knocked the building down straight away, but they never built on the land.'

Bill turned back to the field.

'That wasteland was where it stood,' he finished. 'I wouldn't tell the wife and kiddies that story if I was you. It might scare them a bit.'

Now it was my turn to nod.

'Good job I don't believe in ghosts,' I said.

Bill laughed.

'Me neither,' he said. 'It's the living you should worry about, not the dead. Let the poor buggers rest.'

After this we continued to chat about the inconsequential things in life for a few minutes, mainly the weather and how it looked like we were in for a good summer. There was no way in Heaven or earth that summer could be described as good.

We said our goodbyes and Bill invited us over for a drink once we were settled. As he walked back towards his house, I heard the sound of a lorry pulling up outside. The removal men had arrived. I searched the garden for Mojo. I had not been aware of him running around for sometime. When I spotted him I should have known something was amiss. He was stood about four foot from the back fence in the soil, digging. What was so odd about this you might ask? I, at the time, didn't give it a second thought. I just shouted at him to stop and he went back to running in circles. The thing I realised much later was that in the four years we had owned Mojo, even when he was just a puppy, he had never been the kind of dog that would dig in the garden.

CHAPTER THREE

Moving day had gone off without a hitch. Our first few weeks in the house were almost idyllic. Izzy believed that she was now officially a princess due to the size of her room and the new bed we had bought for her. It was a small double, a white four poster thing with pink netting around it. She would spend hours sitting in the bed having royal audiences with her teddies and dollies.

Anna was excited about the fact that a few of the girls from her class had also just moved onto the estate. They were two of the nicer girls. This pleased me and Rachel greatly. She would visit them regularly, or they would be round ours. They spent much time in the garden, huddled up giggling. Rachel told me they would be talking about boys. This, as her father, was an idea that absolutely terrified me. Although she was growing into a young woman, she would always be my little girl. I thought of her the same way I thought of Izzy. Rachel laughed at me for this.

'If you're this bad now,' she asked me once, 'what are you going to be like when she starts bringing boys home?'

'Are you trying to send me to an early grave?' I asked.

'It'll happen,' she said with a smile. 'Sooner rather than later. How do you think my dad felt the first time I brought you home?'

'If it was anything like I feel, then I'm lucky to be alive.'

She smiled and nodded.

'You're just lucky that Dad knew he could let go, and one day you'll have to as well.'

I looked out of the window at the group of girls huddled in the garden, and try as I might, I could not see Anna as anything other than my little girl.

'I know,' I said, 'but not yet.'

Rachel kissed me on the cheek.

'No,' she said. 'Not yet.'

Anna and her friends also spent a lot of time walking and playing in the field behind the house. The first time I saw them I remembered the story that Bill Jenson had told me. It made me uncomfortable to think of them playing in what was, essentially, the scene of such horror at first. Then my rational mind took over. I was a scientist. The field wasn't cursed, it was merely a place where something terrible had happened a long time ago.

Rachel was in her element decorating the house. I had very little say in what she did, of course. As she often reminded me, I would not have known what good taste was if it had come up and introduced itself. She was probably right. I even tended to leave it to her to buy my clothes, trusting her opinion over my own. She was also writing a lot. One night after the girls had gone to bed she told me that she thought it was time to finally start work on writing her novel. I was delighted for her. She had been putting it off for so long I was worried that she would never do it.

I was feeling very contented. The school year was coming to an end. The summer holidays were always a much more casual time. Though people seem to have the misconception that teachers have the entire six weeks off like the kids, it is fair to say that we do not work very hard during the summer. I would usually take two or three weeks off completely, then the rest of the time I would do half days or half weeks.

It felt good coming home to such a content household. We were all so much happier than we had been in years. Bill Jenson and his wife Mary did invite us over for a drink that first week. She was a lovely woman, all smiles and laughter. Though she was in her forties like her husband, she had a glint in her eye that made her look so much younger. She subscribed to several of the magazines that Rachel wrote for and remembered some of her stories. It was safe to say that the two of them would quickly become good friends.

Bill kept the girls entertained with stories about catching robbers. Izzy quickly took to calling him Uncle Bill, although no one had told her to.

After that first time it became a regular thing for us to go over to the Jenson's or for them to come over to ours. They soon became part of our extended family.

We met some of the other neighbours too. At Number 4, on the other side of us to Bill and Mary, was a young solicitor called Laura Taylor, her four-year-old son Leo, and her Dutch au pair, Mikkala. Laura was a widow. Leo's father had been a barrister who had died in a car accident before he was born. The money he had left them bought the house on Blackfriars Crescent out right. Laura seemed friendly enough, but she had an air of sadness about her. Izzy took to Leo as her little play mate. They would chase each other around the garden, giggling nonstop. Leo would bring his toys over to show her. Izzy would coo over all of them to make the little boy happy, even though she would later tell me they were silly boy toys.

'Then why did you tell Leo you liked them?' I asked her.

'Because Leo is so proud of them,' she said. 'I didn't want to hurt his feelings.'

That was Izzy. Even though she was only six, she already cared so much about other peoples feelings. I was so proud of her.

At Number 7, next door to the Jensons, were the Marklews. He was a doctor at the hospital in Boston, some kind of surgeon I believe. He worked long hours and we rarely saw him. She was a lady who lunches. Everyday she would set off, in her Range Rover, about eleven in the morning, and return around half three in the afternoon. Mary told Rachel that local gossip was that Mrs Marklew was having far more than just lunch on these afternoons. She had often been seen in the company of a young man. You know the type, all muscles and designer clothes, with little to nothing going on upstairs.

Mary thought that she was only staying with Dr Marklew was because of the money he must earn as a surgeon.

'Really?' I asked Rachel when she relayed the gossip to me later. 'Because I would say that the money is the only reason she can manage to be messing around with a handsome young man.'

Rachel laughed loudly at this.

'You're awful!' she said.

I stood by my comment though. Mrs Marklew was tall and slim, with a great figure for her age, but she had been graced with a face that made her look stern and miserable all the time. She looked a good ten years older than she was due to the wrinkles caused by her permanent frown.

Two doors down from Laura and Leo was a house that was being rented by a group of postgraduate students from the university in Lincoln. They kept themselves to themselves and seemed so awkward and nervous when you did speak to them it made me glad that I had not gone into research. Two of them were studying archaeology. The third was studying engineering I believed, but more about them soon enough.

There were, of course, other neighbours, but they have little to do with the events that were about to occur. We did not speak to them much, only the neighbourly pleasantries.

The only problem we had was Mojo. His behaviour didn't change. He was still the same loving dog he had always been. It was just that he became obsessed with digging in the same spot in the back corner of the garden. We all had to keep shooing him away from the spot. I even tried putting down some of that powder that is supposed to keep animals away from an area. All it did was make him sneeze all day until he had dug through it. He was starting to make quite a big hole. I told Rachel that when the school broke up I would fill in the hole and sow some grass seeds, hoping that removing the temptation of the fresh earth would stop him from digging. None of us were sure why he was digging there. We thought that maybe he was trying to dig a hole under the fence so that he could get out and play in the field behind the house whenever he chose.

Suffice to say that those first few weeks were amazing. Rachel and I felt like we had made the right decision by moving to Glenley. Of course, little did we know what was about to happen. As I said earlier, it was all to start with our dog, Mojo. It was the last Saturday before the summer holidays, and the good weather had hit epic proportions. Earlier in the week, I had invited Bill and Mary, and Laura, Leo and Mikkala over for a barbecue that weekend. When the day came everyone was in good spirits. That was the day that changed it all. That was the day we discovered why Mojo had been digging.

CHAPTER FOUR

I was manning the barbecue, assisted by Bill. We both had beers in our hands. It always strikes me as strange that when it comes to cooking on an open flame the men would take charge. I was as guilty as any other man. In all the years we had been married, I couldn't remember a single time that I had let Rachel cook on the barbecue. I mean I was willing to let her cook in the kitchen anytime; however, as soon as there was fire involved it was man work.

I pointed this out to Bill, who had his own view on the reasons why this happened.

'Well, Dan,' he said before pausing to take a swig of his Grolsch. 'It takes us back to our roots. It's the only connection that modern man has to his primeval ancestors. Getting a steak and cooking it on the barbecue is the equivalent of killing a mammoth and cooking it on a camp fire.'

Though it seemed too simplistic, I think he had something.

'Perhaps you're right,' I said.

'Oh I know I am,' he said with a smile. 'No matter how evolved we become as a species, no matter how civilised or cultured we think we are, the past is always there. As much as we might try, we can't escape our history.'

It was an interesting premise. A little deep for a barbecue, though, so we moved on to lighter topics.

As we talked and cooked, Rachel and the other three women prepared salads, while chatting and drinking copious amounts of wine. Anna had her school friends round, and despite their normal cool teenage girl persona, the three of them were running around playing silly games with Izzy and Leo.

Occasionally I would hear Anna shout at the dog.

'Mojo! Stop digging, you silly mutt!' This made the other children laugh so much that Izzy felt the need to repeat the 'silly mutt' part over and over.

Mojo did briefly look up from his digging and run over to them panting. For a while he joined in the game, chasing them all round. It was a game he had always loved playing with Izzy and Anna, but with the three extra children, he was finding it hard and confusing work. Within a few minutes, he had slinked off back to work on his hole.

'You didn't invite the Marklews then?' Bill asked me.

'No,' I said. 'I haven't seen his car there all week. I think he must be away, and I thought that this might be a little low brow for a lady of her standing.'

This made Bill roar with laughter.

'Oh yes. She has probably never eaten a barbecue sausage in her life,' he said.

'She's more into designer sausage from what I hear,' I said.

Bill erupted into another deep belly laugh, at which point his wife wandered over with another two chilled bottles of beer for us.

'It sounds like you don't need another one of these just yet,' she said whilst mock frowning at her husband.

'Oh come on, love,' he pleaded. 'I'm just letting my hair down.'

She shook her head and then reached up and stroked his short-cropped, thinning grey hair.

'Well, don't let it down too far, William,' she said with a smile. 'You haven't got much left.'

'Cheeky mare!' he said as he swatted her bottom as she walked away. It was the kind of playful gesture that showed a couple who were still utterly in love despite twenty odd years of marriage.

'We were just talking about the Marklew woman,' Bill said.

'You pair of gossiping old women,' Mary said laughing.

'I get most of my information from you, don't forget,' Bill said.

Mary laughed, then she pointed at herself and pulled a 'who me?' face.

'Mojo! Get away from that bastard hole!' shouted a shrill voice. It was, of course, our beautiful little princess Izzy. Anna and the older girls stood together giggling. Leo was looking at Izzy in open mouth shock.

'Izzy!' I shouted. 'You don't use words like that. Go and sit inside and think about what you've done.'

She sulked off inside, with the kind of dramatics that told me her teenage years would be ten times worse than Anna's had been so far. I glanced over at Rachel who was managing to look embarrassed whilst glaring at me. Yes, I admit it. Izzy had learnt that one from me just the night before. Of course, I hadn't been aware that she had been listening at the time.

'Sorry about that, everyone,' I said, feeling Rachel's shamed eyes burning into me.

'It's all right, mate,' Bill said, slapping me on the back. 'They all do it.'

After everyone had finished eating, Anna went back to Holly's house. Izzy stayed inside and watched *Beauty and the Beast* for the thousandth time, her earlier faux pas now forgotten by her and forgiven by everyone else. Mikkala took Leo home, bathed him and put him to bed. She then came back with a baby monitor for Laura, who thanked her and put it on the garden table in front of her. Mikkala herself was taking the night off. She was headed into Darton for a night out with friends, but promised Laura she would be back by lunchtime the following day. Laura told her to take her time and enjoy herself. Laura told us how hard the girl worked looking after Leo and the house for her. She put in far more hours a week than she was contracted to. Laura, though, knew that she needed some time to herself. She was a young woman, only twenty years old, and living in a foreign country.

'Have a good night,' Laura said.

Mikkala smiled.

'I will,' she said. 'There is so much to do in town.'

We all laughed at her sarcasm. It was true. Darton had never been great for a night out, but over the last few years, two of the three nightclubs had closed completely and the third opened only occasionally. There were only two pubs that were left on the high street, and usually one or the other had trouble on any particular night.

'Where you going?' I asked.

'The Nags Head,' she replied. 'It is, how you say, a shithole, but it is better than the Black Bull.'

This was true. 'The Bull,' as the locals called it, was populated mainly by chavs and drug addicts, leading to most people I knew calling it 'The Jeremy Kyle Show.'

'It will be nice to catch up with the girls, though,' Mikkala continued, 'but I will be back for lunch.'

'Don't worry about it,' Laura said with a smile. 'Go and be young, free and single.'

Mikkala bid us all good night and thanked me and Rachel for the food and then she left.

The air in the garden finally started to cool as the sun began its evening descent. The five of us that were left sat around talking. Bill and I had already made a hefty dent in the first crate of Grolsch, and God only knew how many bottles of wine the women had gotten through. I was starting to feel that warm, happy and relaxed state of mind that always seemed to precede drunkenness for me. Bill, probably due to his sheer size, didn't seem to be even remotely drunk. His wife Mary, on the other hand, was three sheets to the wind. Her cheeks were almost as red as the wine she was drinking. She couldn't seem to stop laughing for more than a few minutes at a time. Her laughter, though, was very contagious. Each time she set off again, it was not long before everyone else was joining in.

Rachel seemed on the outside to be holding up fine with the alcohol. As far as any of the others knew she wasn't even tipsy, but after fourteen years of marriage I could see the signs. Whenever she had drunk too much Rachel would constantly play with her hair, winding those loose, deep brown curls around her index and forefinger. It was something that always reminded me of the eighteen-year-old girl I had met all those years ago. The other sign was the fact that whenever she thought no one else was looking she would wink at me or blow me a kiss. God, I loved her so much. Through all the years and the hardship that was one thing that had not changed.

Laura was quiet, not to the point of being rude. She would laugh at jokes and respond when asked something directly. The rest of the time she would just sit there looking at the rest of us. Some times she seemed to be looking past us. It must have been hard for her. I couldn't dream of what it would be like to lose someone like that. I only knew that if it had been me, had I lost Rachel so early and been left to raise Anna on my own, I would have fallen to pieces. Anna would probably now be living with her grandparents, whilst I lived in the bottom of a bottle. Just imagining it nearly broke my heart in two. So it was fair to say that I admired Laura more than she would ever know.

As the sun began to set, Rachel disappeared inside to get Izzy to bed. Anna came home and sat outside with us for a while. She asked if she could have a small glass of wine. At first I said no.

'Oh come on, Dan?' Mary said with a glint in her eye. 'One little glass won't hurt her.'

This was true. We had let her have a few small glasses of wine in the past, at weddings and other special occasions.

'Fine,' I said in defeat. Mary poured a small amount of the Merlot she was drinking into a glass and passed it to Anna, she thanked her and then came over and plonked herself down on my knee. I groaned in mock pain.

'My God,' I said. 'You are getting too big for this Anna.'

She laughed and punched me gently in the arm.

'Are you calling me fat?'

I shook my head and hugged her. She squirmed away. Despite the jokes I loved these moments. They reminded me of when she was a little girl, and it was almost impossible for me to get her off my knee. Nowadays moments like this were few and far between. Most of the time we were just passing ships. There was no major reason for this, Anna and I had had no big arguments that led to this. It was just a combination of her growing up and my inability to accept it. I never wanted her to grow up. I wanted her to stay my little girl forever.

'Where's Mojo?' she asked. Thinking about it I hadn't seen the dog in quite some time.

'Mojo?' I shouted. As my eyes darted across the garden I saw the Jack Russell pop up from the hole he had been digging. The white fur of his legs and belly was black with mud. He looked at me with his head cocked as if he was questioning what I wanted. His tail was wagging with its usual vigour.

'Get out of the bloody hole!' I yelled at him. He ran off into the house. I got to my feet to try to stop him, knowing that if he jumped on the furniture in that state Rachel would probably string us both up. I followed him to the kitchen door. He walked over to his bowl and ate a few biscuits before washing it down with the entire contents of his water bowl. After being fed and watered, he sauntered back outside. Rachel came back down from putting Izzy to bed.

Soon after that, the last rays of the sun began to glow a deep red over the top of the woods at the back of the house. When I looked at my watch, I was surprised to see that it was already half nine. Anna kissed me and

Rachel goodnight. She said she was going to get into bed and watch a DVD. She said it was because it had been a long day, but I suspected it was because the conversation amongst the adults wasn't as exciting as she thought it would be.

'So does anyone know why this is called Blackfriars Crescent?' Rachel asked the others.

'Not a clue,' Laura replied. 'I did always wonder that myself though, because it doesn't fit in the rest of the road names on the estate.'

I had noticed this. Every other street on the estate seemed to be named after some kind of bird. There was Sparrow Way, Kestrel Avenue and Robin Close to name but three.

'It's because the road was named Blackfriars Road when the hospital was here,' Bill interjected. 'This and Raven Street were the only roads that were here then. Raven Road ran straight through the middle of all the hospital buildings until it joined Blackfriars Road here, which cut across the back of the complex in front of the mental hospital.'

Bill was, it appeared, a fountain of local knowledge. Then, he had lived here most of his life. He had been born in Glenley Hospital and raised in Darton. The only time he had spent away from the area was when he had done his police training at Hendon. That was where he had met and fallen in love with Mary. After those seventeen weeks he had spent with her on the outskirts of London she had agreed to marry him and move back to Lincolnshire with him.

The sound that stopped our conversation and got us all to our feet was one that has been scarred onto my memory. Even now when the lights go out at night I sometimes hear it in my mind. It always seems to foreshadow a restless night of nightmare-haunted sleep.

It sounded like a yelp, followed by a hollow thud that seemed to echo around the garden forever, disrupted only by the reverb-soaked howl of pain that followed. It was a sound that I had never heard Mojo make before, and it chilled me to my core.

Bill and I were the first up. We sprinted across the garden, both of us knowing exactly where the sound had originated. When we reached the hole I couldn't see Mojo, but I could hear him whimpering distantly. The hole went down into blackness. At first, I couldn't figure out why. Yes, the hole had been big enough for Mojo to disappear in, but that wasn't hard. The dog only stood about ten inches off the ground. He'd only dug down about a foot and a half last time I had looked in the hole.

'He's dug through into a cave or something,' Bill said.

The women arrived behind us. I turned to Rachel.

'Get my torch,' I said.

'I'll go and grab my ladder,' Bill said.

Before either of them could move, the baby monitor back on the table erupted into a scream so loud it distorted the speaker. 'Leo!' Laura nearly screamed. She ran for the house. Bill and I followed.

CHAPTER FIVE

Leo was fine. He had just woken from a nightmare, or at least that is what we all thought at the time. He said that there was an ugly man with a long, black, hooded cloak in his room. There was real fear in his eyes and tears streaked his face. He explained what he'd seen, punctuated by the kind of gulping sobs that only a small child can achieve.

Laura held him close as he told us how he had woken up and seen a scary-faced man in a cloak with a big hood. The man had been stood in the middle of his room with his back to Leo. Then he turned and jumped towards him. This was when Leo had screamed. Though we were all convinced it was a dream, Bill and I made a quick search of the house for Leo's peace of mind. When we were done, we left Laura alone to settle him. We did have another emergency, after all.

Luckily, Izzy was fast asleep by this point and Anna must have been too engrossed in her film to have noticed the commotion. Had they been around they would have been inconsolable and would have made the rescue more difficult.

Bill ran back to his house to get his ladder. Rachel had found my halogen torch, the one I had bought for our camping trip to Wales the year before. I stood precariously close to the edge of the hole. Rachel tried to step forward as I shone the powerful beam down into the darkness below. I motioned for her to stop.

'Stay a few feet back,' I said. ' We don't know how stable the ground is. It could all go crashing down there at any minute.'

'Then why are you stood there?' she said, tears brimming in her worried eyes.

'Because we have to do something to help Mojo,' I said reassuringly, 'but the less weight we put on here the better until we know how safe it is.'

I looked back down the hole with the torch. At first all I could see was more blackness. I have to admit that at that point even I, the rational scientist, feared that our little dog had fallen through to the centre of the earth. Then I spotted a flash of white as the beam moved. I quickly scanned the torch back. There he was. He was sat on the ground looking up at me. He was shaking and whimpering, but on the whole he looked okay. The only problem was how small he looked from here. He must have fallen at least thirty to forty feet.

Bill returned with the ladder. I looked at it then shook my head at him.

'That's not going to reach,' I said.

'What?' he said, shocked. 'This is a twenty foot ladder.'

I explained how far poor Mojo had fallen. Bill had a look of disbelief on his face.

'Should I call for the fire brigade?' Rachel asked.

I was about to tell her yes when Bill interrupted.

'I've got a rope in the shed. We could tie it around you. Dan and I could lower you down.'

Although I didn't like the idea of being lowered down into the darkness of the hole not knowing what I was going to find down there, it sounded like the best plan. There was no way that I would be able to take Bill's weight to lower him down.

Bill and Mary went over to their shed to get the rope. I looked over at Rachel. Despite how warm the evening was, I could see that she was shaking. Tears ran down her face. I walked over to her and put my arms around her. I kissed her forehead and she looked up at me.

'I'm scared,' she said. 'Maybe I should just call the fire brigade.'

I held her closer, feeling her trembling against me.

'We need to get Mojo out,' I said. 'He's fallen a long way. He might be really hurt. This is going to be the quickest way to get him out.'

'But we don't know if it's safe down there,' she said, her voice almost a sob.

'I'm sure it is,' I lied. 'If I get stuck down there I'll just wait with Mojo until you can get the fire brigade here.'

At that moment Bill and Mary returned with the thickest and longest rope I had ever seen. I had been expecting the modern sort of rope, thin and multi-coloured, the kind used for climbing and abseiling. This, however, was the old-fashioned wound rope, the sort that I used to have to climb in P.E. at school. It was almost as thick as my wrist and must have been at least sixty foot long. It was so big that it took both of them to carry it with some still trailing on the floor behind. If time had not been so much of the essence I would have asked Bill why on earth he owned a piece of rope like that. I could not see any reason. Later on I did ask. Bill explained that many years ago he had owned a barge that he often used to take holidays on the Norfolk broads, the rope had been used for mooring the barge at night. When he sold the barge, he decided to keep the rope in case it ever came in useful.

After a little discussion, we decided the best way to proceed was to have Bill take the main strain of the rope, with Mary and Rachel helping him, while I climbed down the rope. This made me feel a little better than being lowered down. At least I was in control of my own descent, rather than feeling like a worm being lowered as bait.

Once the rope was down the hole and I was sure that Bill had a good hold and a sure footing I began to climb. I had the torch tied to my belt. It had been a long time since I had climbed down a rope. The first part wasn't too bad. I held onto the rope and backed into the hole., pushing against the soil of the hole Mojo had dug with my feet. It reminded me of the time that I had abseiled down the outside of the school gym for charity. Once I reached the bottom of where Mojo had dug through, the hole opened out. There was nothing around me; I was just hanging in mid-air. I gripped the base of the rope with my feet. I suddenly realised why the teacher had always made us take off our shoes to climb the rope when I was at school. It was much easier to grip barefoot than in Hush Puppies.

'You alright holding that up there?' I yelled up, aware of the way my voice echoed.

'Yes, mate,' Bill shouted back at me from above. 'No problem.'

I shimmied slowly down the rope. In the darkness I had no awareness of the space around me or how big it was. I couldn't shake the irrational feeling that, somehow, the dog had dug a hole straight out of the reality of our dimension and had fallen into the emptiness between worlds, and here I was dangling into eternity. This was not completely irrational.

Though I was a biochemist, I had house-shared with two physicists at university. Many nights had been spent with Jim and Mark discussing inter-dimensional theories, how our reality was only one in an infinite number of realities. They often discussed whether our laws of physics would only apply in our universe. Theories suggested there were points where the different dimensions met; these were called wormholes. As I slowly descended on that rope, I wondered if one of those wormholes existed in my garden. Though Jim and Mark had always said that they most likely existed in deep space, there was theoretically no reason why they could not exist here on earth.

Eventually I reached the bottom. The floor at the bottom was much more even and solid than I had expected. I felt something warm nudge against my leg. I let out a little scream. I tugged the torch from my belt and switched it on. I should have known that my assailant in the dark was none other than Mojo. I looked down at him. He was still shaking, but upon me reaching down and stroking his head I saw his tail begin to wag, though not as vigourously as usual. He was covered in dust from down here, but on initial assessment, he didn't appear to be bleeding.

'Are you okay?' Rachel shouted from above. 'Have you found Mojo?'

'Yeah,' I shouted back, again my voice echoing. 'He looks all right.'

I picked the dog up. I felt his back and ribs. They seemed fine. His only reaction was to try to lick me to death. I felt his front legs again. They seemed fine. When I squeezed his back left leg, though, he let out a little yelp.

'I'm sorry, mate,' I said to settle him. I looked up to the hole I had come through. 'His back leg seems to be hurting him a little. I don't think it's broken but it might be an idea to take him to the vet.'

'You coming back up with him?' Bill shouted in response. I thought about it, but I really didn't like the idea of being pulled up.

'No, I'll tie him onto the rope and you can pull him up, then throw the rope back down for me.'

'Okay, make sure it's a secure knot you use. Wouldn't want the little bugger falling down again,' Bill replied.

I tied the rope tightly around Mojo's chest. As he got pulled up the loop around him would pull up against his front legs, stopping him from slipping.

'Alright. Pull him up.'

'Okay,' Bill responded. He must have begun to slowly pull the rope out because Mojo began to rise. He looked confused but didn't struggle to get free too much. I stood below him as he rose up through the air, keeping him in the torch's beam. If he did manage to wriggle out of the rope, at least I would be able to catch him. It was amazing he had survived a fall like that once with only minor injuries. I didn't want to risk him doing it again.

As I saw him disappear out of the hole I heard Rachel shout ecstatically.

'Mojo!' I imagined her running over to him and showering him with kisses, which he would accept and return in spades.

Suddenly I realised that I had not even had a look around. I still didn't know where I was. Bill's initial idea that it was a cave now seemed unlikely due to the smoothness of the floor and the stone work I could see above me when I was watching Mojo rise up. At first, I thought that maybe it was the remains of the hospital basement. Most hospitals built in the last sixty years had cavernous underground areas. They contained all the pipes that worked hard to heat the large buildings. Then I remembered that the larger, more recent hospital buildings had been further into the estate. We were near where the mental ward had stood. That building had been built in the 1800s as a workhouse. It was unlikely that it would have had a basement at all, let alone one this large.

I shone the torch around. It was an enormous space, the size of at least two football pitches, maybe even three. The stonework was all sandstone, not red brick, suggesting to me that it was old. There was a series of carved arches that went up on either side, meeting in the vaulted ceiling. Above my head crudely carved faces were staring down. It was like being in a church.

'Heads up!' came a shout from above, making me jump. The rope came down, hitting the floor with a hard thud. 'Ready to come back up?'

I realised that for the first time since I had climbed down through the hole I wasn't thinking about going back up. The place had me curious.

'Can you hold on a minute?' I shouted back, finally getting used to the way my voice reverberated. 'I want to check this place out.'

'Okay, Indy,' Bill shouted down, laughing.

'Dan,' Rachel joined in. 'Get back up here.'

'It's all right, baby,' I said. 'It's safe enough down here.'

'Be careful,' she said. 'I can't feel a break on Mojo's leg, by the way, and he seems to be walking okay on it. I think it's just bruised.'

'That's good,' I said. 'Better take him to the vet on Monday just to check it out, though.'

'Just give us a shout when you wanna come up,' Bill said. 'Don't just grab the rope. I'm not holding it at the minute.'

I continued exploring the space below. The vast chamber stretched up to about level with the front of our house in one direction and well into the field in the other. I couldn't tell exactly how far, as my torch beam didn't reach far enough to light that end up. I headed in that direction.

The sheer size and grandeur blew me away. It was like I was walking through an underground church, except there were no pews. I remembered the rumours I had heard about the mad doctor in the asylum before Bill had told me the true horror that had happened. In those exaggerated tales I had heard before, people said that the evil Dr Richards was in league with the Devil. They said he was some kind of Satan worshipper. It occurred to me that maybe there had been some truth in those stories and that this was the scene of some kind of evil worship and ritual.

I pushed this thought to the back of my mind. There was, of course, no truth in those stories. Bill had been one of the police officers who had investigated the case. He said that Richards had never said anything about devil worship. He had confessed to everything. He offered no reason. He said that the idea had just come to him when he had started working at the hospital.

Ahead of me I saw the end of the room. It opened up into three concave arches. The two on either side were shorter and thinner than the central arch which went almost to the ceiling. I had seen similar structures in many churches in the past. The word chancel popped into my head, though I was not sure that it was exactly the right description.

In front of the central arch stood a squat stone structure. At first I thought it was an altar. This brought the idea of Satan worship back to the front of my mind. What if this had been the altar used for human sacrifices?

Then I realised that the main structure was round. I estimated it had a diameter of about six or seven feet. On top of it was placed a large, smooth stone. It must have been at least a foot thick and, I presumed, weighed a tonne.

The stones that made up the circular structure were darker rock than any of the other stone work down here. Whereas everything else was made of smoothly carved sandstone, this was made of various kinds of stone, that were all irregular sizes and shapes. It reminded me of the dry stone walls I had seen when walking around the Yorkshire dales and moors. I don't know why, but I got the feeling that this structure was older than anything else down here.

I reached out my hand to touch it. I had barely grazed the surface with my finger when I jerked my hand away. It was freezing, the kind of cold that hurts. Pain shot up from my fingertips like an electric shock jumping up my arm. The air down here certainly was cooler than it had been back up in the garden, but these stones were unnaturally cold.

A wave of nausea came over me. Years ago Rachel and I had taken a ferry over to Ireland. On the way out the weather had been fine and so had I. On the way back, though, a storm had hit and the waves were vicious. The boat rocked violently. Rachel had taken it in her stride. I, on the other hand, had turned green and spent the rest of the trip throwing up. The feeling I felt now in my stomach was exactly the same. I turned to head back to the rope. Panic grabbed hold of me. At that moment the only thing I wanted was to get away from there and never return. There was no reason for this, but I felt in a state of pure terror. I took no more than two steps before I dropped onto my knees. I started to wretch. Nothing would come. It was just that dry heaving that pulls your stomach and chest muscles so much they hurt for days.

I began to crawl back to the rope, the hole, the real world. When I was a few feet away from the stone structure the feelings were gone, both the nausea and the pain. The panic faded. Perhaps the whole incident had been my imagination. I looked back at the circular stone structure. I felt compelled to touch it again.

'Dan? Are you okay?' came Rachel's voice from above. 'You've been down there ages.'

The thought of touching the stones again was gone. It was time to leave. I started heading back to the rope.

'I'm fine,' I shouted. 'Just coming back now if you wanna get hold of the rope, Bill.'

'Will do, mate,' Bill shouted in reply.

I virtually ran back to the rope and grabbed hold of it. I kicked off my shoes and took off my socks. I tucked the socks into the shoes and then tied them to my belt by the laces. I climbed up the rope as quickly as I could.

CHAPTER SIX

After getting out of the well and hugging Rachel for what felt like an eternity, Bill and I set to work securing the area around the hole. I helped him back to the shed with the rope first. Once inside the shed he started handing me things. He had some thick bamboo garden stakes and some chicken wire. We decided that if we hammered the stakes into the ground in a square about twice as big as the hole and then used his staple gun to attach the chicken wire to them, this would be secure enough to stop one of the kids accidentally falling in the hole until I could sort out something more substantial the next day. Mojo would have to stay in the house for the rest of the night, just in case he decided to dig under the wire. Rachel and Mary had taken the dog inside to bathe him and check him more closely for injuries.

I carried the rubber hammer and the stakes back across to our garden, while Bill brought the chicken wire and staple gun. It only took us about fifteen minutes to do the job. Looking at the temporary fence we had made around the hole made me feel slightly more secure.

Our wives were still inside bathing the dog when we finished our task. I looked at Bill. He was dripping with sweat. The job had been a hot one in the warm evening air.

'Another beer?' I asked.

Bill considered this for a moment.

'After everything that has happened tonight, I have to ask if you have anything stronger?'

'I think I have a half bottle of rum I've had since Christmas,' I said. 'Want a rum and Coke?'

He nodded. As I went over to the kitchen, Bill went to the table and sat down heavily. The rum was Morgan's Spiced and there was just over half a bottle left. I grabbed it, a couple of glasses and the Coke from the fridge and headed back outside.

'Sorry, no more ice,' I said as I walked back to the garden table, 'but I think the Coke should be cold enough.'

'Not a problem,' Bill said.

I poured out the drinks. I think they were somewhere between double and treble measures, topped up with Coke. We sat there in silence for a while, savouring the taste of the rum, and finally relaxing from all that had happened. I took out my cigarettes and lit one. I saw the look of longing on Bill's face.

'How long since you quit?' I asked, knowing the look all too well.

'About three years,' he said. 'Don't suppose I could pinch one? I think I need it tonight.'

I smiled and handed him the packet. He took out one of my Marlboros and ran the length of it under his nose, inhaling deeply as he did it.

'I always loved the smell of these things before you light them,' he said. Then he put it into his mouth. I passed him the lighter. He struck it and inhaled deeply on the cigarette. He closed his eyes and held the smoke in for a long time then blew it out in a long plume from his nose. He reminded me of a dragon doing this. He sighed with pleasure.

'What the bloody hell is down there, Dan?' he asked.

I had been waiting for this question. We had been so busy since I got back up to the garden that we had not had time for the conversation.

'I don't know, to be honest,' I said. 'I thought at first it might have been part of the old hospital basement, but that wasn't right.'

'How can you be so sure?' he said with another plume of smoke coming from his nose.

'It didn't look right,' I told him. 'It was old. Really old. It looked more like a church.'

Bill frowned at that.

'I've lived here my whole life and I've never heard about any sort of church out here, especially not an underground one.'

'Well, that's what it looked like. There was even some weird round altar.'

'A round altar?' Bill asked.

'There was a round stone structure. Like a stone cylinder. Sticking out of the ground about three foot. It had a big slab of stone on top of it,' I said.

'Sounds like a covered well to me,' Bill said.

Of course. It was so obvious when I heard Bill say it. It looked like an old well. I would have recognised that instantly if I'd found one in normal circumstances and if it hadn't had the stone on top of it, but in the madness that had happened tonight and the strangeness of the location, my mind had been unable to make the connection.

'Whatever it is, you should report it,' Bill said.

'Who to?' I asked. In all honesty, I had no idea who to report this kind of thing to.

'I'd let the police know,' Bill said, 'and probably the council. See if they can get that hole sealed up for you.'

I thought about this. Certainly having a hole in the garden that dropped thirty-odd feet to a stone floor was not the safest thing in the world.

'I guess,' I said, 'but that thing has been covered up for God knows how long, Bill. It might be some kind of important discovery and I, for one, would love to know what the hell it is.'

Bill nodded.

'True, maybe you should get those university boys down the road to take a look.'

The research students. Two of them were archaeologists. They would probably be able to shed some light on it.

'Good plan,' I said. 'I'll pay them a visit in the morning then report it to the council on Monday.'

After Bill and Mary left I felt exhausted. Rachel and I got ready for bed. We laid in bed. I could tell that Rachel was going to ask the same things as Bill. I gave her the same answers, explaining that I would get the archaeologists to take a look the next day, then report it on Monday in my lunch break. The council offices where only a five-minute walk from the school so this would not be a problem. She still seemed anxious.

'I think it could be dangerous,' she said.

'The fence Bill and I built will stop anyone accidentally falling in it,' I reassured her. 'We'll tell the kids to stay away from that end of the garden, and watch Mojo when he's outside.' I looked around the room. 'Where is he anyway?'

'Oh after I dried him off he went and curled up with Izzy,' she said. 'But what if more of the garden caves in?'

'I don't think it will,' I said. 'The stonework on the rest of the roof seemed okay. I think there must have been a weak spot there.'

She frowned at me. She knew that my knowledge of stonework was limited. Then she smiled.

'I guess I'll have to trust your opinion for now,' she said. 'I suppose it is kind of exciting having an archaeological discovery in our garden.'

This was true. I, myself, was fascinated by the chamber and desperate to know more. There was at the back of my mind, though, a niggling sense of unease. I had not told either Bill or Rachel about what had happened to me when I touched the well. I was pretty much convinced that my mind had created the whole thing. After all, I had just been through some serious stress. Yet still I could not shake that last hint of fear, the remnants of the panic that had grabbed me like an iron fist down there in the darkness.

'Are you all right?' Rachel asked. Over our sixteen years together she had developed a sort of sixth sense to my moods and thoughts, something I had never been able to do in return. Her mind was still an impenetrable puzzle to me and her moods as unpredictable as ever.

'Yeah,' I said, not wanting to worry her. 'Just wondering what it is down there.'

We made love that night. Then we fell into a deep peaceful sleep in each other arms.

The noise woke me up. I looked at the red display of the alarm clock. 3:33 AM, the little screen read. I listened carefully. I was not sure whether the sound had been real or the last part of a dream I had been in and could no longer remember. Then it happened again. A faint creak. Like someone slowly stepping across a floorboard, trying to be quiet.

I sat up in bed. I looked at the door. There was no light seeping in from the bottom of the door. Izzy had a habit of walking really slowly when she got up to use the toilet in the night, but she always put the light on. Anna on the other hand would leave the light off, but like most teenagers she was quite heavy-footed.

There was another creak. It was closer to our door this time. If it was Izzy deciding to brave the toilet without the light, she was on her way back to her own room. However, Izzy had a fear of the dark that was severe enough to require us to leave a night light on in her room all night. Another creak, this time level with our door. Another thought suddenly leapt into my mind. Burglars. My heart was suddenly racing. I could feel it pumping against my chest.

There was a slow scraping noise from the other side of the room. It was one that I couldn't quite place until I noticed that the door knob of our bedroom door was turning slowly. I looked around the room. I was searching it for a possible weapon to use if the intruder entered. I saw what I needed in the corner near the window. It was the torch I had taken down in the hole. It was one of those heavy duty, metal cased ones. Swung with enough force I was sure it could do some serious damage. I slid slowly out of bed. I tried to be as quiet as I could. As I put my weight on the floor, though, there was a telltale creak. I froze on the spot. The doorknob stopped turning. There were no creaks or footsteps though. Perhaps the burglar was unsure if they imagined it. I tiptoed over to the torch and picked it up. Its weight felt reassuring in my hand. Suddenly Rachel stirred.

'What are you doing?' she asked, looking at me with bleary eyes.

I put a finger to my lips to silence her.

'I think someone's in the house,' I whispered.

The intruder heard this. Suddenly there was a scurry of footfalls heading back the way they had come. I ran for the door and stepped out into the dark landing. I flicked on the light switch beside our door. The brightness of the light burned my eyes. The sound of the footfalls was already heading down the stairs. I gave chase.

Our intruder must have been quick on their feet because when I reached the top of the stairs they were not in view downstairs. Instead, I could hear them on the wooden floor of the kitchen, heading for the back door.

I ran so fast that I nearly fell down the last four stairs. As I turned the corner toward the kitchen, there was a loud knock like someone had run into the back door. I flew to the kitchen door and flicked on the lights. At first I could see no one. Then I spotted Mojo. He was stood at his water bowl, his mouth wet.

'Jesus. Was that you, Mojo?' I said in a sigh of relief. Then I felt a chill run down my spine strong enough to make me shiver. Although it was possible that Mojo could have been responsible for the footsteps I had followed, he was fast enough on his feet that was for sure, and could maybe even have caused the thud on the back door, but there was no way on Earth he could have been the one turning our bedroom door knob.

'Mummy! Daddy!' The shout came from upstairs. It was Izzy. I knew at that moment that Mojo had unwittingly led me in the wrong direction. The intruder had not come downstairs at all. He was in my six-year-old daughter's room. Fear left me at that instant and rage took over. I flew back to the stairs. I climbed them in three giant bounds. I was on the landing when I saw Rachel coming out of our room. I ran past her, holding my hand up for her to wait there. I ran to Izzy's door. Anna opened her door, which was opposite Izzy's. She looked half-awake.

'What's going on?' she said.

'Get back in your room!' I screamed at her, more aggressively than I had intended, but my body was surging with adrenaline. Anna went wide-eyed and then slammed her door.

I raised the torch in the air above my head and grabbed the doorknob. I pushed the door open and entered the room in one push. I looked at Izzy's bed. It was empty. I felt like my heart was about to explode. I turned and saw her stood by her window looking out. I lowered the torch and ran to her, swooping her up in my arms and holding her tightly.

'What's wrong, baby?' I said, kissing her hair.

'The men with hoods,' her words made me spin round. I was searching her room for signs of the intruder or, by her use of the word men rather than man, the intruders.

'Where are they, honey?' I asked, unable to see anyone in the room.

'In our garden,' she said.

I spun back to the window and peered out into the darkness. The only thing I could make out was the chicken wire fence that Bill and I had erected earlier.

'Where?' I asked, noticing Rachel was now at our side.

Izzy looked out of the window and frowned.

'Oh,' she said, confused. 'They must have gone.'

Rachel saw how tightly I was holding on to Izzy. She gently eased up my grasp and took her off me. She took our daughter back to bed. I kept peering out of the window, staring into the darkness, looking for any trace of the 'men' that Izzy had seen, assuming that they were our intruders.

'It was probably just a bad dream,' Rachel said, tucking Izzy back in her bed.

'I was awake and looking out of the window,' the six-year-old protested.

'Maybe you thought you were awake,' Rachel said in a soothing tone while stroking her hair. 'Perhaps you've started sleepwalking.' Rachel turned to me. 'Maybe that's what you heard?'

I nodded, though I didn't entirely believe this. Anna had been prone to sleepwalking when she was younger, but had long since stopped. Izzy had never shown any of the signs of following suit.

'If so,' Rachel continued, 'we really need to make sure that hole is safe.'

'What hole?' Izzy asked, sounding like she was starting to drift off again. I stepped away from the window, unable to see anyone, and walked over to her bedside. I bent over and kissed her forehead.

'Oh, nothing to worry about, princess,' I said gently. 'You go back to sleep.'

'Okay, Daddy,' she said and rolled over.

I took Rachel's hand and led her out of the room. I pushed the door to and stopped in the landing.

'It could have been her walking around,' I said, thinking about it rationally. 'But the hole is secure enough, plus we don't keep the keys in the doors, so it's unlikely she'd get out of the house.'

Rachel nodded, and the looked down at my hand. I was still holding the torch, my knuckles white from gripping it. She smirked and shook her head.

'My hero,' she said and kissed me gently on the lips. 'Let's get back to bed.'

I was about to follow her to the bedroom when I heard the faint sound of sobbing coming from Anna's room.

'I'll be there in a minute,' I said and pointed to Anna's door. Rachel nodded and walked down the landing. I stepped over to Anna's room and knocked gently on the door.

'Come in,' she responded, her voice shaky.

I opened the door and stepped in the room. She was sat up on her bed rubbing her eyes with tissues to try to hide the fact that she had been crying. I felt instantly guilty, the harshness of my words earlier had made her cry. Seeing her like that reminded me of when she was little, the way she would sit there and sob silently when she was told off. She never cried out loud, she never shouted back, she would just sit there crying quietly and looking ashamed. I walked across the clutter on the floor and sat on the bed next to her.

'What's up, Dad?' she asked, trying to sound perky.

'Oh, nothing much. We think Izzy might have started your old tricks,' I said.

'Sleepwalking?' she asked.

'Yes,' I said, 'but I thought it was someone else in the house. Like a burglar or something. That's why I shouted at you. I just wanted you to be safe.'

'Okay,' she said with a little smile.

'I'm sorry I upset you,' I said. I leant over and hugged her and gave her a kiss on the cheek. She pretended to rub it off in disgust.

'Eww! Dad!' she said, then looked at me and kissed me back on the cheek. 'It really is okay, Dad.'

'What is?' I asked.

'That you yelled at me,' she said. 'You were just trying to protect us.'

I smiled and stroked her hair.

'Well, that's my job,' I said, then laughed and puffed out my chest. 'Super Dad to the rescue.'

Anna laughed and kissed me on the cheek again.

'You are,' she said. 'Because you'd never let any one hurt us.'

I kissed her forehead.

'No, I never would.'

Anna smiled at me.

'Get back to sleep, kiddo,' I said. getting up and walking back to the door. 'I've got something to show you in the morning.'

CHAPTER SEVEN

'Mojo did that?' Anna asked, looking from behind the fence, in disbelief, at the hole.

'I don't think so entirely,' I said. 'I think the ceiling had caved in a little down there and all the earth that had been packed down on top of it had started to shift. I think maybe Mojo noticed this and just kept digging.'

'Wow,' she said. Unless you have, or have had, a teenage daughter, I don't think you'll be able to appreciate how wonderful it is to leave them speechless, if only for a few minutes.

It was nine o'clock Sunday morning. We'd had breakfast early and Rachel had taken Izzy off to her dance class as was the routine. Princess Izzy had recently decided she wanted to be a princess and a ballerina, not to mention a vet and a builder. After they'd left, I'd asked Anna to come out into the garden so that I could show her the hole.

'I need you to stay away from this part of the garden though,' I warned her. 'At least until I know how safe it is. If you're out here with your sister I need you to make sure she stays away, and Mojo, too, for that matter.'

At the mention of his name the Jack Russell came running over, his tail wagging with its usual enthusiasm. He seemed all right after his adventure the previous evening. I thought he'd just bruised his leg. Rachel, though, insisted that she would take him to the vets on Monday just to be sure.

'You went down there?' Anna asked.

'Yeah,' I said. 'It was the only way to get Mojo out, and we couldn't leave him down there, could we?'

'What's it like down there?' she asked.

'It looks kind of like an old church,' I said, still unable to think of a better description, 'only without windows or pews.'

'Sounds spooky,' Anna said. Then her eyes glinted with a trace of smile. 'And cool.'

She had reached that age where spooky things had stopped being just plain scary and become in some way interesting, the age where you like the feeling of being scared, where you enjoy hearing ghost stories or watching horror movies.

'Yeah, it's certainly interesting,' I replied, 'and quite exciting that it's in our garden.'

'Can I go down there?' This I was not expecting.

I shook my head.

'Uh-uh,' I said. 'No way. Your mother would kill me.'

She looked up at me with her beautiful big brown eyes that had always been able to get whatever they wanted out of me.

'Certainly not until I know it's safe,' I said, backtracking a little, 'and not until there's a better way to get down there than shimmying down a rope while Mr Jenson holds it.'

We went back inside and Anna started up the computer, probably to tell everyone on Facebook about the secret chamber under her house. I prayed to God I wouldn't be inundated with teenagers all wanting to go down there.

'Hey, honey? Perhaps it's best if we don't tell too many people about it yet,' I said as a preemptive strike. She looked a little disappointed.

'At least until you've been down there yourself,' I said.

As I expected, this made her eyes sparkle with excitement.

'Okay, dad,' she said and then mimed zipping her mouth shut.

'Will you be okay for a few minutes if I just nip and see the neighbours?' I asked.

'Uh huh,' she said, already engrossed in what she was doing on the computer.

It was yet another warm day as I walked the short distance up the crescent to Number 2. The sun was rising quickly. The front lawns of the houses on the crescent were all well-kept, with fairly expensive cars in the drive. Number 2 was the exception to this rule. The lawn was not messy, but the grass was considerably longer than the others. Ours would probably look the same in a few weeks due to my lack of interest in gardening. My rule was that if I could still see Mojo's legs then the grass was okay for another week. The driveway held a couple of older cars, a red Ford Fiesta that had seen better days and a Volvo 340. There was also a battered old VW camper van, not one of the classics but one of the eighties models. It had been decorated with a few daisies painted under the front windscreen.

I walked up the path to the front door and rang the bell. I looked at my watch and saw that it was still only half nine, far too early to get a response from any self-respecting student on a Sunday. I decided that if there was no answer in a few minutes I would not ring the bell again; instead I would come back later. Just as I thought this, the door was opened. I was greeted by a well-dressed man probably in his mid twenties. He was wearing chinos and a white cotton short sleeve shirt. He had glasses and a thick crop of wiry brown hair that I could see he needed to use a lot of products on to gain some semblance of control over.

'Can I help you?' he said in an accent that had a slight Birmingham twang to it.

I held out my hand.

'Hi,' I said as he took my hand and shook. 'My name's Dan Martin. I live at Number 5.'

'Oh yes, of course,' he said. 'I thought I'd seen you around. I'm Paul West.'

'Nice to meet you, Paul,' I said. 'I was wondering if you could help me with something, if you have a few minutes.'

'Sure,' he said, stepping aside and motioning me into the house. 'Please come in.'

The house was still decorated in the same magnolia our house had been when we moved in. This was a rental property after all. They all seemed to be decorated like that these days. It was tidier than I ever remembered any of my student houses being. In the living room there was a large leather sofa and a couple of leather swivel chairs. There was an enormous television and an array of games consoles. Also there was a bookcase that spanned the entire wall; it was full to bursting with large hard back volumes. As I looked at it, Paul laughed.

'What's really bad is we have another three that size upstairs.'

He motioned me to sit down. I sank into the big leather sofa. He sat on one of the swivel chairs opposite me.

'So how can I help, Mr Martin?' he asked.

'I was told that a couple of you guys were archaeology research students.'

He nodded.

'Rick and I are both working towards our PhDs in archaeology.'

'Well, last night my dog uncovered a hole in my garden that led into some kind of underground chamber.'

Paul leant forward. I had caught his interest.

'Some part of the old hospital?' he said, resting his elbows on his knees and in turn his head in his hands.

I shook my head.

'No, it seems much older than that,' I said. 'It looks more like an underground church.'

Paul sat back in his chair and looked contemplative for a few moments then turned his head back towards the door.

'Rick?' he shouted.

'What?' came the muffled reply from upstairs.

'Get down here!' Paul shouted.

A few moments later there was the sound of heavy footfalls on the stairs. The young man who entered was tall and well built. His shoulders nearly scraped the doorframe as he came in. He looked more like I remembered students looking, in scruffy jeans and a faded black T-shirt. His hair was almost to his shoulders and he had a good few days of stubble on his face.

'What's up?' he said, entering the room. He then noticed me and put up a hand in a wave. 'Hi. Number 5, right?'

I stood up and shook his hand.

'Actually my name's Dan.'

He sat down on the sofa next to me. Paul retold what I had told him. Rick listened intently, a smile creeping in the corners of his mouth. I could tell they were both excited by the prospect. It was obvious why; it is rare these days that major archaeological discoveries are made, especially not in your neighbour's garden. They were thinking of the significance it could have for their research. Rick turned to me.

'Is it safe down there?' he asked.

'It was a little dicey getting down there,' I admitted, 'but once I was down there the structure seemed sturdy enough.' I left out my encounter with the well, still telling myself that it was a creation of my own imagination.

'Has Thom still got that spelunking gear in his van?' Paul asked Rick.

'I presume so,' Rick said, then realised that Paul wanted him to find out. 'I'll go ask,' he said, jumping to his feet and leaving the room.

Paul turned to me.

'Our other housemate Thom is into spelunking.'

'What happened to calling it potholing?' I asked. It showed my age a little. The terms potholing and caving were quickly being replaced by the cooler-sounding word, spelunking.

'Yeah, he has loads of gear. Ropes, winches, rope ladders. We might be able to figure out a safer way to get down into it.'

I looked at my watch. I'd been out of the house for about half an hour now. I thought about Anna sat at home on her own. I knew she was safe enough, but you never stop being a father even as your kids get older.

'I better get home,' I said, standing up.

'We'll see what Thom has in his van and then pop over this afternoon and have a look if that's okay?' Paul said, getting to his feet to show me out.

'Tomorrow would be better for me, me and the girls have the day off,' I said.

'Okay. Tomorrow afternoon it is then,' Paul replied.

'That's great,' I said. 'I'm as curious as you are.'

I walked back to the house. The sun was getting hotter. I waved at Mikkala and Leo who were getting out of Laura's car carrying shopping bags. The little boy looked happy and excited. He came running over to me.

'Hello, Mr Martin!' he yelled, waving as he approached me.

'Hi, Leo,' I said, waiting for him to reach me. I bent down to speak to him. Mikkala waved and then headed inside with the bags.

'How are you today, Leo?' I asked.

'I went to the shops with Mikkala,' he said, in the way that only a four-year-old can, where they answer a question you didn't ask rather than the one you did.

'Did you buy anything nice?' I asked.

'Ice cream, ice cream, ice cream!' he chanted whilst doing a little dance.

'Yummy,' I said.

Mikkala came back out of the house and headed over to us.

'Leo,' she said when she arrived, 'Mummy wants you in the kitchen.'

'Ice cream!' the boy yelled then ran off inside.

'Did you have a good night?' I asked Mikkala.

'It was okay for a while,' she replied. 'Then there was a lot of fighting, so I got a taxi home.'

'Probably the best idea,' I said. I had seen first-hand how bad Darton could be when trouble kicked off.

'I will never understand why you English get so drunk and go out looking for a fight,' she said. I suddenly felt a little ashamed. I was never that kind of person myself, but I could understand why it looked like we were all that way to a foreigner.

'I don't understand it either,' I said, shaking my head.

'It does not happen back home,' she said.

'It's not the best part of our culture,' I said. 'We're not all like that.'

Mikkala laughed.

'Oh I know that, Mr Martin,' she said. 'It is just the, how you say, fucking idiots.'

Now I laughed.

'That sounds about right,' I said.

'Will Izzy be coming around to play to today?' she asked.

'I have no idea,' I said. 'She's out at her dance lesson at the moment, but I'm not sure what she's doing after that. We'll give you a call if she wants to come over.'

'Okay, well we'll be in all day,' she said. 'See you later.'

'Bye,' I said as she wandered off. I was glad to see Leo looking so cheerful. He had obviously forgotten the nightmare. It made me think of Izzy and the events last night. The more I had thought about it, the more sense it made that she had indeed been sleepwalking and that it was a combination of her and the dog I had heard roaming the house, not burglars. Still, something jarred me, how awake and with it she had seemed when she was stood at the window.

Anna had started sleepwalking as soon as she could climb out of her cot. She would get up in the early hours of the morning and wander downstairs. We would hear her talking to herself in the kitchen, the lights out. Even then, though, we had always been able to tell she was asleep. Her eyes were open, yes, but they were vacant, and her voice was slurred and distant.

Once, just after Izzy was born, we heard the baby crying in the night, but the sound was coming from downstairs, not in the room with us. Both Rachel and I had leapt out of bed and run down stairs. We found Anna sat on the sofa holding Izzy in her arms, staring into space. When we asked what she was doing, she answered in her usual sleep voice.

'We're watching *Lion King*.'

The television was not on. Anna was just watching a blank screen.

The worst time, though, had been the last time it really happened, just before Anna turned ten. She somehow managed to unlock the door and leave the house, something she had never done before. Neither of us heard her leave. I got up for a pee in the night and saw that her bedroom door was open and that she was not in her bed. At first, I didn't worry as this had always been a common occurrence. As I headed down the stairs to find her, I saw the front door was wide open. I cannot find the right words to describe the terror I felt at that moment. All I know is that I only ever felt that scared once more in my life, but I will get to that soon enough.

In blind panic, I screamed to Rachel that Anna had wandered off. She began to cry, waking Izzy, who at two had no idea what was going on. Without even stopping to put on my shoes, I grabbed my car keys and headed out of the open door. I was only wearing my jogging bottoms, and I was barefoot. It was a cold November night. However, even if it had been the middle of summer, I think the fear I felt inside would have kept me cold.

I didn't even know where to look. She could have gone in any direction. Then I remembered that it was common for sleepwalkers to walk places they knew well when awake, so I started to drive towards her school.

Sure enough, halfway there I spotted her walking down the side of the road. She was only wearing her nightie but had her Barbie backpack slung over her shoulder. She had one hand up in the air slightly. It looked like she was holding hands with someone who wasn't there. I pulled up slightly ahead of her and ran to her. I threw my arms around her and lifted her up.

'Anna! What are you doing?' I said, tears running from my eyes with relief.

'Mummy was just taking me to school,' she said.

I patted her back and carried her to the car. By the time I had put her in the front seat she was properly asleep.

From that night on I would always hide the keys after I locked up at night.

I got back to the house and opened the front door. As I did so I heard Anna gasp. She poked her head through the door into the dining room. She looked shocked when she saw me.

'Where have you been?' she asked. There was suspicion in her voice. I shut the door and walked over to her.

'To see the neighbours, like I said.' I was confused.

'You've only just got back?' she said and I could see that she had started to tremble.

'Yes,' I said, hugging her. 'Why?'

'Then who came in fifteen minutes ago and went straight upstairs?'

I looked down at her and she looked up. Not at me, but at the ceiling above my head.

CHAPTER EIGHT

I told Anna to wait downstairs while I checked it out. She was shaking like a leaf. I saw the walking stick I had used when I sprained my ankle last year, in the corner of the hall. I grabbed it. It was not as heavy as the metal torch, but it was a better weapon than nothing. I said to Anna that if I didn't come down in a few minutes or if she heard any kind of struggle she was to run next door and get Bill. She nodded silently.

I took the stairs slowly, careful not to make any sound. The first floor was where all of our bedrooms were. When we had moved in we had considered letting the girls have this floor for their rooms and having a guest room. Instead we took the room down here with the en suite. We were worried about not being able to hear Izzy if she had any problems in the night.

The first room I came to was the family bathroom. I pushed open the door slowly. There was no one in there, I even checked behind the shower curtain, feeling foolish as I did. That was the sort of thing that the foolhardy hero would do in a horror movie, only to be greeted by the masked killer and his knife. I, on the other hand, was greeted by an empty bath.

I carried on down the hall to mine and Rachel's room. It, too, was empty. I checked the wardrobes—nothing but clothes, far more of Rachel's than mine. I didn't bother looking under the bed, knowing that we had so much stuff stored under it that no one could possibly have got under it.

I walked on down the landing and entered Anna's room. There was no way that anyone could have found somewhere to hide in all that mess. Izzy's room was clear, too. I was guessing that Anna must have imagined the sound.

Then I heard it, the scurrying above my head. I ran back to the staircase up to the third floor. Up there was our guest room with en suite, the largest room in the house by a long way and the one we had considered taking as our own. The other room up here was a study. I used it for marking and planning my lessons, and Rachel used it for writing.

I raced up the stairs and swung open the door to the study. There was no one visible. I crouched down and peered under the heavy antique desks. There was nothing to be seen.

I then moved quickly across the landing, to the guest room. As you opened the door, the en suite was to the right. I poked my head inside and saw no one hiding in there. I proceeded into the bedroom; it was hot in here. Warm air rises, and this room got the best of the morning sun. I scanned the room and saw nothing amiss. I checked the wardrobe; it was empty except for some extra bedding. I looked over to the bed; with the way that the covers draped all the way to the floor, there was no way of seeing under it without getting closer, but it was clear that something was not right. Rachel prided herself on her skill at making a bed. In our entire marriage, it was one job that she had never left me to do. Her reasoning was that if I had done it, I would have done it wrong, meaning she would have to redo it. It made more sense for her to do it in the first place.

Rachel had made this bed up and as yet not a soul had slept in this room, though we were planning to have my mother over for a few weeks in the summer.

The way the covers draped to the floor should have looked immaculate, but they didn't. They were all crumpled up at the foot of the bed on one side, as if someone had moved them to get under the bed.

I could hear my own breathing as I crept across the room. I inched slowly closer to the bed. I knelt down near where the covers had been moved. I knew I should have lifted them with my free hand, ready to strike with the stick when I needed to, but I was too afraid. Instead, I kept a little distance between myself and the bed and used the stick to slowly lift the covers.

There was the sudden sound of movement from under the bed and then it leapt for me.

'Fuck!' I screamed as I fell backward. I heard the front door slam as Anna went running to Bill and Mary's next door, while I was left flat on my back with Mojo vigourously licking my face.

By the time Bill burst through my front door with a cricket bat in his hand I was sat on the bottom step stroking Mojo. Mary and Anna were stood out on the drive way.

'Jesus Christ! Dan!' Bill said, relaxing and putting the bat down. 'Anna said someone had broken in.'

'Yeah,' I said, still stroking the dog. 'My fault. I told her to come and get you if she heard a struggle. The bloody dog jumped out from under the bed and scared me half to death.'

Bill laughed.

'Wow, that dog has been causing a lot of trouble lately.' he said, leaning over to rub Mojo's head. The dog in turn licked Bill's hand.

Bill walked over to the door and shouted.

'All clear!'

Anna came running in and threw herself towards me, almost crushing poor Mojo, who wriggled free and ran off to the kitchen.

'I thought they'd got you,' she said, kissing me on the cheek.

'No, it was only Mojo,' I said with a grin.

She looked confused.

'There was no one up there?' she asked.

'Nope, just the dog.'

'But I heard someone come in and walk up the stairs.'

I stroked her hair.

'No, baby,' I said gently. 'It must have been Mojo, maybe he ran into the door and then went up the stairs. He was under the bed in the spare room.'

She stood up and shook her head.

'No,' she said. 'I heard the door.' She walked over and pushed the front door shut. She pointed at the latch. 'That sound, when it closes, that click. Then I heard footsteps going up the stairs. Not like Mojo, like a person.'

I looked at Bill, who shrugged.

'Anna,' I said, 'there was no one up there. You must've made a mistake.'

'I know what I heard, Dad,' she said angrily then stormed past me and ran to her room.

I smiled apologetically at Bill and Mary.

'She hates it when she thinks someone is calling her a liar,' I said, excusing my daughter's tantrum.

'Don't we all?' Bill said.

'I'll go and talk to her,' Mary said, patting me on the shoulder as she passed me. I stood up and walked to the kitchen. Bill followed me. We stepped into the garden, the sun had not risen to its full height yet and a long shadow of the house stretched across the lawn. Stopping just before the temporary fence Bill and I had erected the previous night. The chicken wire glinted in the sun. I took out my cigarettes and lit one. I offered one to Bill. He put his hand up.

'Only when I've had a few beers,' he said. 'She'll be fine, probably just heard the dog like you said.'

'Yeah,' I replied. 'It's the only thing I can think of. Damn mutt did it to me last night. I thought there was someone in the house. Turned out it was a combination of Mojo running round and Izzy sleepwalking.'

At mention of his name, Mojo came trotting over to me. He rubbed his head at my legs until I bent down and stroked him. It was one of his little quirks, so often he would behave like a cat, rubbing around your legs until you gave him the attention he wanted. Of course, the movement was not as delicate as a cat would have been. Once he was satisfied he wandered off to get a drink.

'Well, you can see how easily it's done then,' Bill said. 'Let me tell you, when you're a copper and you spend all of your days looking for criminals, the slightest noise at night has you convinced you're about to be murdered in your bed.'

'Yeah,' I said. 'It didn't help that Izzy had some kind of dream where she thought that there were men with hoods in our garden. She was convinced she'd seen them out of the window.' I smiled at Bill. I saw the frown on his face, and it troubled me a lot. 'What's wrong?'

'Oh, it's probably just a coincidence,' he said, trying to make light of whatever he was frowning about.

'No seriously, Bill. What's wrong?' I asked.

'Well, doesn't that remind you of someone else's nightmare?'

'Leo,' I said. I hadn't made that connection, but this could offer a possible explanation. 'Maybe the older girls were telling ghost stories at the barbecue yesterday.'

'Perhaps?' Bill said, but he was still frowning.

'There's something else isn't there?'

'Last night, Mary got up for a glass of water and said that she saw a couple of kids in long coats and hoodies walking across the flower beds on the island out front.'

Could it be possible that these were who Izzy had seen? After all, at six years old, if she had seen a group of teenagers in hoods she would have called them men as they would be so much bigger than her. It was one thing them walking over the flower beds out front of the houses, but why had they been in my back garden? Anger gripped me a little, it felt like a violation of the sanctuary of my home. Then I thought about how I had not seen anyone; it seemed unlikely that a group of kids could have moved quickly enough for me to have not seen any trace of them.

'That's quite a coincidence,' I said with a nervous laugh.

'Yeah,' Bill said. 'I think maybe we should consider starting up a neighbourhood watch scheme around here.'

'Thing is I looked out of the window just after she said she was watching them, and I didn't see anything. I work with kids everyday, Bill, and I don't know any teenagers who can move that fast.'

Bill laughed.

'You've obviously never spent any time chasing kids who were up to no good,' he said with a smile. 'They can be quick little buggers when they want to be. Besides, if they were up the far end of your garden they could have just jumped the fence and hidden behind it or even run into the field. At night you wouldn't be able to see them within a few yards, it's so bloody black out there, and if they were nearer this end they could have come towards the house, then you wouldn't have been able to see them either.'

I thought about this. It was certainly a reasonable explanation of what had happened. The only thing was, how had they known to hide at that exact moment? Izzy had her night light on all night, so it wasn't like they saw that light come on. Unless they'd seen me put the kitchen light on a few moments earlier. Yet Izzy was acting like they were still there when I had rushed into her room.

'Don't worry about it too much, though,' Bill said reassuringly. 'We don't get many bad kids round here. They might have just been exploring, don't suppose they meant any harm.'

'I hope so, Bill.'

After that, Bill asked if I'd been to see the students at Number 2. I told him that I had, and that they were excited to get a look at the chamber. I told him that they were coming round this afternoon, and that the other housemate had lots of caving gear so he might be able to find a safer way of getting in and out of it. Bill laughed.

'Good,' he said. 'I don't think my arms could hold on that rope for every one to get down there.'

Mary came out into the garden followed by a sheepish looking Anna. She walked over to me.

'Sorry I yelled, Daddy,' she said. It was funny that whenever she was apologising for something or trying to get something she wanted she would still call me Daddy, the rest of the time now she would say Dad.

'It's okay, baby,' I said, hugging her. 'I wasn't calling you a liar. I was just saying you must have made a mistake.'

'I guess,' she said, sounding unsure. 'I'm so sure that I heard the door.'

'I'm just saying that it's easy to hear something and imagine it was something else. I did it last night, remember?'

She frowned slightly.

'Maybe,' she said. She hugged herself as though she was cold, despite how warm it was. 'It was just a bit creepy.'

I rolled my eyes.

'I don't think ghosts haunt brand new houses. In fact I don't think there are ghosts at all.'

She looked at me.

'How do you know?' she asked.

'Because no one has ever proved they exist. There's been no real measurable data. If they existed there would be some far more credible evidence than badly shot video and photographs of dust.'

Suddenly Izzy ran into the garden, still wearing her tutu she wore for her ballet class.

'I can pirate!' she yelled excitedly and began spinning quickly and unsteadily on her tiptoes, chanting loudly as she did. 'Pirate, pirate, pirate!'

Rachel stepped out into the garden.

'It's called a pirouette honey, not a pirate,' she said. 'Hey, everyone?' she added, noticing Bill and Mary.

CHAPTER NINE

The rest of Sunday was fairly uneventful. We ate lunch and then watched a film as a family. This was always a major task, finding something that everyone would enjoy was always difficult. As always, though, if in doubt put on a Disney film.

After that, I went out for a smoke. I sat in the garden looking at the hole. The chicken wire fence around it reminded me of one of those old war films like the great escape.

Rachel came out with a glass of wine and sat opposite me.

'I thought you were going to give those things up?' she said, smiling and pointing at my cigarette.

'I am,' I said. 'When I'm ready.'

'She laughed and watched the sky above her.

'There goes another flying pig,' she said. She looked over to the hole. 'Did you get any luck from the archeology students?'

I nodded.

'They seemed fascinated,' I said. 'They wanted to come and have a look at it this afternoon. I told them tomorrow was better.'

'They could have come today,' she said. 'It's not like we've done a lot.'

'I know,' I said. 'It's just after last night I just wanted to relax.'

'Amen to that,' she said, raising her glass in a mock toast before taking a sip.

That night was peaceful. Nothing disturbed our sleep. I got about eight hours straight of sleep, more than I usually managed. When I woke the next day I felt refreshed. The stresses of Saturday seemed a long time ago. It was Monday morning and I didn't have to go to work. God bless teachers unions and their love of one-day strikes.

I spent the morning playing with Izzy, then took Anna into town to buy some new clothes. She didn't need them, but I felt like I owed it to her. Twice in the last two days I had upset her. After she had spent a small fortune on two pairs of jeans, a top and some trainers we went home to eat.

About half twelve, just after we had finished our lunch, the doorbell rang. I answered. There on my doorstep stood Paul and Rick, both carrying bags on their shoulders. Behind them stood another young man, I guessed that this must have been Thom the spelunker, owner of the camper van. He was tall and muscular, I could tell from his physique that he did a lot of sport. From his spiky, bleach blond hair and his attire of long shorts, vest and wooden bead necklace, I could guess that one of his favourite was probably surfing.

'Hey guys,' I said. 'Come on in.'

'Hi, Mr Martin., Paul said politely. 'It's probably best if you unlock your gate, we have a lot of stuff to bring in and we don't want to drag it through your house and make a mess.'

'Sure thing, Paul,' I said. 'And please, I'm a secondary school teacher, only my pupils refer to me as Mr Martin. Just call me Dan.'

'Okay, Dan,' he said awkwardly.

'Head over to the gate and I'll go round and unlock it,' I said.

'Thanks,' said Rick.

They wandered off towards the gate at the side of the house that led to our back garden. I walked through the house to the kitchen, where Rachel was loading the dishwasher and Izzy was sitting on the worktop, still in her tutu.

'The archaeologists are here,' I said. 'Can you keep the kids and Mojo out of the way for a while?'

Rachel looked up at me.

'Sure, we'll take a drive over to the park in town and take Mojo with us,' she said.

'Great, I'll see you later then,' I said opening the back door.

'Just all of you be careful,' Rachel said. I could see the concern on her face. I walked back over to her and took her face in my hands.

'We'll be fine,' I said before kissing her on the forehead.

'Get a room!' came Anna's voice from the doorway.

'Hey, honey, you and Mum and Izzy are going to take Mojo to play in the park,' I said, letting go of Rachel.

I left Rachel to explain the details as I went out into the garden. The sun was now high enough that nowhere in the garden offered any shade. I walked to the side of the house and unfastened the gate, Paul was waiting in front, Rick behind him and Thom bringing up the rear holding two very large bags.

'Come on in,' I said, stepping aside. They entered the garden and walked to the centre of the patio. Standing near the table, Thom set the two bags on the ground.

'They look heavy,' I said to him.

'Yeah, about three stone each,' he said in a soft, well-spoken voice that didn't suit his appearance.

'Do any of you guys want a drink before we start?' I asked.

They all said yes so I went back in the kitchen to fetch a six-pack of Cokes out. I was greeted by Anna,who was practically drooling at the door. So much so that she didn't even notice me trying to get in; her eyes were fixed in the direction of Thom. I knocked on the glass and she jumped and stepped back, opening the door as she did.

'See something you like?' I said, teasing her. She blushed and started shaking her head.

'No. I was just interested in what they were doing,' she stammered.

I walked over to the fridge and pulled out the cold cans of Coke. I walked back to the door and smiled at Anna.

'Have fun at the park,' I said as I stepped out of the door.

'Yeah, okay,' she said, shutting the door behind me and resuming her place up against the glass. Hormones were beginning to take over my little girl. I was terrified and not prepared for this stage at all.

I walked back to the table and handed round the drinks. They all opened their cans and took big gulps, then Paul set his can down on the table.

'Is that the hole?' he asked, pointing at the fence that Bill and I had made.

'Sure is,' I said. 'Want to take a look?'

I led them over to the fence. The hole itself was only just visible from this point.

'I'm not sure how safe the ground around it is,' I told them. 'I'm sure it's fine, but if you want to step over one at a time and take a look, I think that's the best idea for now.'

They all nodded. Paul looked to Rick who motioned that he could go first if he wanted. Paul stepped over the chicken wire and knelt down at the edge of the hole. He looked inside, then pulled a torch from the bag he was carrying, He switched it on and shone the beam down into the darkness below. I could see from his face that he was impressed. He put the torch back in the bag and pulled out one of those laser tape measures. He pointed that down the hole for a few seconds until it beeped, Then he looked at the digital display on the side of it. He got up and hopped back over the fence.

'It's thirty-six feet down to the bottom,' he said, showing the readout to Thom.

Rick took out his own torch and went over next to check it out. He was more vocal in his amazement as he looked down into the chamber.

'Wow,' he said, looking back at us. 'This is awesome.'

He leapt back and let Thom take his turn. He looked down with a torch then reached in an arm and seemed to feel around the inside of the chamber. He pulled out his dust-covered arm and brushed it off.

'Looks like the stonework around the hole is secure enough,' he said as he came back. 'I can't feel any loose bricks or soil seeping through. I think it'll take all of our weight around it,' he said before jumping over the fence. He then took a few steps across the lawn and got down on his knees and began thumping my lawn with his hand. I was a little confused.

'What are you doing?' I asked.

'Oh,' he said, realising how his behaviour must have looked. 'I'm just seeing how firm the soil here is. I have a fifty-foot rope ladder in one of those bags. If the ground is solid enough, I could drive in a series of pegs to hold it in place, and that would take our weight as long as we all went down one-by-one.'

This made sense. It would also certainly beat shimmying down Bill's old rope.

'Once we have it checked out,' Thom continued, 'I could erect a scaffold down there for people to get up and down, That would be a lot safer.'

Thom and Rick set to work setting up the rope ladder. Paul asked if he could just do a quick taped interview with me about how I'd found the chamber. So I went inside with him to do this.

I explained to him all about how our dog had been digging in that spot constantly for the few weeks we had lived here and about the events of the previous night, about Mojo falling in the hole, my rescue of him and my investigation of the chamber. I told him again how it had reminded me of a church. I explained that I had even thought that there was an altar down there until, thanks to Bill, I had realised that it had been a covered well.

'A well?' Paul asked.

'Yeah,' I replied. 'It seemed that it was older than the rest of the chamber.'

'In what way?'

'Well, the rest of the chamber seems like it's made of well-smoothed sandstone, whereas the well is made of various stones, that haven't been smoothed. The only smooth thing is the slab that's resting on top of it.'

Paul switched off the tape recorder.

'Thanks,' he said. 'I can't wait to get a look down there, and I really want to see the well.'

'Why?' I asked. I would have thought the huge underground chamber, covered up for God only knew how long, would have been more interesting than the old well.'

'It just seems strange,' he said. 'Wells weren't usually built inside of basements, for fear of them flooding. The fact that you say it looks older than the rest of the chamber suggests that the land level was lower here when the well was built, and that this chamber was built around it. It's fascinating.'

Paul's eyes lit up as he talked. I could see in them his passion for his subject. It made me wish I had carried on into research. Maybe I would feel the same way when I talked to someone about the molecular structure of the human body; instead, I spent my days telling kids who weren't that interested what would happen if you put magnesium in water. When I could, I would show them the reaction created by a small amount, it would always lead to someone asking where they could get some, and me telling them they couldn't. I guessed they wanted to try the old block of magnesium down the toilet to see if they could destroy the whole of the schools plumbing. What they didn't know was that at university I had tried this one myself and nearly got myself thrown out in the process. The result, though impressive, was not as grand as I had expected. It didn't destroy the whole of the building's plumbing, it merely caused a lot of damage to that particular toilet.

Rick came in looking rather hot and sweaty.

'We have the ladder down, Dan,' he said. 'Do you have a couple of long extension leads?'

I told him that I did and that I'd bring them out. He smiled and went back outside. Paul followed him and I headed to the cupboard under the stairs and pulled out my two twenty-metre extension leads. I took them to the kitchen door.

'Will these do?' I shouted out to the guys who were stood near the hole. Rick ran over to me.

'Yeah, they're perfect,' he said. 'Can you plug one in here and attach the other one to it and see how far they stretch?'

I did so and walked over to the young men. There was still at least fifteen metres of the second one left to unwind when I reached them.

'That's awesome,' Thom said, taking them off me. He unwound it the rest of the way, then attached one from his bag and unwound that.

'What are they for?' I asked.

Thom rustled in one of his bag and pulled out a couple of large lamps, the kind that workmen would use off a generator when working on the electrics somewhere.

'These!' he said with a smile. 'Once we can get a scaffold up and get a generator down there we can set up enough to light the whole place, but these will give us enough light for now.'

I looked down at the rope ladder. It was made of much finer rope than Bill had brought last night, but as it was designed for caving, it must have been tough enough. The rungs themselves were made of aluminium, with a grip surface on them. They had secured it to my lawn using about eight of the biggest pegs I'd ever seen. These were not the sort of thing I'd experienced when I had been camping in the past.

'So, who wants to go first?' Rick asked.

I could see on all of their faces, even Thom who was not an archaeologist, that they all wanted to be the first down there, but none of them wanted to admit it.

'Maybe we should let Dan go first,' Thom said. 'It's his house after all.'

I liked the gesture, but felt bad for them as I had already seen what it was like down there. I decided what I thought was the best option.

'Why don't you go first, Thom? After all, this is your caving gear,' I said.

The others nodded, realising that this meant that neither of them would be able to claim they were the first.

'All right,' he said. 'I'll take the bag with the lamps in down on my back. When I get down there if you throw me down the extension lead I'll start setting them up.'

We all agreed this would be a good plan. I then decided to let Paul and Rick descend the rope ladder next. Paul let Rick go first, he took the extension leads down with him, tied to his bag, thinking this would be a safer option than to risk throwing them down and Thom missing them.

'Here goes,' Paul said as he approached the ladder. I could sense he was nervous. I was not sure whether it was because he was worried about using the ladder or if he was scared of going underground. Neither of these, though, were good fears for an archaeologist to have. He was going to spend much of his life doing things like this.

'I thought you archaeologists were only scared of snakes,' I said, joking about the fact that most of what I knew of the subject had come from watching Indiana Jones films.

'No, snakes don't bother me,' he said, laughing. 'Just heights. I'll be fine when I get down there.'

With that he took a deep breath and began to descend. As I looked down to keep an eye on his progress I could clearly see the floor below. Thom and Rick must have got a few of the lamps up and running.

When I saw Paul step off at the bottom he looked up and gave me a thumbs up, it was my turn to once more enter the chamber. At that moment I was excited by the prospect of finally getting some answers. All these months later, though, as I sit here in this comfortable but lonely room, I wish I had never seen the damned place.

CHAPTER TEN

It seemed smaller. That was my first impression of the chamber as I stepped off the ladder. The first time I had come down here, the night before, the place had looked almost never ending. Now that Thom and Rick had got five lamps set up, all pointing in different directions, the boundaries of the chamber could be seen.

'Wow,' Paul said next to me. 'I know you said it was big, but this is immense.'

'You should have seen it by the light of a torch,' I said.

He nodded, as if he understood how impressive the size would have seemed at the time.

A sixth lamp came to life, pointing directly towards the well. With the lamps being angled up from the floor, the beam created a vast dark shadow of the well onto the wall behind it. I felt a shudder run down my spine. I put it down to remembering the strange feelings I had the previous night on touching the unnaturally cold stones. In hindsight, though, I think my feelings were some kind of premonition. Part of me, the part I would have completely denied the existence of before, was telling me to leave the well alone.

Rick patted me on the back, and at his touch the feeling of dread dissipated and was instantly forgotten.

'Nice find, Dan,' he said, a broad smile across his face.

Paul came over and joined us.

'Indeed!' he agreed.

Thom was just looking around, taking in the atmosphere of the chamber. He pointed to the area above surrounding the hole.

'What do you make of that?' he said.

We all looked up to see where he was pointing. I, for one, could not see what he meant. I looked to the others. At first they seemed as dumbfounded as I felt. Then I saw realisation dawn on Rick's face.

'We're not the first people to find this,' he said, with a hint of disappointment in his voice.

'What do you mean?' asked Paul, still confused.

'The area around the hole is made of red brick, Thom said. 'Whereas the rest is made of sandstone.'

'Meaning at some point someone else found this chamber,' Rick added, 'then bricked it back up.'

'If so, they didn't document their find,' Paul said. 'Something like this would be common knowledge if they had.'

'Maybe it was when they built the hospital,' I said. 'That was a red brick building. Maybe some builder accidentally knocked through and then bricked up the hole without even looking.'

They considered what I was saying. They began to smile, this was an explanation they wanted to believe, it meant that we were still the first people to explore the site.

'That's probably what happened,' Rick said.

'It makes sense,' Paul added.

'Okay, let's go with that,' Thom said, sealing the deal.

'Any idea what it is yet?' I asked the two archaeologists.

Paul looked around, sizing the place up. Rick jumped in.

'It looks like an undercroft to me,' he said.

'What's an undercroft?' I asked, knowing that the word was somewhere in my memory but with all definition long forgotten.

'It's a church's basement!' he said. 'That's what the architecture suggests to me.'

'I thought a church basement was called a crypt?' Thom said, joining us.

'Only if there are bodies buried down there,' Paul replied, still looking around. 'There's no evidence of tombs or gravestones down here.'

'Right,' agreed Rick. 'Making it an undercroft, like any basement it would have just been used for storage.'

'It can't be an undercroft,' Paul said.

'Why not?' Rick asked, looking a little offended at being questioned.

'Look at the size of the place,' Paul said, pointing from one end to the other. 'There's no evidence of there ever having been a church up there, let alone one the size of a cathedral that would have had an undercroft this big.'

'Granted,' Rick said. 'But there's very little evidence of a hospital being up there, but we know damn well it was. Besides, they could have flattened the land when they built the hospital, destroying all evidence of the church.'

'Even in the 1800s when the hospital was built they didn't go around knocking down cathedrals,' Paul responded. 'As far as I'm aware, they never did.'

'Oh, that's rubbish!' Rick said, his temper beginning to flare. 'You know as well as I do that several cathedrals were destroyed during the dissolution.'

'Yes, but most were rebuilt, or at least some reference to their existence was noted on the site,' Paul argued.

I looked to Thom, who was watching them closely. He sensed it, too, there was an undercurrent of violence in their exchange of words. It felt like it could erupt at any moment. I felt a sense of unease. It brought back the memory of the panic I had felt down here on Saturday night. I looked over to the well, for a split second I felt the hairs on my arm raise, the way they often did when I was caught outside in a thunderstorm. I imagined some strange energy emanating from the well, spreading, like long cold fingers. I saw it burrowing into the heads of Paul and Rick, twisting their minds, filling them with rage. It would tighten its grip until one of them lashed out and attacked the other. I forced myself to look away from the well and back to the two young men arguing.

'Well, if it's not an undercroft, what the fuck is it, Paul?' Rick shouted, taking a step towards Paul. 'I mean architecturally it's a perfect example. Big, yes, but spot on. I know we'd have to do more work to find out for sure, but just looking at the stonework I'm pretty much convinced it was built sometime between 1066 and 1160 AD.'

Suddenly a thought popped into my head.

'A monastery!' I blurted out.

'What?' Paul said, turning to me. I could still see anger burning in his eyes.

'We live on Blackfriars Crescent,' I said calmly, trying to pacify the situation. 'It used to be called Blackfriars Lane. No one knows why, perhaps it's a reference to there being a monastery here.'

Paul looked at me, then to Rick, they nodded at each other, and at that moment the tension between them was gone. So, too, was my sense of the strange energy creeping across the room from the well. It remained buried in my memory until now as I piece together the events again.

'It could certainly have been the undercroft of an Abbey,' Paul said.

'That would explain the size,' Rick agreed.

'So many were destroyed during the dissolution that it's possible it could have been down here undisturbed since the 16th century,' Paul suggested.

'There were many monasteries built in Lincolnshire then,' Rick added.

'Benedictines?' Paul asked.

'Yeah, they were the only black-robed monks in the country at that time,' Rick said, grinning.

'This could be a really significant discovery,' Paul said.

With this solved, the two archaeologists began measuring the room with the laser. Rick did the actual measuring whilst Paul took notes. They also measured the size of the stones on the walls, and noted any interesting features. In all, their initial assessment of the undercroft took about forty-five minutes. During this time I stood and watched, as well as taking a closer look at the chamber.

I spotted Thom heading towards the well. I felt like I should warn him not to touch it. This would make me look like a madman, though, instead I followed him over there. He brushed the slab on top of the well with his fingers. His hand jerked back like he had been shocked.

'What's wrong?' I asked.

'It's cold,' he said. 'Really cold.'

This part, then, had not been my imagination. So what of my nausea and dizziness? Had that been real, too? I shook the thought off. I refused to let myself believe such nonsense. There had to be a rational explanation.

'I felt it last night,' I confessed. 'Why would it be so cold?'

'I'm not sure,' Thom answered. 'Maybe the cold air is coming up from below. Perhaps the water source is deep underground and frozen.'

I thought about this, but I knew that warm air rises, not cold, and that the deeper you go into the earth the warmer it gets. If we had been up in the highlands of Scotland in winter, I could perhaps have conceived of the water coming from a frozen source nearer the surface, but we were not. This was Lincolnshire in the middle of what was turning out to be a warm summer.

'I don't think so,' I said.

'Then I have no idea,' Thom replied.

He knelt down and examined the stones on the side. I could tell from the look on his face that these, too, were as cold as I remembered them, but this time he was expecting it and did not jerk back. He continued to stroke the stones. I continued to watch him, waiting for some sign of him feeling what I had felt. Instead, though, his eyes seemed to glaze over, as though he was deep in thought. He continued to caress the stones, his vacant eyes staring into space.

Something was happening to him, something I didn't understand. I felt like I should alert Paul and Rick, but I could not find my voice. The words stuck in my throat, almost choking me. I tried to turn to them and attract their attention by waving my hands, but my feet were rooted to the spot and my arms hung limply at my side. All I could do was watch as Thom stroked the rocks. His head tilted towards them, as though he was listening to them whisper to him. His eyes still fixed on nothing, but seeing something, of that I was certain. A smile began to creep onto his lips, a dark smile, the kind of smile worn by a cruel child torturing some defenceless animal.

'We're about done for today,' Paul's voice from behind me broke my paralysis and whatever spell was upon Thom. He shook his head and looked at me, confused, then the feeling of fear left me. I forgot having any sense of distrust of Thom or the well.

'We should try to get that slab off,' Rick said, joining us.

'What?' I asked.

'The slab on top of the well. See if we can find out how deep it is,' he replied.

I knew that this was a bad idea. Something in my subconscious was screaming at me to stop it from happening. I pushed my fear deep into myself. It was irrational and I was not the kind of man to put faith in the irrational; I only believed in what could be seen, measured and examined.

Thom walked over to one of his bags that was on the floor near the ladder. He bent down and came back with an enormous crowbar. There was an unusual gleam in his eyes

'Why do you have that?' Paul asked.

'Well, if I'm ever in a cave and a rock falls and blocks my way, I want to be able to at least try to move it,' he explained.

He slid the flat end of the crowbar under the slab. He looked at us all.

'Paul, you come and join me pushing on this,' he said and Paul nervously went over. You could tell from looking at Paul that he was not one for much in the way of physical activity. 'Rick, you and Dan pull the rock back as we push. Hopefully, we should be able to slide it far enough to get it off.'

On the count of three, we all did as he asked. He and Paul pushed down hard on the crowbar. Paul was straining so hard that a vein bulged above his right eye. Rick and I pulled at the slab with all our might. Nothing happened; it didn't move an inch.

'Everyone rest,' Thom said, letting go of the crowbar.

Paul put his hands on his knees and panted; Rick and I leant on the slab. Both of us had sweat on our brows. Thom was the only one of us who seemed unaffected by the effort of trying to move the slab. I felt again a sense of unease. Even considering the fact that he was in far better physical shape than the rest of us, he should have shown some signs of fatigue from the sheer effort of trying to move the slab, yet he hadn't even broken a sweat.

He knelt down in front of the well. He was examining the spot where he had placed the bar under the slab. He tried pushing it in further, it wouldn't go. He got up and wandered back to his bag. He brought out the mallet he had used to drive the pegs in the ground to hold the ladder. He hit the curved end of the crowbar hard with the mallet, it slid in a little further. He did the same again, and again, until it would go no deeper into the crack. Then he set down the mallet.

'All right, let's try again,' he said.

We did try again, and even though it felt like my muscles were about to snap away from my bones, the slab would not move. Eventually, Rick gave up pulling and slumped on the floor. Paul and I quickly followed suit.

'It's not going to move,' Rick said in a breathless voice.

'Yes, it fucking will!' Thom said, his voice tinged with anger, though I could not tell if it was directed at us or the slab. All I did know was that he was evidently determined to move the slab. He picked up the mallet and hit the crowbar repeatedly, sliding it further under the slab.

'Again!' he yelled at us.

We all took up our positions and waited for Thom to count to three.

'One, two, three.' On three, we used all of our combined strength. Looking at Paul it looked as though he was straining so hard this time that the vein above his eye was about to explode. I pulled back on the slab, feeling the burn in almost every muscle in my body. It felt like an eternity we were straining, with no result on the slab. I was about to give up when I felt the movement, it was less than an inch, but it was moving.

'It's coming!' Thom shouted.

We kept up working on it. I felt like my arms were about to fall off. Then there was another jolt of movement.

'Keep going!' Thom ordered us.

There were a few more almost endless seconds of straining, and then it began to slide freely. We uncovered half the well before we stopped, Thom and Paul came round to join us. With each of us holding a corner of the slab, we lifted it off the well and leant it against the side of the well. We all looked at each other, there were smiles all around, we were proud of our achievement. All trace of anger and the almost obsessive determination had gone from Thom's face. He looked like the laid back young man I had met earlier again.

Then we smelled it. The excitement of moving the slab must have stopped us from noticing it at first. All at once, though, we all caught scent of it. Even now, I don't have the words to describe the smell. The nearest I can get is once, years ago, I went to a slaughterhouse that had been closed down. I went there to take soil samples as part of my research. The smell that lingered there was a pungent mix of old death, blood, shit and piss. It was a thick smell. It stuck in your nostrils long after you left. The smell coming out of the well was similar, but so much worse. It was the smell of the old slaughterhouse multiplied by a thousand. Paul retched loudly then violently threw up over the side, down into the well.

'Fuck!' exclaimed Rick, covering his nose. 'It smell's like something died down there.'

'No,' Thom said. 'It smells like everything died down there.'

This was closer to the truth. If you can imagine the smell if everyone on earth died at the same time and rotted in the street, that might get somewhere near describing the smell that was surrounding us.

'Well, God knows how long this thing has been sealed up,' Paul said, before vomiting into the well again.

'Wait a second,' Thom said, before running over to one of his bags and rummaging through it. After a few moments, with me and Rick stood covering our noses, he came running back holding something in his hand.

'What you got?' Rick said, though with his nose covered by his hand it came out more like, 'Wad you god.'

'These aren't ideal,' Thom said, handing us each a paper facemask, the kind you are supposed to use when spray painting or cutting MDF. 'But they might make things a little more bearable.'

We each put on a mask. Thom was right, though not completely getting rid of the stench, it made it a little easier to cope with. Paul had finally stopped throwing up and composed himself.

'Okay, let's get on with this.'

He leant over to look down the well.

'Pass me a torch,' he said, his words echoing down the well.

I handed him my torch, he shone it down the well. Despite the smell we were all curious and leant over to see the bottom. The only problem was that we couldn't see the bottom, the stone walls of the well just kept going into the darkness. I knew just how powerful the beam on that torch was. The well was incredibly deep.

'Can't you use that laser tape measure?' I asked.

'I can try,' Rick said, pulling the device out of his pocket. He held it over the well and pressed the button on the side until it beeped. When he looked at the display, his eyes widened.

'Jesus!' he said. 'According to this, it's too deep to measure.'

CHAPTER ELEVEN

After the revelation about the depth of the well, we decided that there was not much more that could be done on a Sunday afternoon. We headed back up to the surface. I got us all a beer and we sat at the table in the garden.

Paul said that he and Rick would try to get permission from their university to properly investigate the site. They explained that this would mean them heading up a team of undergraduate students. I didn't like the idea of a constant stream of students coming through my house, but if it would get us some answers then I would deal with it.

Rick said that starting the next day he would also try to do some research to see if there was any mention of an abbey or monastery on the site. He figured that if there had been such a thing here then there would have to be a record of its existence somewhere.

Thom said that he'd talk to the engineering department and see if he could borrow the equipment to build the scaffold for easier access to the undercroft. If there were going to be that many people working down there it was the safest option. He also said he would see if he could get hold of a motorised winch to check out the well.

When we heard this, we all laughed and told him that he was welcome to go down there if he wanted to, but we would not be joining him. The smell emanating from down there was bad enough at the top of the well. We hated to think what it would be like down below. Thom's strange behaviour down near the well, and my own distrust of it, had completely faded away.

Before they left, Rick and Thom helped me put the fence back up around the hole. I still didn't want Mojo or, God forbid, Izzy to fall down there. Thom said that he would also try to get something a bit more secure to fence the area off, something with a gate to allow easy access but stop accidental falling.

The three of them left after they had finished their beers. Paul promised that he would be in touch the next evening, and hopefully they would be able to start examining the site properly by the middle of the week.

Not long after they left, Rachel and the girls returned from the park with Mojo. The rest of the day was spent fairly normally, watching films with the girls, making sure they had done whatever homework they needed to do. I went out into town and brought us back pizza for tea.

After that, we let Anna take a shower in our en suite while Rachel bathed Izzy in the family bathroom. I took this time to sit out in the garden having another beer and a cigarette.

'Any news yet?' Bill asked from over the fence.

'Looks like it's an undercroft,' I said.

'Really?' Bill sounded confused. 'I don't remember ever hearing about a church being here.'

'They think it could have been a monastery, destroyed in the 16th century. It would make sense of...'

'The Blackfriars in the road name,' Bill said finishing my sentence. 'Well, I've always wondered where that came from.'

Bill and I had a little general chitchat after that, then he went back in. I heard Izzy in the kitchen; I went inside to find her getting herself a bowl of Coco Pops for her supper. It was nearly time for her to go to bed. Anna was back on the computer chatting to friends on Facebook. Rachel was stretched out on the sofa reading a magazine.

After Izzy had finished her cereal, I took her up to bed and read her a chapter from our current bedtime book, *Peter Pan*. I kissed her good night and went to leave the room.

'Daddy?' she asked as I opened the door. I turned back to her.

'Yes, princess?' I replied.

'Will those men be back again tonight?' she asked, her voice getting sleepy.

'Which men?' I asked. 'The guys from down the road?'

'No,' she said. 'The ones with hoods.'

'I don't think so, honey,' I said. 'That was just a dream, remember?'

She didn't answer; she had already drifted off to sleep. I shut the door silently and headed back downstairs. Her words stuck with me, it wasn't a dream though. The truth was that some kids in hoodies had been messing around in my garden. Bill had told me that he was planning to keep an eye out for them tonight; he was planning to sit up late and watch out of darkened windows. This made me feel a little more secure, but not completely. I had a bad feeling about it.

When I got downstairs, I informed Anna that she only had an hour left until she had to go to bed. We had an agreement on school nights. She would go up to her room by nine, but she was allowed to watch one film before she went to sleep.

I lifted up Rachel's legs and sat down next to her, letting her rest her legs across my lap, and turned on the television. As per usual there was not a lot on. I ended up watching an old episode of *Only Fools and Horses* for probably the hundredth time. Yet it still made me laugh. Rachel laughed at me laughing. She was always amazed that I could watch something repeatedly and enjoy it every time.

'How many times have you seen this one?' she asked with a grin.

'Not sure,' I answered. 'Somewhere between ten and fifteen maybe.'

'And you laugh at it every time the chandelier falls to the floor?'

'It's funny!' I defended myself.

'The first time maybe,' she said. 'Even the second or third, but the fifteenth?'

'How many times have you read *Wuthering Heights*?' I asked, turning it on her.

'That's completely different,' she said, sitting up.

'How many?' I repeated.

'Once a year for the last seventeen,' she confessed.

'And don't you enjoy it and get emotional every time you read it?' I said, grinning.

'*Wuthering Heights* is one of the classic works of English literature,' she said. 'It's a work of art.'

'So is *Only Fools and Horses*,' I replied. 'It's the most classic example of the Great British situation com...'

I was cut off by the cushion hitting me in the face.

'Twat!' she said, grinning.

'Oh, you are in trouble now,' I told her and then leapt across the sofa and began to tickle her. She laughed and pleaded with me to stop. This was her weakness, her Achilles heel. She was so incredibly ticklish that she became incapable of anything. I had once made her sick just by tickling her. Since then I had figured out when to stop, we weren't there yet. She wriggled to try to get free of me, but I kept going. Tears ran down her face.

We were disturbed by the sound of Anna clearing her throat behind us. I stopped tickling Rachel and we turned around to face our daughter.

'You guys are so weird,' she said, looking at us quizzically. 'Anyway, I'm off to bed.'

She kissed us both goodnight and went upstairs at nine. Rachel went off to make herself a hot chocolate and asked me if I wanted a tea. I did. So we sat watching *CSI Miami* until it was time to go to bed. I fell asleep quickly that night. All the exertion from uncovering the well had taken its toll.

I knew I was dreaming, it was a weird sensation. Usually at the moment I figured out I was dreaming I would wake up, I was incapable of lucid dreaming. That was not what this was though. Even though I was fully aware that nothing around me was real and was just a creation of my subconscious, I was unable to control it.

I was falling. It had been years since I had a dream like that, but there I was falling through darkness. I could not see my hand in front of my face. All that was left were my other senses, I could smell death in the air as I fell, its tang burning into my sinuses. Then there was the sound, a terrible scream, high-pitched and full of fear. I realised with some distress that this sound was escaping from my own mouth. I stopped screaming and then I could hear another sound. It was a low frequency rumble, its formation sounded like words, it was as if thunder had learned to talk. I could not make out the words, and somehow I knew that even if I could they would have been in a language unknown to me.

I remembered that I was holding a torch. As I switched it on, I knew what I would see. There all around me was the stone wall of the well, above me and below me was nothing but darkness. I could not see the entrance to the well, nor the bottom, only the walls surrounding me.

Until this point my biggest fear had been hitting the floor at the bottom and feeling every bone in my body shatter before I died. Now, though, I knew this was not what would happen. Something was waiting for me at the bottom of the well, something hungry. Like a dragon, its jaws gaping at the bottom ready to swallow me whole as I fell into its mouth.

I was terrified. I tried to scream again, but now I was unable to. All I could hear was that low rumble of a language getting closer and closer. It was the language of the dragon. The language of the beast that was soon to devour me, body and soul.

I woke up screaming and fell out of the bed. A light came on and Rachel was above me.

'Oh my God, Dan! Are you okay?'

My heart was beating faster than I had ever felt it go before. I looked up at her concerned face and smiled. I crawled back into the bed.

'Just a bad dream,' I said, pulling her to me and holding onto her.

'It must have been really bad,' she said, stroking my hair. 'I've never known you to scream in your sleep before.'

We held each other for a long time. I could feel my heartbeat starting to settle. I looked over Rachel's shoulder and saw the alarm clock. It was 2:54 AM.

There were several loud bangs from downstairs. I felt Rachel jump in my arms. My first thought was the kids in the garden. They were trying to get into the house. Then there were several more loud bangs; I realised what it was.

'Someone's knocking on the front door!' I said, getting to my feet.

'Who would be banging on the door like that at this time of night?' Rachel said, and I could pick up on the worry in her voice.

'Only one way to find out,' I said, trying to sound calm, despite my own concern.

I opened the bedroom door, aware that Rachel was getting up and throwing on her dressing gown to follow me. As I stepped out into the hall, there was another barrage of knocking on the door. This time I could also hear the muffled sound of a woman's voice in distress.

I ran down the landing to the stairs. Rachel followed me but stayed at the top of the stairs as I charged down them. I could hear before I got to the door that it was Mary. I ran to my jacket, which was hung up near the door. I searched the pockets for my car keys. Once I had found them, I went to the door. When I opened it Mary was stood on my doorstep in her dressing gown, her hair was a mess and her face was wet with tears from her glistening red eyes.

'Mary?' I said. 'What's wrong?'

I could hear Rachel running down the stairs. Mary threw herself into my arms.

'Buh, buh, Bill!' she cried out. I pushed her away from me and looked her in the eye.

'What's wrong with Bill?' I asked.

'He's not moving!' she sobbed. 'I think he's dead!'

Rachel took over holding Mary.

'Where is he?' I asked.

'Our garden,' she cried into Rachel's shoulder.

'Go and see if the doctor is home next door to them,' I said to Rachel as I ran out of the door. I ran across our front lawn and jumped the small hedge that separated ours from Bill and Mary's. I looked back and saw Rachel leading Mary down the path. They were heading to the doctor's house.

As I crossed their lawn, I could see that Mary had left the front door open. I raced through it. I had been in their house several times, but even if this had been my first visit I would have known where to go. The layout of all the houses on Blackfriars Crescent was the same. I ran to their kitchen, the door that led out to the garden was open. I could see him lying there at the edge of the patio. He was motionless. I ran outside and slid to my knees next to him. As I have already mentioned, Bill Jenson was a giant of a man. He was lying face down on the grass, his arms underneath him, as though he had tried to break his fall.

'Bill!' I yelled.

There was not even an attempt to answer, not even the most slightest of movements to suggest he had heard me. I had to turn him over. I put my arms around him and tried to pull him towards me. It reminded me of the way that I had been trying to pull the slab off the well that afternoon. My muscles still ached from that, but I managed to roll Bill onto his back. I don't know how I managed it. They do say, though, that at moments of stress the human body is capable of near superhuman strength.

I looked down at him. His eyes were closed. I couldn't tell if he was breathing. There was no perceptible movement from his chest. I stuck two fingers into his neck trying to find a pulse. I couldn't detect one. This didn't mean it wasn't there; after all, I was not an expert.

I didn't know what to do. All I could do was to wait here for the doctor to come if he was home. If not, we would have to call an ambulance. Just sitting there next to him was making me feel useless. I decided to check again for a pulse. I put my fingers all around his throat to no avail. I then tried to find it in his wrist; still I couldn't find it.

I leant over, putting the side of my face next to his blue lips, hoping to hear some hint of a breath.

All of a sudden, Bill's hands grasped mine. I looked at him. His eyes were wide open, staring at me intently.

'Bill!' I yelled. 'Hold on mate, the doctor's coming!'

He rasped in a breath. The sound was like sand paper on rough wood.

'Not kids!' he said in a croaking voice.

'Try not to talk, Bill,' I said, looking around to see if help was on it's way.

He let go of my hands and grabbed my head, turning it to face his own.

'They're not kids!' he said.

'I don't know what you mean, Bill,' I said. Panic was gripping me now.

'The ones in your garden,' he spat. 'They're not kids!'

I realised what he was saying. He was talking about the people Izzy had seen the night before, the ones Mary had seen out the front of the house. She had thought they were teenagers in hoodies and long coats. Now Bill was trying to tell me she was wrong.

'Who are they, Bill?' I asked.

He groaned, pain in his eyes.

'Bill, for the love of God, who was in my garden?' I yelled.

'Mmmm, mmm, mmm,' he tried to say something, 'men' maybe, and then his eyes glazed. I saw the life leave them. He was still once more. I began to sob, crying for the friend I had just lost and out of fear of what he was trying to tell me. Had grown men been in my garden wearing hoodies? Kids could be put down to a harmless bit of fun, but if these were adult men then it suggested they had more sinister intentions. I rested my head on Bill's lifeless chest, crying so hard I could feel my tears soaking the material of his T-shirt.

'Bill!!!!" Mary screamed. I looked up to see her dropping to her knees on the patio, falling so hard I'm amazed she didn't break her knee caps. Rachel knelt down next to her and held her as she wailed. Dr Marklew came running towards me. He had his mobile phone to his ear. He gently pushed me away from Bill's body and began to exam him.

'He's not breathing!' he said into the phone. His hand grabbed Bill's wrist and checked for a pulse as I had done a little while ago. I knew what he would find though, nothing. I had seen Bill die with my own eyes.

'No pulse either,' Marklew said into his phone. He got up and wandered to the other end of the garden to carry on his conversation. I assume it was to save us all the pain of him telling the ambulance not to rush. The man was dead. He hung up and walked back over. He patted my shoulder as he passed me, it was a gesture of warmth that suggested despite being a surgeon the man still had some bedside manner. He walked over to where my wife was knelt cradling the poor widow in her arms.

'I'm so sorry, Mrs Jenson,' he said in a soft voice. 'There's nothing I can do. He's gone!'

Mary started to wail again and the doctor stood up.

'Thank you,' Rachel said to him. He offered her a kind smile and then walked back to me.

'Mr Martin?' he said. I looked at him and saw that he was offering a hand to help me up. I accepted and got to my feet, aware that tears and snot were all over my face from where I had been crying.

'Thank you for coming so quickly, Doctor,' I said.

'I wish I could have done more,' he said. 'I didn't know Bill that well, but he always seemed like a nice man.'

I nodded. This was true, in the short time I had known him Bill had become one of my closest friends. It was hard to accept that he was gone, not as hard as it would be for Mary of course. She had to face the horror of telling their children that their father was dead.

'One of the best,' I said honestly.

'The ambulance is still on its way. Someone will have to contact the undertakers to pick him up from the hospital as soon as possible. They'll take him to the Pilgrim Hospital in Boston,' he said.

'The one you work at?' I asked.

'That's right!' he said. 'I'm going to nip home and get Mrs Jenson a sedative to calm her down and help her sleep. I think it's for the best if someone stays with her tonight.'

'I'm sure my wife wouldn't want to leave her like this anyway,' I said with certainty. Rachel had always been one of the most caring people I knew and if someone needed her she would always be at their side.

'Good,' Marklew said.

He looked uncomfortable for a few seconds then spoke.

'I know it seems insensitive but I'll need some information off Mrs Jenson.'

I nodded. Knowing what he was trying to say.

'I can ask her for you,' I said. 'What do you need to know?'

'If you could try to find out if she has a preference as to which funeral directors to use that would be a big help. If not, the hospital will recommend a good one.'

'All right,' I said.

Marklew again patted me on the shoulder. This was more of a stretch for him now that I was stood up as I was a good six inches taller than him, but the gesture was appreciated. He left to go and fetch a sedative for Mary. I wandered over and knelt down next to the two women on the patio. Mary's wails had become more subdued sobs. Rachel's face was tear-streaked, but she made no sound; she was being strong for Mary. I did the only thing I could think to do and threw my arms around them both.

CHAPTER TWELVE

Rachel did spend the night with Mary. I left after the doctor brought back a few tablets for the grieving woman. I told him that Mary had said that she had no preference when it came to undertakers. It was not something they had ever even thought about. I had felt awful having to ask at a time like this. Mary, though, had told me not to worry, she knew these things had to be done. The doctor said he would ring the hospital and tell them to call the best people for the job and would bring around the details in the morning. I thanked him again for coming so late, he said that it was nothing, and that he only wished he could have done something for poor Bill.

I walked out with him. We said goodbye and I watched him walk back to his house. I suddenly felt sorry for him. He seemed like a really nice guy; he deserved better than his unfaithful shrew of a wife.

When I got home I was glad to find that all of the commotion had not woken the girls, I would, of course, have to tell them. They would be distraught. As much as I had come to see Bill as one of my closest friends, they had come to see him as a kindly uncle.

I decided I would not tell them until they got home from school the next day. I would let them have one more day before grief set in. Anna, I knew, would take it badly, but she had at least encountered death before when my grandmother had died seven years ago. Anna had loved her great-grandma with all her heart. What was not to love? She was one of the kindest and sweetest women you could hope to meet. It was all the qualities I loved in her that I fell in love with in Rachel.

A year after she died our second daughter was born and there was no debate over what to call her. She was named Isabella after my grandmother.

In her life Izzy had not yet had to face death, not even in the form of a pet. So I was worried about how she would take the news of Bill's passing. The main reason I decided not to tell them until after school was that I had not yet figured out how to break it to them, and I was hoping by tea time Rachel would be here to help.

I, of course, was going to have to take the day off work. There was no way of knowing if Mary would be in the state of mind to do all the things that needed doing. She had not called their kids before going to bed, so it was unlikely that they would be able to get home before tomorrow afternoon. Me taking the day off presented problems with keeping things hidden from Anna. She was a pupil at the school I taught at. Although I didn't teach her this year, word would get round to her of my absence and then she would panic.

I spent the next half an hour laying on our bed trying to come up with a solution for this. I could ring the headmaster first thing in the morning and explain the situation to him, tell him not to let Anna know as we were planning to tell her after school. When the girls woke up I would tell them that Rachel was in bed not feeling well. I would say that I was going to drop them off at school then come home and take her to the doctors. If they asked to see her before leaving, I'd tell them she was asleep and needed rest. This would satisfy Anna and she would help get it across to Izzy.

Once I figured out that little problem I was left with nothing to concentrate my mind on. I just laid there in bed playing the evenings events over and over in my head, thinking of the way Bill had looked as the lights went out behind his eyes. I have told you many times already that I am a rational man. I didn't put much faith in religion or superstition. In fact, I saw the two as the same thing. One thing I have always believed is the old saying that the eyes are the window to the soul. I didn't believe in the soul per se, but I did believe that you can see life in the eyes. There is something that lights up in the eyes of a human being, an intelligence and awareness that is not there in most animals or in the eyes of those poor unfortunates who are virtually brain-dead through accident or some birth defect. It is something that is impossible to replicate. Every time I watch a film that claims to have the greatest computer generated beings to date, I can see it is missing. No matter how perfect the skin, or the individual strands of hair, no matter even how good the animation of the eyes themselves is, those lights are missing, The beings created on screen look hollow and lifeless to me.

I thought about the words he had spoken to me just before. It troubled me to think that men were in our garden. So many possibilities as to what they were up to went through my head, each more disturbing than the last. I worried for the safety of my home. My wife. My children.

Then a voice spoke up in the back of my head, a voice I didn't hear very often. It was the part of my mind that was open to possibilities of those things that are outside of nature. I thought that voice was dead and gone, killed by years of studying science, years of trying to rationalise and quantify everything in existence, and denying all those things that did not fit.

I don't know whether it was the shock of seeing Bill die in my arms that had brought this voice back to life, but its presence unsettled me.

'*He didn't say men!*' this voice whispered deep with in my mind.

'No, but that's what he was trying to say,' I said out loud to myself.

'*He could have been trying to say anything that began with M,*' the voice hissed back at me.

'Like what?' I said, laughing at my own inner voice. 'Murderers?'

'*Maybe?*' said the voice. '*Maybe it was monsters, or maybe, just maybe, it was monks!*'

'Shut up!' I yelled, the sound echoed around the room.

I sat there trying to push this thought away. The voice in my head was only saying this because of what I'd found out about the undercroft today, the connection it made to the name of our street. There was no use running off with thoughts that ghostly monks were now prowling the streets, it was madness. I refused to listen to any more of that sort of nonsense, even from my own mind, especially from my own mind.

Soon after that, I must have fallen asleep. This time, fortunately, it was dreamless as far as I could remember. I woke to the sound of the alarm, which I had set for six, half an hour earlier than I would usually get up but allowing me time to call Matthew Webber, the headmaster, at home.

Matthew was understanding as always. He told me that my classes would be covered and to ensure that nothing was said to Anna he would not tell anyone else the true reason for my absence. He said not to worry if I needed the next day as well, and that Anna may as well take the rest of the week off after today to get over the shock. This would take her up to the summer holidays.

After my conversation with Matthew, I went upstairs to wake the girls. First I knocked on Anna's door. I heard a grunt from inside. I opened the door and walked over to the curtains. I opened them and let the morning sun stream into Anna's room.

'Rise and shine, kiddo,' I said as I shook her.

She looked up at me with bleary eyes and then to the clock on her wall.

'It's too early,' she said. This was true, it was only quarter to seven, and usually we left the girls in bed until seven.

'Well, honey,' I said, 'your mum's not feeling too good this morning, so she's staying in bed. I need you to help me get Izzy ready. Okay?'

'Okay,' she said begrudgingly.

'Thanks,' I said with a smile. 'I'll go and wake her, then I'll go downstairs and sort out breakfast while you get her dressed.'

Anna agreed to the plan and I left her to get herself dressed. I walked across the landing to Izzy's room. I opened the door and saw her snuggled up in her bed, her favourite bear cuddled up under her chin. She looked like an angel in these moments; it always made it hard for me to wake her. You see, if it was up to me that was the way she would stay for the rest of her life. Safe and content, and never any older than six.

I went over to her curtains. They were already open halfway. I remembered that I had shut them completely when I put her to bed the previous night. I worried that she had been looking out of the window again. I reassured myself with the fact that if she had seen any of what happened with Bill she would have come and told me in the night. I pulled the curtains open all the way and walked over to her bed.

I bent over and kissed her on the forehead. She woke with a beaming smile.

'Hi, Daddy,' she said, putting her arms around my neck and hugging me.

'Good morning, princess,' I said. 'I need you to let Anna help you get ready for school today. Mummy's not feeling very well so we have to leave her in bed, can you do that for me?'

'Yes, Daddy,' she said, giving me a kiss. 'I'm a good girl!'

'That's right!' I said, walking towards the door to head downstairs to make breakfast.

'Mr Jenson told me I had to be a good girl when he came round last night.'

I froze on the spot. She must have dreamt it I kept telling myself. It must be one of those weird coincidences, but the voice that had woken up in me last night was already trying to tell me different.

Anna was a star that morning. She got Izzy washed and dressed, she brushed and plaited her hair, then made sure she ate her breakfast while I claimed I was going upstairs to check on their mother. A few minutes later, I came down and said that she was fast asleep so we'd better let her rest. The girls agreed with no arguments. I took them to school, explaining to Anna that I wouldn't be staying today as I had to take Rachel to the doctors. She believed every word. It made me feel guilty for lying to them, but I was doing it with the best of intentions.

By the time I got back to the house, I could see that the curtains were open next door. Rachel was stood at the window waving at me. She was still in her dressing gown and had a steaming cup in her hand. She pointed at it, then me. I knew she was offering me one so I went straight round to the Jensons', or Mary's place as I would have to get used to calling it. Rachel answered the door. Her eyes looked red and puffy.

I took her in my arms and kissed her.

'How are things?' I asked.

'Mary finally cried herself to sleep about five this morning,' she said. 'I haven't woken her yet, Dr Marklew came around and told me that the hospital had called Goodwins funeral directors in Boston and they had collected Bill's body and taken it to their chapel of rest.'

I was a little shocked at this news.

'That's quick isn't it?' I said. 'Don't they need to do an autopsy or something?'

'That's what I said,' Rachel replied. 'But Dr Marklew said that given Bill's age and history of heart problems there was no need.

'That's good!' I said. 'At least Mary doesn't have to deal with that this morning.'

'How are the girls?' she asked. 'I take it from the fact you've just come back on your own, they're at school and you haven't told them yet.'

I shook my head, a little ashamed of my own cowardice.

'I didn't know what to say,' I said. 'Plus I thought it might be best to have them out of the way today until everything is sorted out.'

She nodded.

'Yeah, you did the right thing,' She said with a tired smile. 'We'll tell them later.'

We went inside and Rachel made me a coffee. I sat down on the sofa. My wife sat next to me. She put her head on my shoulder and began to sob gently. I guessed that she had been holding so much in all night for the sake of Mary that now she needed to let it go. I stroked her hair. Neither of us spoke for quite some time. It wasn't that we weren't good at telling each other how we felt. The fact was that we didn't have to. Rachel and I could have entire conversations without opening our mouths. It was done with a combination of facial expressions, body language and touch. It could be annoying for people who spent time with us, but to us it was the most natural thing in the world.

Eventually Rachel sat up and rubbed her eyes dry on the sleeve of her dressing gown.

'I suppose I should wake her up soon,' she said. 'She has to call her kids.'

I nodded. I told Rachel that I was going to nip back home and sort a few things out there, it felt a little cowardly. There was nothing to do at home that couldn't have waited, but I didn't want to face Mary just yet; I couldn't. Rachel would be better help to her than I could be. Then there was the chance that she would ask me if he'd been conscious when I got to him? Whether he had said anything? I hadn't decided how to answer that question yet. The kindest thing would have been to either say; he had been unconscious when I got to him and had remained so; or that he had come round briefly and said her name. These would be things that might bring her some comfort, if not right now then certainly in time. I couldn't tell her the truth. That her husband's last words were to inform me that the people who were hanging around my garden were not kids, as we had all first assumed, but men.

'*Or monks!*' The voice of the irrational waking up again.

'Nonsense!' I told this voice in my mind. There was no way that Bill was going to say monks; he was going to say men. This idea was disturbing enough without descending into paranoid fantasy. What were these men doing in my garden? For the first time, I realised another question. What had they done to Bill? Last night, knowing that Bill suffered from angina, I had simply assumed that his death was due to a heart attack. Now I began to wonder if there was more to it. Perhaps upon seeing these men he had given chase and over-exerted himself. Bill had seemed fit as an ox, but he did have a heart condition.

'*Or maybe he saw a ghost and it scared him to death!*' The voice in my head interrupted my chain of thought.

'I don't believe in ghosts!' I shouted at my empty living room. I sank down into an armchair and put my head in my hands. I felt like I was starting to lose my mind. Here I was arguing out loud with a voice in my own head, a voice that was part of me. I was arguing with myself. I began to laugh, just a little chuckle to myself at first, but quickly it became louder. The more I thought about how inappropriate it was to be laughing, and how ridiculous I must have looked, the more I laughed. Soon I fell from the chair to the floor, rolling around, roaring with laughter. Tears ran from my eyes down my reddening cheeks. I was beginning to choke on my own laughter. I was unable to take in enough breath. I began to panic, yet still I couldn't stop laughing. I began to feel light-headed, and the room around me began to fade away to darkness.

I was back in Bill and Mary's garden. Bill was lying in my arms, dying.

'They weren't kids in your garden,' he rasped at me.

'Who were they Bill?' I asked him.

'They were...' He looked at me. 'Mmm...'

He closed his eyes. He began to shrivel in my arms, drying out like a prune in the sun, his skin stretching tight over the bone and turning grey. Bill's massive body was wasting away before my eyes. I wanted to scream, but I couldn't, all I could do was watch in mounting horror as the skin on his face began to peel away like paper, exposing his skull. The bones began to crumble and soon all that was left of Bill was dust.

I looked up and saw them.

There at the bottom of Bill's garden was a line of hooded figures. Their black robes hung to their feet. The massive hoods obscured most of their faces, but I could see their hideous smiling mouths, lined with razor sharp teeth.

The figures, there were nine of them in all, began to approach me. They moved in unison, each step exactly the same.

I did not want to be here anymore.

CHAPTER THIRTEEN

I came to nearly an hour later lying next to a small puddle of my own vomit. My eyes were dry and itchy, the way they often are when you have been crying a lot. I pushed my self up onto my hands and knees. I still felt a little dazed, but things were getting better. My chest felt tight, like it used to when I was younger and smoked a lot more, and my sides hurt. I ached from laughing so much, in all my life I had never encountered anyone who had laughed so much they passed out. Yet I had just done exactly that. I couldn't see anything that was funny enough to send me into that state. I supposed it must have been brought on by the stress of the last few days. Thankfully, the fear induced by the dream did not linger the way it sometimes does.

I got to my feet and cleaned up my puke. My clothes were sticking to me. I had sweated a lot during the deranged bout of laughter. I decided to take a shower and get changed and then head next door and see how Mary was doing, and relieve Rachel for a while so she could come home and do the same.

The shower felt good. I have never liked hot showers, even in winter I would have the water lukewarm at best. On a hot summer's day like this, I would have the water verging on cold. Rachel could never understand it. Then I in turn could never understand her reasoning behind having the shower so hot it felt as though it was peeling off your skin. I had always found a cold shower invigorating; it woke up the mind and the body in a way that nothing else could.

I dried myself off and dressed in a pair of light-weight cargo pants and a linen shirt. I felt so much cooler. I left my hair wet, hoping this would keep me feeling refreshed longer. I did indeed feel refreshed. The stupid voice that wanted me to believe in ghosts was buried again with all the other things I had believed in as a child. The hideous dream had faded in my memory. I had decided to tell Mary that Bill had come round while I was with him last night and that he had simply said her name before closing his eyes again, and I had decided that there was no reason to be afraid. Bill had not said that there were ghosts in my garden, nor men, he had merely said, 'Mmmm.' Perhaps he was going to say 'Moles' for all I knew, and all I would ever know. There was little point worrying about it until I saw someone myself. The house was always secure at night, and woe betide anyone who tried to get in and hurt my family.

I walked back next door. Rachel saw me coming and opened the door for me as I reached it. I felt guilty for feeling so rejuvenated when I saw her. She looked drained. I gave her a big kiss.

Inside the living room I found Mary dressed and with her hair and make up done. I had expected her to look awful. Instead, she looked dignified in her grief. She got up when I came in and hugged me and kissed me on the cheek.

'Thank you for last night, Dan,' she said as she held onto me.

I said nothing, merely patted her on the back.

'I'm going to make a cuppa. Would you like one, Dan?' she said.

'Yes, please, Mary,' I said.

I told Rachel to go home and get some rest and a shower. I said that I would stay with Mary. At first she protested, then Mary came back into the room and told her not to be silly and that she would be fine. Rachel eventually agreed and went home.

Mary brought me a cup of tea which I sat on the sofa and drank. She sat in one of the two arm chairs opposite me, not the one nearest the door. That had been Bill's seat. As a mark of respect I thought it would be a long time before anyone sat in that chair again.

Mary told me that she had called their children when she got up this morning. Their daughter, Maggie, who had moved to London recently to live with her boyfriend, was devastated but had told her mother she would get the first train she could. I assumed she would be here by about 4 PM. Their son, Alex, who was at university in Manchester, said he would be back in a few days. He had to go and see some lecturers and take his exams. If it was me, I would have rushed home the instant I heard the news, but different people react in different ways. Perhaps he needed to come to terms with the death of his father himself, before he could face his mother and be of any help to her.

The conversation began to dry up a little. It was at these quiet moments I could really see the pain in her eyes. It was as if a part of Mary had died out there last night, a part she would never get back. She would, of course, carry on for the sake of her children, but she would never be the same woman.

'Was he gone when you got to him last night?' she asked. It was the question I had been waiting for since my arrival at her house.

'He was unconscious when I got to him,' I said. 'I was checking for a pulse, but I'm no expert and I couldn't find one.'

'You tried your best, though, dear,' she said.

'Then he did come round briefly,' I said. I saw a tear fall from her wide eyes as I told her this. 'He looked up and said your name. Then he just closed his eyes, and that was it.'

She began to weep again, gentle tears. I felt bad for lying to her, but thought that I had made the right decision. I stood up and took her over a box of tissues from the coffee table. She took one and dried her eyes. I was about to walk back to the sofa when she grabbed my hand.

'Thank you, Dan,' she said through her tears. 'It would have meant a lot to him to have someone he was so fond of with him at the end.'

'His last thoughts were of you,' I said. Perhaps I wasn't lying. Maybe Bill's last word was going to be Mary. It began with M as much as men or monk. I had only assumed that he was going to say men, thinking he was responding to my question.

Mary told me how much Rachel had helped her the previous night. She said that she didn't know how she could ever repay her. I told her that she didn't have to. We knew she would have done the same for us.

She told me about how she and Bill had met in Hendon. That he had been such a dashing young man, especially in his uniform, and how after a chance meeting in a pub, he had seen her everyday for the rest of his stay at the police college. On the day before he was due to graduate, he had proposed and asked her to come back to Lincolnshire.

'I didn't have a single doubt in my mind when I said yes,' she told me. 'My friends thought I was mad running off to the country with a man I had barely known for three months. It just felt right. You know?'

I told her that I did. That the moment I saw Rachel for the first time I knew that we were meant to be together. She smiled, it was good to see Mary smile. Their story had been so much like our own. A chance meeting in a pub was not unlike mine and Rachel's chance meeting in the students union. I wondered how many people's marriages were based upon chance meetings. It made me wonder if there was such a thing as fate? Would Rachel and I have met somewhere else had I not literally bumped into her that night? Would our paths have never crossed? I began to think there was such a thing as destiny, because I could not imagine myself loving anyone else the way I loved her. So I must have been meant to meet her that night. Just as Mary must have been destined to meet Bill.

Now he was gone. If there was such a thing as fate, it was cruel. It can give the greatest love of your life and then take it away at any given moment.

A little while later Rachel came back looking refreshed. She was dressed in a light summer dress. It was the sort of thing she wore when we first met. Sixteen years and two kids down the line, she still looked amazing in it.

'We should really consider heading off to get the kids from school,' she said.

I looked at my watch, I was amazed at how much time had gone by. It was half two in the afternoon. Izzy's school was only about six minutes away in good traffic. However, good traffic was rare in Darton in the afternoon.

'Will you be all right?' I asked Mary.

'I'll be fine,' she said, standing up and hugging me and then Rachel. 'Your girls need you more than I do. Maggie will be here soon.'

'I'll call in later,' Rachel said. 'Call my mobile if you need anything.'

'I'm fine,' she said again. 'I'll see you later.'

We said our goodbyes and left the house. We headed back to our own drive. As we did, I saw Paul and Rick approaching from their end of the crescent. Rick was carrying a ring binder. He put up a hand and waved at me. I waved back.

'I need to pop to the loo,' Rachel said. 'I'll bring the car keys back out with me.'

She went inside and I stood waiting for the two archaeologists at the end of my drive. When they arrived they looked both happy and nervous.

'Hey, Dan?' Rick said. 'We heard about poor Mr Jenson. Is his wife okay?'

'As good as can be expected, I suppose,' I replied.

'Could you pass on our condolences?' Paul asked. 'We don't know her very well and don't want to intrude at a time like this.'

'I'm sure she'll appreciate them,' I said. 'How has your day been?'

'Busy,' they replied in unison.

'Did you get the go ahead?' I asked Paul.

'I had loads of meetings with lecturers in the department,' he said. 'The head of the department wanted to come over tomorrow to check the site out for himself before he gave us the go ahead.'

'That's great,' I told him, although my enthusiasm for finding more out about the undercroft had waned slightly since the previous night.

'But once he heard what Rick had learnt he gave us the approval on the spot,' Paul said excitedly.

'And have I found some serious shit out!' Rick joined in.

'Really? So there was an abbey here?'

Rick began nodding frantically as he opened the ring binder and began to flick through the pages.

'I've spent all day in libraries, on the phone and on the internet and I found out there was a monastery here built in....' He paused to look through the binder once more. When he found what he was looking for he tapped the spot on the page as he spoke. '1139. So we were spot on with the period of the undercroft. The place has a really fascinating history, it was built by...'

I put a hand up to stop him. I felt bad, the poor guy had put a lot of work in, but I didn't have the time for this now.

'I'm sorry, Rick,' I said. 'I really want to know all about it, but I have to go and get my kids from school. Could you pop over later this evening and give me the full story?'

'Sure. Sorry. I was getting carried away,' Rick said. 'You are not going to believe the history this place had.'

Rachel returned with the car keys. I told the guys to come around about seven.

CHAPTER FOURTEEN

Telling the girls about Bill's death was as heartbreaking as I had expected it to be. Anna threw herself into my arms, crying softly. Izzy screamed hysterically for ten minutes, fighting off any of Rachel's or my attempts to soothe her. It hurt me so much to see them in this sort of pain. As a parent all you want to do is shield your children from anything that can hurt them, but life creeps in anyway. It's life that hurts you, just when you think everything is going great it throws something in to devastate you.

Once Izzy had calmed down to just gentle sobbing, we drove home. Anna sat in the front with me. Izzy sat with her head on Rachel's lap in the back.

'Daddy? Is Uncle Bill in Heaven now?' Izzy asked from the back.

How could I answer this? I was an out-and-out atheist. I had never tried to encourage religion in the children. I agreed with Rachel when we said we should let them make their own minds up. Secretly, I had always hoped they would follow me down the path of atheism. Not that Rachel was religious, she was a self-proclaimed agnostic; she was undecided what she believed.

Right there at that moment, though, there was nothing I could think to say. My daughter was looking for some comfort in a difficult time. She was just a child, did that mean I should lie to her? Lucky for me ,Rachel jumped in to save my skin.

'Do you think he is, princess?' she said softly. I could see her stroking the girl's hair in my rearview mirror.

'I think so,' she said. 'He was a nice man and nice men go to Heaven.'

'Then I guess he must be,' Rachel said.

She looked towards me to support this statement.

'If that's what you think, Izzy,' I said.

Anna was just sat staring out of the window as the fields between Darton and Glenley went passed. Her eyes were red from crying.

'How you doing, kiddo?' I asked.

She looked at me and offered me a half smile.

'I'm all right, Daddy,' she said softly. 'Just sad for Mrs Jenson.'

'Me too!' I said.

When we got home, Rachel set about making dinner for us all. Not that I, for one, was feeling very hungry. Anna went to her room to wait for the meal. Izzy, who was still crying a little, wouldn't leave her mother's side. I sat on the sofa and switched on the television. The doorbell rang. With everyone else occupied, I went to answer it. I was greeted by a tall, attractive, young woman in her mid-twenties.

'Hello, Mr Martin,' she said, holding out her hand. I took it and noticed that, like so many people I knew today, her eyes were red from crying. From her height and the shape of her nose there was no mistaking who she was. 'I'm Maggie Jenson!'

'Hi, Maggie. Come in and please call me Dan,' I said, standing aside to let her in.

Maggie walked into the hallway and stayed there. I pointed towards the living room, though considering the fact that the layout of our house was the same as her

134

parents, I'm sure she could have found it. She sat down. Rachel stepped into the room with Izzy hanging around behind her. She introduced herself and apologised that she was in the middle of cooking dinner. Maggie said not to worry. Rachel left us to it.

'I just wanted to thank you for all that you and your wife did for my Mum last night,' Maggie said.

I told her that it was nothing, and that we considered her parents to be our friends.

'Yeah. Mum has nothing but good things to say about you,' she said. 'She told me that you were with my Dad when he died.'

I nodded. I was preparing myself to have to lie again.

'I just wanted know whether it was quick,' she said, her voice cracking a little as she tried to choke back the tears. 'I hate to think that he suffered.'

'He was unconscious when I got to him,' I told her. 'I don't know if he suffered before that. He came round and then slipped away very quickly and quietly,' I said.

Her tears took hold and she took a tissue from her pocket and mopped her eyes.

'Thank you, Dan,' she said when she had composed herself a little. 'I have to get back to Mum. We're in the process of letting everyone know what has happened. We heard back from the hospital that he died of a massive heart attack, brought on by his angina.'

I led her to the door.

'We'll pop over and check on you and your Mum in a while,' I said as I opened the door.

'Thanks, she'll appreciate that,' she said, stepping outside. She turned back to me. 'Oh, I forgot Mum told me to let you know that the funeral was on Friday at noon at St Leonards. She wanted to know if you would like to speak at the service?'

I was shocked at this. The fact that the funeral was booked so soon made it all feel very real. It hit me that Bill really was gone. The fact that Mary wanted me to speak at the service was touching.

'Oh, I don't know,' I said. 'I really hadn't known him that long.'

'Mum said that the two of you had become really close in the little while you had known each other and that he would have really liked you to do it.'

'In that case tell her I'd be honoured,' I said.

We said our goodbyes.

We all sat in silence during dinner. Each of us, Rachel included, picked at our food, not really eating much. After we had finished, Anna asked if she could go pop round to her friend Holly's. We said that it was fine as long as she was back by eight o'clock. Rachel took Izzy upstairs for her bath. We had decided to put her to bed early, hoping that sleep would help her feel better the next day.

I was loading the dishwasher when the doorbell rang again. I answered it and found Rick and Paul outside. I led them into the living room. I asked if they wanted a drink, both of them accepted a coffee. I was in need of something stronger and poured myself a rum and Coke. When I returned to the living room, Rick was flicking through his folder again.

'So there was a monastery here?' I said as I placed their drinks on the coffee table and sat down with my own.

'Yeah, it was called St Martins,' Rick answered. 'It was built in 1139. There was only a very small settlement here at the time. The town of Darton was still a few hundred years away from forming. The monastery was founded by a group of Benedictine monks; it was essentially an over spill for the much bigger monastery at Boston. There were too many monks there at the time and a group of them decided that there were smaller communities south of Boston that needed help.'

'Very noble,' I said. 'Then that's what you expect from monks.'

'Well, quite. At least you should,' Rick replied.

'What do you mean?' I asked.

'Whether their motives were noble at first I don't know. The church must have thought so to fund the building of the abbey here. Things didn't stay so honest for long.'

'Why? What happened?' I asked, leaning forward in my chair.

'The monks here were vicious. For the next four or five centuries they were responsible for some terrible atrocities. They were robbing and murdering rich travellers who came to the abbey looking for a rest for the night. They were even going out at night and committing highway robberies.'

'Jesus!' I said.

'There were many other things over the years. In 1226 the head monk of the monastery and eighteen other brothers were excommunicated by the Pope himself. It was after an incident where a group of forty nuns on a pilgrimage stopped here on their journey. They were subjected to months of rape and torture at the hands of the monks, kept here as prisoners. All but one was murdered, mutilated and buried in the grounds. One got away, she made it to Boston despite her injuries. She told the monks there everything that had happened. Then she died.'

I sat back in my chair an exhaled loudly. My head was spinning. The story that Ricky was telling me was unbelievable.

'My God, how could all of this have been forgotten?' I asked. 'A story like that and no one round here even knows there was a monastery.'

'Because it was covered up. Yes, the church excommunicated those responsible, but the crimes weren't reported to anyone like the local Baron or the King. They didn't want the bad press, as it were. The excommunication meant that the monks would never get into Heaven. That was the worst punishment for holy men. Later on, around 1410, the Benedictine monks took in a group of Dominican friars.'

'What's the difference between a monk and a friar?' I asked.

'Monks were attached to a specific monastery, the way priests were attached to churches and parishes,' Paul explained. 'Friars, on the other hand, were free to preach wherever and to whomever they chose; they survived mainly by begging.'

'So they weren't very important then?' I asked.

'Not to the church,' Rick said. 'But they were very popular with the people. The church at the time was very rich and very powerful; the friars were far more of and for the people. So in 1410 this group of Dominican friars were traveling the country and got caught in a storm. There were ten of them in all. They asked for shelter at the monastery. The monks welcomed them in. They gave them food and wine. It was drugged. When they came around they were all bound and gagged. The monks took it in turns to torture and sodomise them. Their ordeal went on for days. Finally nine of them were executed. The tenth was released and told to tell the Pope what had happened and dare him to do something about it.

'The friar did as he was told. He traveled to Rome and gained an audience with the Pope. He explained all the vile things that had befallen him and the rest of his group at the hands of the monks of St Martins.

'The Pope decided it was best to leave these evil monks to their own devices.

Back at the monastery, the nine dead friars were impaled along the road leading up to the monastery as a warning to all other clergy to leave them be.'

'My God,' was all I could say.

'Dominican friars wore black robes, they were called the Blackfriars. Somehow I think that the name of this road came from the line of nine dead friars impaled here.

'The records of the incident didn't become known until Henry VIII and the dissolution. When the monks were driven from the monastery and the records seized, the local Baron and the Archbishop of the new Church of England reported the history of the place to the King. By this time Darton had become quite a sizeable market town. They decided that letting the facts become public knowledge may effect trade and things in the town. So

139

they razed the place to the ground, wiping it from history. The records from the Monastery were kept by the local Baron. Eventually they ended up in the possession of the university.'

'This is really fucked up,' I said. 'All of that horror happening on this land.'

'It was a long time ago,' Paul joined in. 'This means that the undercroft is a really significant find. I mean part of a monastery wiped from history on the orders of Henry VIII himself. It's astounding!'

'Yes, it was a long time ago, but I'm not just talking about the monastery.'

Rick and Paul looked at each other, confused.

'What do you mean?' Rick asked.

'The scandal at the mental hospital in the eighties!' I said.

They still looked confused.

'What scandal?' Paul asked.

I forgot that they were not from round here and didn't mix in the kind of circles likely to pass on even the urban legend version of events. Over the next twenty minutes, I filled them in completely on the story of Dr Richards. First, I told them about the exaggerated local folk lore version with its devil worship and human sacrifices. Then I told them the true account I got from Bill. I told them about the rapes, the abuse for profit ring he ran, and the murders.

When I was done, they were the ones looking shocked.

'Christ, I had no idea,' Rick said.

After they had left I thought about telling Rachel what they had told me, but I decided that it was not what she needed to hear after the few days she had been through. Instead I just sat on the sofa holding her.

Izzy had fallen straight to sleep after her bath. We sat in silence just enjoying the embrace. When Anna returned home we asked her to keep an ear out for her little sister while we nipped round to check on Mary.

'Okay,' she said. 'Don't be too long.' She headed into the kitchen.

Rachel and I had one of our silent conversations. We could both tell that there was something wrong with Anna. She had never seemed nervous about being left on her own in the house with Izzy. Rachel looked at me in a way that told me I should go and talk to Anna. I stood up and followed her into the kitchen. She was stood drinking Coke straight from the bottle. Usually I would tell her to get a glass, but I didn't want to start this conversation with a confrontation.

'Are you all right kiddo?' I asked.

She nodded.

We're going to head next door in a minute,' I said. 'Why did you ask us not to be long?'

'I don't know,' she said. 'I just don't like being left alone here for too long.'

'Is this about Bill?' I asked.

She shook her head. I was starting to feel like I was trying to get blood from a stone. She wasn't opening up to me, but it was clear that something was bothering her.

'What's up then?' I persisted.

'I don't know, Dad,' she said. 'I just don't feel safe.'

This stung me, I had always thought that the one thing I could do was make my family feel safe and protected. I began to wonder if Anna had also seen the men in our garden and this was why she felt this way.

'Why not?' I asked. I didn't want to ask her if she had seen the men. If she hadn't then me revealing it to her would make her even more nervous.

'I don't know,' she said again. 'Sometimes I just feel scared here, and I don't know why.'

I frowned and stepped over to her. I put my arms around her and kissed her on the top of her head.

'You don't need to feel scared or uncomfortable, baby,' I said as reassuringly as I could 'You know I'm here to protect you. I'd never let anyone hurt you.'

She sobbed a little against my chest.

'Hey, Anna, it's okay,' I said soothingly.

She looked up at me.

'Do you promise, Daddy?' she pleaded through her tear-reddened eyes. 'You promise you won't let anyone hurt me?'

'Of course I promise, baby,' I said. 'What is bothering you?'

'I really don't know,' she said shaking her head. 'Maybe it is because of poor Uncle Bill.'

This was what I had suspected all along.

'I know that it hurts that he's gone,' I said. 'But you shouldn't bottle it up, you have to let these things out or they'll drive you mad.'

She hugged me tight and then pulled away.

'I'm okay now,' she said, wiping her eyes. 'You should go next door, we'll be fine.'

With that she headed up to her room.

Rachel wandered into the room.

'Is she okay?' she asked.

'She was a bit upset about Bill,' I explained. ' She seems okay now.'

'Well done, super dad,' she said with a smile.

'I have no idea how I made her feel better, but I did,' I said, laughing.

'Let's head next door.'

Maggie opened the door. She greeted us warmly and led us into the living room where Mary was sat looking through old photo albums. She had tears in her eyes but a smile on her face; she stood up and hugged both of us. Maggie asked us if we would like a drink then went off into the kitchen to make coffees. Mary sat in-between Rachel and me on the sofa. She showed us the albums. First was their wedding photographs, they showed a young, attractive and happy couple. You could see from the snapshots that the way they looked at each other, it was a look of utter love.

Then there were family albums, both of their children as babies, children and teens and photographs of family holidays. I smiled as I looked through them; they showed the steady progression of Bill's baldness from a full head of hair to the hair round the sides that he had when I knew him.

Maggie sat opposite us, drinking her coffee. When she was done, she stood up.

'I'm just going to nip outside for a smoke,' she said.

'I'll join you,' I announced, realising that I couldn't remember the last time I'd had a cigarette. We went out into the back garden. I felt a chill as I stepped out of the kitchen door, despite the warm summer air.

The last time I had come through this door into the garden I had found Bill, less than a few moments away from death, on the grass just beyond the patio. The memory was so strong that for a split second I could see him lying there.

Maggie sensed my feelings, stopped, and turned to me.

'Perhaps we should have gone out the front,' she said. 'I forgot that you found him here.'

I shook my head and smiled as I took out one of my cigarettes.

'It's alright,' I said. 'I just haven't been out here since then. I'll be all right though.'

I offered her my cigarettes. She took one and I lit them both with my Zippo. We stood there in silence for a little while, just inhaling the smoke, until she finally broke the silence.

'I wish I'd had more time with him,' she said. 'I wish I hadn't been so eager to move away, if I'd have just waited a little longer.'

'No matter how long you have with someone, you will always wish you had another day with them,' I said, trying to comfort her.

'Maybe!' she said. 'But I was so far away.'

'He was so proud of you. You and your brother, he was happy for you.'

'Thank you,' she said.

When we went back inside we found that Mary and Rachel had picked out a few photos of Bill to get blown up to display at his funeral. I offered to take them into the school the next day to get them enlarged in our art department. This would save some money,

Mary thanked me, saying that she did not know what any of them would do without us.

Mary, Maggie and Rachel agreed to go shopping the following day to get the outfits they would wear for the funeral. They would take Izzy and Anna with them. I thought this might help the girls feel better. I was going to have to go into work the next day, but promised that I would take the Friday off for the funeral. It was the last day of the school year so I would not miss much. I decided that I would take my first few weeks of holiday for the following few weeks.

Before we knew it we had been sat there for nearly an hour. Rachel and I suddenly felt guilty for leaving Anna alone with a sleeping Izzy for so long, considering what she was going through. We made our way home to find Anna asleep on the sofa. Usually we would wake her up and send her to bed. She looked so peaceful, however, that for the first time in years I picked her up and carried her up the stairs and put her into bed. She stirred a little as I laid her down.

'Shhh. Go back to sleep, baby,' I said, stroking her brow.

'Okay, Daddy,' she mumbled before rolling over.

When I came downstairs I found that Rachel had brought the bottle of rum and the bottle of Coke into the living room. She had poured us both a drink. We snuggled up on the sofa, not saying much, just enjoying the closeness, both of us thinking how we couldn't face the thought of losing the other. By half ten we were both feeling quite tired so we headed to bed for a more peaceful night's sleep, or at least that was what we had hoped. It was not going to happen.

CHAPTER FIFTEEN

An hour after falling into a deep and peaceful sleep I was woken by the sound of footsteps on the landing, slow foot steps like before, I felt my body tense, the fear of an intruder gripping my mind again. I turned my head and saw the landing light spilling in under our closed door. I was relieved, it was only Izzy on her way to the bathroom. I listened to her slow progression down the landing. She reached our door and I expected her next footfall to pass the door on her way to the bathroom. Instead, though, I heard our doorknob start to turn. I sat up as the door opened and Izzy's little silhouette came into view.

'What's wrong, princess?' I said. Rachel woke up at the sound of my voice and sat up as well.

'You okay, baby?' she said.

Izzy ran into our room and jumped up onto the bed with us. We pulled the quilt over her and both cuddled up to her.

'You sad about Uncle Bill?' Rachel asked.

'Yes,' she replied. 'But I can't sleep because of all the people in the garden.'

Rachel and I looked at each other. They were back. My mind instantly brought back Bill's dying words. They weren't kids; they were men. Then the irrational voice came back into my head. '*No, they're not kids, they're ghosts of evil monks,*' it said. I shuddered, trying to push the thought out of my head. I got out of bed and pulled on a t-shirt.

'You stay here with Izzy,' I said to Rachel. 'I'm going to check this out.'

Rachel nodded, pulling Izzy closer to her.

'Be careful,' she said nervously.

'I will,' I said, pulling on my trainers. I grabbed the torch again and left the room.

I went quickly, but quietly, downstairs without turning on any lights. I went to the kitchen door. I peered through the glass, but all I could see was darkness. I opened the door as quietly as I could, but the click as it unlocked sounded deafening in the silence of the night.

I stepped out into the night, it was still warm, yet I was shivering. I turned on the torch and scanned the garden. There was no sign of anyone. The only thing I could see was the glinting of the chicken wire around the hole that led to the undercroft.

I stepped across the grass, sweeping the beam of the torch back and forth as I went. I looked back at the house as I reached the end of the grass. I could see a dim light coming through our bedroom window where I had left the door open. Though I had not put anymore lights on, I had not turned off the landing light that Izzy had put on. There was a brighter light coming from Izzy's room, where her night light was still on. Her curtains were open where she had been looking out into the garden.

I walked the rest of the garden, passing the hole. I felt cooler as I passed it; it seemed that the air at this end of the garden was a few degrees colder than near the house. I walked to the fence and shone the torch into the field behind the house. The beam was powerful enough to illuminate the land all the way to the edge of the wood. I could see no one visible, it was, of course, possible that someone was hiding in the long grass of the field.

'Who's there?' I shouted into the field. There was a sudden sound of movement. I braced myself. I saw birds scattering into the night. I let out a sigh. There was no one out there; Izzy had just been dreaming again.

I walked back to the house, feeling the air warm up again as I stepped back onto the grass. I took one last look into the field; still no one could be seen.

When I got back upstairs, Rachel was still sat up in bed. Izzy had fallen asleep nestled up against her mother. Rachel looked at me to ask if there was anyone out there. I shook my head.

'I couldn't see anyone,' I whispered, not wanting to wake Izzy up. 'I even checked the field behind the house. I guess she was dreaming again.'

I could see the relief on Rachel's face.

'Shall we leave her in with us tonight?' she asked. I thought about it.

'No, I'll carry her back to her own bed,' I answered. 'We won't get a good night's sleep with her in bed with us.'

Rachel smiled. She knew that it was true. Izzy had a habit of wanting to sleep across the bed, taking up so much room that Rachel and I were clinging onto the edge of the bed.

I picked Izzy up, trying not to wake her. She stirred though.

'Did you find them, Daddy?' she asked in a sleepy voice.

'Nope, princess,' I said softly as I carried her down the landing towards her room.

'But I saw them,' she said as we entered her room. I laid her down on her bed and pulled the covers up to her. I kissed her on the forehead. Then I went over to the curtains. I was planning to close them, but I found myself instead staring out into the darkness. I still couldn't see anyone.

'Was it the men with hoods again?' I asked, thinking of Bill's words.

'No,' Izzy said. 'They were ladies.'

This news took me aback. I had been so worried there had been these hooded men in our garden and now she was telling me they were women. Perhaps she had been dreaming after all. I went to her bed and sat down on the edge stroking her hair.

'What were ladies doing in our garden?' I asked.

'I don't know,' she said. 'They were just wandering around in funny dresses.'

'Why were they funny?' I asked.

'They were all white, but when they turned round they were tied at the back, but I could see their bums.' She laughed as she said this. She was, after all, six and saying the word bum was still hilarious.

I did not feel like laughing though. I said goodnight and left the room. I stood outside her door listening to her start to snore. Her words describing the dresses the ladies were wearing troubled me; to me they sounded like hospital gowns.

'The ghosts of Dr Richards' victims!' the irrational voice said.

I refused to believe this. I did not believe in ghosts. It was just coincidence. Izzy was just having really vivid dreams.

'Dreams about hooded monks and female patients!' the voice began to scream in my head. She doesn't know the stories. How could she pick two such

random things to see in the garden that fit with the history of the area?

'I don't believe in ghosts!' I said out loud. 'It's not possible!'

The landing light above my head suddenly flickered off and on several times. I looked up at it, trying to rationalise it, maybe the bulb was on its way out. I was tired and a lot had happened in the last few days. I went back to bed. Rachel was already back asleep when I got there. I snuggled up next to her and soon drifted back into a deep sleep.

A few hours later I was woken once again by a knocking on our bedroom door. Rachel and I sat up, knowing that it was Anna. Izzy never knocked, she would just open the door and wait for us to acknowledge her.

'Come in,' Rachel said, and Anna opened the door. Her silhouette was stooped like she was only half awake.

'What's up, kiddo?' I asked.

'I can't sleep,' she said. 'There's a weird noise in my room.'

I got up and went back to her room with her. I stood there listening. Nothing. For a moment I considered the possibility that Anna had been dreaming the sound. It was also possible she was still dreaming. Though it had been years since her last episode of sleepwalking, it was possible that the stress of everything that had happened recently had triggered a new bout.

I looked at her closely. She looked tired, but she didn't have the glazed look in her eyes that had always accompanied her sleepwalking. I was relieved. With everything else that was going on, I didn't need to be worrying about that as well. I carried on listening in silence for a while longer.

'I can't hear anything,' I said.

'It comes and goes,' she said. 'Just wait a minute.'

We stood there together in silence for what seemed like ages. There was no sound at all. Then I heard footsteps coming down the landing. Rachel stepped into the room.

'What is it?' she said. I shrugged. There was no sound to be heard except for the faint sound of Izzy's snoring coming from her room. We all continued to listen for a while. There was nothing.

'Well, whatever it was it's stopped now,' I said. 'Maybe you should just get back into...'

'Shh,' Anna said, cutting me off. 'There it is.' I listened carefully. It was a soft scratching sound, like nails on stone.

'What is that?' Rachel asked.

'I don't know,' I said, trying to pinpoint the origin of the sound. It seemed to be coming from the wall opposite Anna's bed. 'A mouse, maybe?'

'In a brand new house?' Rachel asked in disbelief.

'Well, there is a lot of wildlife in the fields behind the house,' I said.

I put my ear to the wall. I expected to hear that the sound was coming from the bottom of the wall, behind the skirting board maybe. Instead, though, it seemed to be coming from higher up, near the middle of the wall. I went along the wall trying to find where exactly it was happening.

Eventually I found that it was coming from behind a large poster of the boyband JLS that Anna had put up.

'It's coming from behind here,' I said, and the sound stopped.

'What is it?' Anna asked. I could hear in her voice that she was a little afraid.

'I don't know,' I said. 'Let's take the poster down and see if we can see any clues.'

Anna nodded. We carefully took the pins holding the corners out and pulled the poster away from the wall. I was looking for somewhere to put the poster on the floor when I heard Anna let out a yelp of shock and Rachel gasp. I looked up.

There on the wall, carved into the plaster in an elegant script was a phrase in a language I couldn't quite make out.

OCCIDERE MERETRICES

'Who did that?' Anna asked, almost crying.

'What does it mean?' Rachel asked.

All I could do was shake my head. I had no answers. The only thing I knew was that maybe I was going to have to start listening to the irrational voice that had been troubling me. There was no logical explanation I could see at that moment.

CHAPTER SIXTEEN

Anna spent the rest of the night in our room with Rachel, too scared to sleep in her own room. I slept on the sofa in the living room; well, when I say slept, I think there were only a couple of hours of actual sleep. Most of the night was spent going over the events of earlier. First, there was the fact that Izzy had seen women in hospital gowns wandering around our garden. Like the irrational voice had said earlier, it seemed to be pushing it that it was a coincidence that she had seen female hospital patients and hooded figures in the garden. There was no way that Izzy could have known the stories about what had happened around here. The facts of what Dr Richards had done in the hospital were kept fairly quiet, replaced by outrageous folklore. These urban legends were passed around freely by older children, but I doubted they were told by six-year-olds.

The facts of what had happened at the monastery had been kept locked up in vaults and libraries for over half a millennia; it was impossible that Izzy could know anything about it. No one even knew there had been a monastery here, let alone that it was home to monks of dubious character, until Mojo discovered the undercroft.

It was becoming more apparent by the second, as I slept fitfully on the sofa, that something was happening here that I did not understand, something that I had spent most of my life denying even the possibility of.

The incident in Anna's room was even more perplexing. We had heard the sound of those words

153

being etched into the plaster by unseen hands, their meaning was still a mystery to me. OCCIDERE MERETRICES. I was not sure, but I suspected it was Latin. I decided I would try to find out the next day. Even though Latin wasn't taught in most schools anymore, I thought someone at the school might have some knowledge of it.

In all my life, I had never experienced anything that had forced me to reconsider my understanding of the world; studying science had always reinforced what I thought. Everything I believed in could be proven by some form of experiment or equation.

I was woken from one of my short bouts of sleep by Rachel. She was holding two cups of coffee. I sat up and gave her room to sit down next to me. She smiled, but it was an effort. Her eyes were bloodshot and she had bags underneath.

'How did you sleep?' she asked.

'Not great,' I replied. She yawned and I smiled. 'I take it you didn't either?'

'No. I kept thinking about what happened upstairs, it was so strange. When I did manage to sleep Anna would turn over in her sleep and elbow me.'

This made me laugh out loud.

'Well, we all know where she gets that from,' I said with a grin.

Rachel smiled and elbowed me playfully in the ribs.

'Did she sleep all right?' I asked.

'Yeah, eventually. It took her a while to stop crying and drift off. I don't think we'll ever get her back in her room though, she's terrified.' She looked at me. 'So am I. What are we going to do?'

I didn't know what to tell her. The truth was that in the space of one night I had gone from being a sceptic, who always looked for the rational answer, to a believer. I had no rational explanation for what had happened. The writing had not been carved into the wall before we moved in, there was no way that Anna could have done it herself, her handwriting was not that great with a pen on paper. Beside which we all heard the sound, that scratching noise as the words were gouged into the wall by an unseen hand.

I had no idea what was the right thing to do. I had always scoffed at the people who called in psychics or priests to rid their homes of spirits; I couldn't see my self doing this.

'I don't know,' I answered. 'I'll try to find out what the words mean, that's the first step. Then after that I guess we look for some kind of scientific way of finding out what is going on.'

'Like what?' she asked.

'I don't know for sure,' I said. ' I think I'll give Jim Roberts a call?'

'Your old housemate from Uni?' she asked looking confused.

'Yeah,' I said. 'He's one of the cleverest men I've ever met, and he was always into these sort of things.'

'What about our family, Dan?' she said. 'Are the girls safe here?'

I took her hand in mine.

'Of course they are,' I said, and at the time, I believed this completely. 'Although I've had to reevaluate my position on whether or not ghosts exist, I still know that there is no way they can hurt you.'

'How can you know that?' she said harshly. 'If it can scratch words into a fucking wall, how can you know it can't hurt us?'

This I couldn't answer; I just looked down at the floor, hurt a little by the tone of her voice. She picked up on this instantly.

'I'm sorry, Dan,' she said, taking my hand in her own. 'I know none of this is your fault. I'm the one who wanted this fucking house.' Tears welled in her eyes. With my free hand, I stroked her cheek softly.

'We both wanted the house,' I said softly. 'I know this is frightening, but I won't let anything hurt you or the girls.'

She kissed me. Gently at first, but rising quickly in passion. I don't know whether it was the build up of pressure from all the events of the last few days, but we soon found ourselves making frantic love there on the sofa. If I had known then that it would be the last time, I would have savoured it more, but blissfully unaware of the coming events as we were, we lost ourselves in the heat of the moment.

Afterwards we held each other for what seemed like hours. Neither of us spoke. What more was there to say? We had no explanation for the strange occurrences in our home, neither of us knew how to proceed. So for now the best we could offer each other was the warmth of our embrace.

At about half seven I had a shower and got dressed for work. Rachel made me a few bacon sandwiches for my breakfast. I appreciated the gesture, but had to admit my appetite was suffering from the stress of last night. I forced one of the sandwiches down, wrapped the other up in cling film, and promised Rachel that I would eat it later. She told me that she planned to let the girls sleep as long as they needed today. I agreed. Anna had had such a shock the night before that she needed the rest. Undoubtedly, Izzy would rise earlier. Rachel would be able to find some way to entertain her easily enough. Once both girls were up and dressed, she planned to take them next door to see if Mary and Maggie needed anything.

I kissed Rachel goodbye and took my briefcase and box of books out to the car. As I was placing the box into my boot, I heard Paul's voice behind me.

'Morning, Dan,' he said. The sound gave me a start, I was still so on edge.

'Jesus!' I exclaimed as I dropped the box into the car. I spun around and saw Paul.

'Oh, sorry I made you jump,' he said.

'It's alright,' I said smiling. I put a hand to my chest and felt my heart thumping faster than normal. 'I'm just a little tense today.'

'Anything the matter?' he asked.

I considered telling him about the events of the night before. About the scratching sound and the message etched into the wall, after all he was an archaeology student. There was a good chance he would be able to read some Latin but, like I had been my whole life, Paul was a man of science and I did not want him to think I was losing my grip on reality. I would wait until later and show him the phrase if no one at school could decipher its meaning.

'No, not really,' I lied. 'Just the whole thing with Bill and not getting enough sleep.'

'Yes, it's terrible about poor Mr Jenson,' he said and looked down at the floor. It was a look I had seen before, the discomfort of the young on how they should talk about death when someone had just died. The older you get the more of a reality and a part of you life, death and grief become, but in youth it seems so far away and alien. I decided to let him off the hook and change the subject.

'So what can I do for you this early, Paul?' I said, and saw the relief on his face that the previous subject was over.

'I just wanted to let you know that Rick and I will be starting to examine the undercroft this morning. Thom and a few of his spelunking friends will join us later in the week, they are thinking of checking how deep the well is.'

With the strange happenings in the house last night I had almost forgotten about the hole, the undercroft and the well, even though at the back of my mind there was some connection between it all. I felt like we had disturbed something, something that should have been left to rest, but as a man of science, I craved answers.

'Fine,' I said. 'Just let Rachel know what you're doing so she can keep the girls out of the way. I'll be home about half four, we can catch up then.'

Paul agreed and we exchanged farewells, and then I set off for work.

CHAPTER SEVENTEEN

'Occidere Meretrices? Occidere Meretrices?' Jeff Weston repeated to himself as he looked at the scrap of paper in his hand. It was the same note I had copied from the wall of Anna's room the night before. It was lunchtime and I had approached Jeff in the staff room. He taught Spanish, French and German, and was the most qualified languages teacher we had in the school. I had asked him if he could translate the phrase for me. I followed him back to his classroom, where he had left his reading glasses, and he began to examine the words.

'Well,' he said eventually. 'It is definitely Latin, that much I can be sure of.' He handed me the note. I had guessed as much, dealing with science you pick up some Latin names along the way.

'What does it say?' I asked.

'That I can't really help you with,' he said apologetically. 'It's been nearly forty years since I studied any Latin and that was only very basic stuff. It seems to be saying something about death, but I can't be certain.'

My heart sank when he said the word death. I needed more than that. Was it a threat? Were the lives of me and my family at risk?

'Where did you find such an obscure phrase?' Jeff asked, as I slipped the note back into my pocket.

'Oh, it was written on a wall of an old ruin near my house,' I said.

'Well, I can't think of anyone here who might speak Latin well enough to help you,' he said. 'You could try a church, particularly a Catholic one. They don't often use Latin in their masses anymore, but an

159

older priest might be able to help you with it. There are translation sites on the internet, but I'd advise you against using them. Most of them aren't all that accurate, sometimes the kids use them to do their homework and I can always tell as they basically end up writing gibberish.'

I thanked him for his help and headed back to my own classroom. There was still half an hour of the lunch break to go, but I did not feel like sitting in the staff room making idle conversation with my colleagues. I thought about what Jeff had suggested to me. I knew there was a Catholic church in town, somewhere near the girls high school, but the idea of asking a priest for help seemed ridiculous to me, even if it was just for help with translation. What if the message gave some indication of its source? Surely if I went to a priest and learned of something supernatural occurring in his area, he would have to inform the church and investigate the case.

Though my belief system had been turned on its head in recent days, I was still not prepared to go running into the arms of the church. I had no belief in God and felt that religion had no place in my home or anywhere near my children. I supposed my best option was to try one of these translation sites. Jeff had urged me not to, but even if the translation was not totally accurate, it might at least give me some idea of the general meaning of the phrase.

As I climbed the stairs that led to my classroom, I heard the phone ringing in the little office shared by the science staff. I sprinted the last few steps and went to the answer it.

'Hello, science block, Mr Martin speaking,' I said as professionally as I could muster after my short burst of running.

'Dad?' I recognised Anna's voice instantly. I could also hear the fear in it.

'Anna?' I said. 'What's wrong?'

'Mum told me to call you,' she said. 'Something is happening next door, can you come home please.'

After I got off the phone to Anna I rushed to the headmaster's office. Forgetting completely about my plan to try and translate the phrase on the internet. I told him that I needed to be excused again, that something was wrong at home. He did not look best pleased, but told me to go home and sort out the problem. I apologised and thanked him profusely. I promised him that I would be back the next day, it turned out that that was a lie. I would never go into work again. Not from that day to this, as I sit here writing this account.

I drove home as quickly as I could. Midday traffic in Darton was usually a nightmare and today was no exception. Anna had given me no idea of what was happening next door. I feared the worst. I guessed that in her grief something terrible had afflicted Mary, perhaps a heart attack of her own.

I was shocked as I headed up the towards Blackfriars Crescent that the emergency vehicles were not in Mary's drive, but were on the other side at the home of Laura and Leo. I was also surprised that the emergency vehicles in question were not ambulances, but police cars. As I pulled into my driveway I saw two policemen exit Laura's house. They were escorting

Mikkala, the au pair, to the police car. She had her hands cuffed behind her back, she was struggling and crying, tears streaked her face, and her reddened eyes looked wide in confusion.

'I didn't do it!' she sobbed loudly, her Dutch accent thicker than normal. 'I never touched him. I love Leo!'

I shut my car door and saw Anna and Izzy stood watching from our front room. They both looked at the scene unfolding with an expression of fear and confusion. I waved at them both and mouthed the words 'stay there' to them. Anna nodded and pulled her little sister closer to her in a protective gesture.

I headed across the grass and towards the policemen who were putting Mikkala in the car forcefully.

'What's going on?' I asked, both to the policemen and Mikkala.

'Mr Martin!' Mikkala exclaimed on seeing me. 'Tell them it's a mistake; tell them I wouldn't do that!' She looked at me pleadingly as one of the policemen finally pushed her onto the back seat of the car and slammed the door on her. The other policeman took my arm and moved me away from the car.

'You're Mr Martin? From next door?' he said. He was a tall, powerfully built man, maybe five years younger than me, but with a weariness in his eyes that said he had seen far too much of the evils of this world.

'Yes,' I said. 'What the hell is going on?'

'We have to take Miss Parivnic to the station. My colleagues are inside with Ms Taylor and your wife; they can explain what's happened. Let yourself in.'

I watched as the policemen got into the front of the car. Mikkala turned and looked pleadingly at me as they drove her away. I looked after the car as it headed down the street. Once it was out of sight, I just stared into the space it had been. My head was swirling with confusion. Eventually I steadied myself and walked into the house. There were two police officers inside, one stood by the door as I entered. The other, a policewoman, sat next to Laura who was sat on the sofa crying. On the other side of her sat Rachel. When she saw me enter, she got up and ran to me, alerting the others to my presence. Rachel hugged me.

'I'm sorry for calling you out of work,' Rachel said. Her face was streaked with tears. 'I just didn't know what else to do.'

I let Rachel lead me to the sofa opposite the one that Laura and the policewoman sat on. We sat down.

'What's going on?' I asked, perplexed. 'Where's Leo?' Suddenly I was aware of the child's absence.

'Mr Martin,' the police officer said. 'Leo is at the hospital. His mother went in to wake him for school this morning to find him unconscious in a pool of his own vomit. When she couldn't wake him, she called an ambulance. It turns out that at some point during the night, someone had poured rat poison down his throat. We came to investigate the scene and found an empty bottle of the stuff in Miss Parivnic's room, along with the funnel she used to get it down his throat.'

I put my hand to my mouth in shock. I had seen the way that Mikkala had been with the boy. It was clear to me that she had loved him like a little brother; it seemed totally incomprehensible to me that she could have done something so evil to him.

'Oh my God!' I managed to say at last. 'How is Leo now?'

Laura looked up at me her eyes wet and red.

'He's stable,' she said in a choked voice. 'But he's still unconscious, and it's going to be a while before they know what damage it's done.'

'I'm so sorry, Laura,' I said.

'We've arrested Miss Parivnic for attempted murder. We're going to take Ms Taylor back to the hospital now to be with her son, but we might need statements from you and your family,' the policewoman said.

'Of course,' I said. 'We'll help in any way we can.'

The police led Laura out to their car. The female officer was semi holding her up. Laura looked broken. She looked like she had aged twenty years since I saw her last. We agreed to lock up for her, she gave us the set of keys that belonged to Mikkala. As the police car moved down the street we locked the door and stood on Laura's drive watching until they were out of sight. I held Rachel close to me, her cheeks were stained with tears. I knew exactly how she felt. Though we felt sorry for Laura and poor little Leo, we were really thinking about what if something happened to one of our girls. How could we carry on after that? It made me suddenly more concerned about their well-being, with everything that was happening in the house.

'Perhaps you should take the girls and stay at your mum's,' I said. 'Just until we can figure out what is going on.'

She looked up at me and smiled.

'I'm sure you were right this morning,' she said. 'I doubt that there's anything that can hurt us.'

'But until we know...' I began to say, but she put a finger to my lips to silence me.

'Until we know, you'll protect us. I trust that,' she said. 'Besides, how freaked out Anna is about last night if we took her away I think it would scare her more.'

'Well, tomorrow I'm going to try to find us some help,' I promised.

CHAPTER EIGHTEEN

The rest of that day was spent with us all worrying about Leo. Izzy was distraught that her little friend was poorly and in the hospital. We didn't tell her the full details of what had happened. She was fond of Mikkala, and we thought that until it was clear what had really happened it was best not to say too much.

Anna, however, was older and realised that the police wouldn't take Mikkala away for no reason.

'What did she do?' she asked me whilst we were washing up.

'No one knows yet,' I said, then added. 'No one even knows for sure yet if she has done anything.'

'The police must have thought she'd done something,' she said.

'Well, yes,' I admitted. 'There was some evidence that she had poisoned Leo.'

Anna looked shocked.

'Why would she do that?' she asked. 'Why would anyone hurt a little boy like Leo?'

'I don't know, kiddo. Some people just do bad things. It makes me sick to my stomach, but it's the world we live in.'

'I can't believe it,' she said. 'She always seemed so nice.'

'As I said, we don't know that she did yet. This could all be a mistake and what happened to Leo could just be a terrible accident. Innocent until proven guilty, remember?'

Anna nodded. We finished the washing up in relative silence. Anna was trying to process the information, I think. I felt suddenly guilty for moving to this damned house. We had moved with the best of intentions, to keep Anna away from the bad crowds in town and to give both the girls a better life. However, since we had moved here it seemed that the children had been faced with more death and sadness than they ever had before.

After the washing up was done, Anna went to her room to watch a film. Izzy sat in between me and Rachel on the sofa. She rested her head on her mother's lap. We left her there until she fell asleep, and then I carried her up to bed.

When I came back downstairs, Rachel was pouring herself a glass of wine. I pulled out my cigarettes and we headed out into the garden. Without speaking we both looked over the fence at the blackened windows of Laura's house.

'It's terrible,' Rachel finally said, breaking the silence. 'How can something like that happen?'

I shook my head.

'I don't know.'

'You could see that Mikkala loved that little boy so much,' she said, tears welling in her eyes. 'I just can't believe she would just decide to poison him.'

'Perhaps she didn't,' I said. 'Perhaps it's a mistake. Like you say, it's clear to anyone how much she loves Leo. I don't think she did it.'

We sat in silence until Rachel had finished her wine. When we went back inside Rachel said she was going up to bed. The events of the day had taken their toll and she was emotionally and physically drained. I nodded and kissed her.

'Are you not coming up?' she asked.

'No, not yet,' I said. 'I want to call Jim.'

'Oh, yes, of course.' It seemed that Rachel had almost completely forgotten the supernatural events of the previous night. 'Ask after Kelly for me.'

I said I would and then kissed her again. She made her way up to bed.

I poured my self a large rum and Coke and then pulled the address book out of the drawer near the phone. I flicked through to R, and then scanned the page until I saw Jim and Kelly Roberts written in Rachel's handwriting, Jim and Kelly had gotten married not long after me and Rachel. Kelly and Rachel had been good friends while we were all at university. They had stayed in Leicester for quite a few years and had then moved to Nottingham, where Dr Jim Roberts, PhD was a senior lecturer in applied physics at the University of Nottingham.

I typed the number into the phone, but did not press the green button to make the call. Instead, I paused. I was not looking forward to making this call. Jim and I had always remained friends, but in recent years it had become little more than the odd e-mail to each other. Both of us were so busy with work that, even though we only lived about an hour and a half apart, it was never convenient to meet up.

Now, here I was calling him to ask him for his help. Not only that, but I was asking him for help with something that I had always mercilessly taken the piss out of him for.

Jim had always claimed that as a young child he had seen the ghost of an old man in his family home. Rather than frightening him, the apparition had fascinated him and had led him to embark on a lifelong quest to understand the nature of the paranormal. He had learnt as much as he could about physics, neurology and psychology as he could to try to find out what caused people to see ghosts. He found that no one subject had ever given a conclusive answer. He set about using his vast scientific knowledge to investigate haunted places. He believed that there had to be some way to not only scientifically measure and quantify supernatural activity, but also to conclusively prove its existence.

His obsession led to much ribbing from me and our fellow housemate Mark. Both of us took the traditional scientific view that the paranormal was utter nonsense made up a long time ago to explain things that people didn't understand. As far as we were concerned it was only the ignorant and the impaired who could believe in such things. We put the idea forward once that Jim had these beliefs due to some minor brain damage caused by his epilepsy. He, to his credit, took this idea on board and had a complete brain scan. They found no damage in areas of the brain that could have caused him to see or believe in spirits.

Now, all these years later, I had to go crawling to him with my tail between my legs and ask him for his help because I believed my house was haunted. I knew Jim well enough to know that the irony of the situation would not be lost on him. I also knew that he would not let it go unmentioned, he was bound to relish rubbing my nose in it. To be honest, I wouldn't blame him.

Finally, I sighed and pressed the green button. I heard the phone begin to dial the number, and then it rang.

'Hello.' I heard Jim's voice. He answered very quickly.

'Hi, Jim,' I said, 'it's...'

'Dan 'The Man' Martin!' he said, cutting me off. 'How long has it been since we spoke on the phone?'

'It was Christmas I think?' I replied, knowing full well that it had been. 'So how's things? How's Kelly?'

'Things are good thanks, work keeps me up to my eyeballs, plus I'm editing a new book at the moment,' he said. 'Kelly's great, still working for the same company. She virtually runs the place now.'

'That's great,' I said. 'Well, tell her that Rachel sends her love.'

'How about you? How's life treating you? How are Rachel and the girls?'

I took a deep breath.

Jim picked up on the pause.

'Is everything okay, mate?' he said.

'To be honest with you, no, not at all,' I said. 'That's why I'm calling, I really need your help.'

'Anything I can do you know I will, mate,' he said, sounding concerned.

'It's really difficult for me to do this,' I said.

'Do you need some money, Dan? If so, just let me know how much and I'll see what I can do.'

'No, it's not about money,' I said. 'I need your help with something.'

'What is it, Dan?'

'I think my house is haunted.'

To my surprise, Jim did not once try to rub my face in the irony of the situation. Instead, he listened carefully as I explained all the things that had been happening in the house. The discovery of the undercroft, the figures Izzy had seen, the noises we had all heard and most disturbingly the message written on the wall of Anna's bedroom. I told him how I was at my wits end, that I needed answers.

'It'll be okay, Dan,' he said reassuringly. 'I'll come over and do a sweep of the house with some of my equipment. We'll see if together we can come up with a rational explanation and if not, we'll try to find some evidence of what is happening and why.'

'Thank you so much, Jim,' I said.

'Don't mention it,' he said. 'I can come over tomorrow afternoon.'

'That'd be great,' I said.

With that agreed, we chatted for a few more minutes about nothing in particular. He told me that he had heard from Mark the other week. Mark now lived in Florida and worked for NASA. We eventually said our goodbyes and I felt relieved to know that Jim would be there to help the next day.

I decided that perhaps Rachel was right going to bed. An early night would probably do me good. I decided that I would go out and have a smoke and then follow her up to bed. I picked up my lighter and headed into the kitchen. The lights were off in there and, as I approached the back door, I froze for a second in horror.

There, stood in the middle of my garden, was a figure in a long black robe and large black hood. He was tall and thin. The hood obscured most of his face, but I could see the white of his chin shining in the moonlight. He was stood with his head bowed looking down into the hole.

For a millisecond, I thought that my heart had stopped beating, that I was experiencing the last few seconds of brain activity before I died of shock. Then I felt it kick back into rhythm, at least twice as fast as it should be.

As I stared out at the hooded figure, my fear began to mutate into anger. Anger that then grew into full-blown rage. I hated this thing for scaring my family. I hated it for making me feel uncomfortable in my own home, and I hated it for Bill's death.

Without thinking, I flung open the back door and charged into the back garden, yelling as I went.

'Bastard!' I screamed at the top of my lungs.

The figure looked up and then turned to run, human after all. He looked young. Perhaps Mary had been right that it was just a group of teenagers. It was not a robe he was wearing, but a long black overcoat over the top of a hoodie. Still my anger would not abate.

I followed him. He ran to the fence that separated our garden from Mary's. He leapt over it, with an agility that I did not have. I had to put my hands on top of the fence and vault it. He ran towards the house, I feared for Mary and Maggie. I used all of my strength and pushed harder, sprinting to catch up with him. Just as he opened the kitchen door of Mary's house, I grabbed hold of his hood, pulling him back by it. He choked as the collar of the hoodie gathered around his throat. I didn't care. I wanted to hurt him. I spun him round and grabbed his throat and slammed him against the wall.

'You little shit!' I screamed as I pulled back my fist, ready to swing at him.

'Stop! Dan, Stop!' It was Maggie. She was running from the kitchen to the garden. She put herself between me and the intruder.

'Maggie. I was...' I said.

'It's okay, Dan,' she said calmly. 'This is Alex. My brother Alex.'

It took a moment for what she was saying to register, I was still so pumped full of adrenaline and rage. Then it dawned on me what she had said and I let him go. He slumped to the floor choking.

'Jesus,' I said. 'Alex, I'm so sorry.' I held out my hand and offered to help him up, but he swatted my hand away.

'Fuck you,' he sputtered.

'Alex!' Maggie said angrily.

'No, it's okay Maggie,' I said. 'I must have scared the shit out of him. I am sorry if I hurt you, Alex, it's just when I saw you in my garden I thought...' I trailed off. I didn't know how to finish the sentence without making myself sound crazy. I could hardly say that I thought that he was a ghost monk and I had charged at him for all the trouble he had caused in my house.

'You thought what?' he said, standing up, his voice tinged with anger. 'That I was going to steal your shitty chicken wire fence?'

'No,' I said. 'I thought you were a burglar, we've had a few prowlers of late and it has my kids scared,' I explained.

'Whatever,' he said, turning around to go in the house.

Maggie stopped him. She yanked on his shoulder and pulled him back to face us.

'What the hell were you doing in Dan's garden anyway?' she said.

'I just wanted to see that hole,' he said.

'Why?' I asked.

'Mum told me how your dog fell down there the other night, and Dad helped you up and down there.'

'Yeah, that's true,' I said.

'So I wanted to see the hole that killed my father,' he said coldly.

I couldn't respond. I was shocked.

'Jesus Christ, Alex!' Maggie said.

'Think about it,' Alex said. 'Dad has a heart condition. This idiot lets him pull him up on a rope, the next night he has a massive heart attack and dies. Doesn't take genius to join the dots does it?'

This thought had never even crossed my mind. Suddenly I felt ashamed. Why had I let Bill do that? I knew that he had angina. There was no way I should have let him help me rescue Mojo.

'That's rubbish, Alex,' Maggie said. 'Apologise to Dan right now.'

He scoffed.

'No fucking way,' he said. Then he stormed off into the house.

Maggie looked at me; she looked embarrassed. Then she saw the worry on my face.

'Dan,' she said softly. 'What he said just now, it isn't true. That had nothing to do with Dad's death.'

'I don't know,' I said. 'It makes sense.'

'No,' she said firmly. 'Alex is just upset and angry, and he lashed out at you because you were there. I'm sorry about him saying those things, and I'm sorry about him sneaking around your garden, he's such a moron.'

I bid her goodnight and went back over the fence, not wanting to see Alex again, or to face Mary. I went to bed that night with a heavy heart.

CHAPTER NINETEEN

My sleep that night was disjointed at best. Though I had none of the horrific nightmares that had been plaguing me of late, I did keep waking with a deep sense of sadness and regret. Alex's words kept spinning around my head. Had helping me with the rescue of Mojo from the undercroft had anything to do with Bill's death? I didn't know what I would do if this was the case. One thing I was certain of was that there was no way I would feel right speaking at the funeral. I would have to talk to Mary and tell her. I had also decided that I was not going to return to work now until after the holidays had started.

After we got up, I rang the school and told the headmaster that I was going to be off work for the rest of the week, and hence the rest of the school year. He did not take the news too well, even a nice man like him had a limit. When I told him that he was perfectly welcome to advertise for a teacher to replace me he seemed to mellow. He told me to keep him posted on when I would return during the holidays and we would discuss it then.

After the phone call, Rachel took Izzy to the park leaving me to talk to Anna about what had taken place in her room the night before. We sat down together on the sofa.

'Want to talk about it?' I asked. She looked younger today. Yesterday, she had been a girl on the brink of womanhood. Today, she looked like a scared child. She sat huddled up on the sofa with her knees hugged up to her chest. She wore no makeup and her hair was just tied back in a ponytail. It was the look on her face that did it the most. It was a look I remembered.

When Anna had been about eight she had to have a lot of dental work to correct an overbite she inherited from me. During the numerous and painful appointments she developed a severe fear of the dentist. She would make herself physically sick with worry in the days leading up to an appointment. On a day she had to go to the dentist she would be quiet all day and just sit there with a distant and nervous look in her eyes.

It was this look that I was seeing now. She looked at me and shrugged. I don't think she knew whether she wanted to talk about it or not.

'It was scary, wasn't it?' I asked.

She nodded.

'I was scared,' I said. 'Mum was scared, so there's nothing wrong with it scaring you.'

'Was it...' she started, then paused for a few moments, trying to decide whether to continue or not. 'Was it a ghost?'

I looked at her and shrugged.

'I'm not going to lie to you, honey. I don't know,' I said. 'I've never believed in ghosts. Maybe there is another explanation, something more rational, but I don't know what that could be.'

'Do you think our house is haunted?' she asked. I noticed that she lowered her voice. I wondered whether she did not want any potential ghosts to hear her talk about them.

'I don't know, something strange is happening here,' I said. 'It's scary when things we don't understand happen, but I promise you I'm going to find out what's going on.'

She hugged me.

' I never believed in ghosts, you know, Daddy?'

'Me neither,' I said. 'I guess it's not all bad. I mean if there are ghosts it proves that there is something else. That we go on after we die. That's kind of reassuring.'

'I guess,' she said. 'Like it means Uncle Bill might still be around somewhere.'

That thought hadn't occurred to me, but as she said it I felt a warmth spread through me. I liked the idea that Bill was still out there somewhere, maybe next door watching over his family in their time of need. Then I remembered what Izzy had said about him being in her room the night he died and telling her she had to be a good girl. Perhaps Bill was watching over all of us.

'Maybe he is,' I said, hugging her. 'But whatever is going on here it's nothing that can hurt us.'

'Promise?' she asked, her eyes pleading with me for reassurance.

'I promise.' I believed that when I told her. 'Still scared?'

'A little I guess,' she said, but she did look more relaxed. 'Can I sleep in Izzy's room until we know what's happening?'

'Of course you can,' I said. 'I'll move your bed in there later, you can keep an eye on her sleepwalking.'

She laughed. We sat there on the sofa for a while after in silence. I realised that it had been too long since we had spent so much time together. I vowed that from now on Anna could have as much of my time as she needed.

When Rachel and Izzy got back, I decided I had to go next door and tell Mary that I no longer felt that it was right for me to speak at Bill's funeral on Friday.

I knocked on the door and for a moment I was worried that Alex would open the door. Maybe he had calmed down since our little altercation the night before, but if not it could be very awkward. Fortunately, it was Mary that answered the door. She gave me a big hug and ushered me into the living room.

'Lovely of you to pop round, Dan,' she said, heading to the kitchen. 'It gives me an excuse to have another cuppa.'

'Always glad to help,' I said, sitting down on the sofa.

'The kids have gone into town,' she said from the kitchen. 'They don't usually get on that well, but they're making the effort for my sake I think. Well, Maggie is at least.'

She brought me in a cup of coffee; she had made me so many over the few months we'd known each other that she no longer had to ask me how I took it. She sat down opposite me.

'So what brings you over to see me, Dan?' she asked.

'Well, I don't know if you know, but I had a little incident with Alex last night,' I said.

'Yes, I heard about that,' she said, looking ashamed. 'I am sorry about it, he had no right to be wandering your garden at night. He can be a little morbid sometimes. I think it's the music he listens to, and all the black he wears. He calls himself a Goth, I think it's just taking things too seriously.'

'It's all right,' I said. 'I shouldn't have reacted the way that I did.'

'Nonsense,' Mary said. 'You reacted the way anyone would to a stranger in their garden. I know Bill would have done the same, except Bill would have probably roughed him up a bit more than you did.'

I still felt the guilt that had been niggling at me all night. The guilt that was going to eat me up inside if I didn't do something soon. Her mentioning Bill just made me feel worse.

'Mary,' I said. 'Alex said that he thinks that Bill helping me rescue the dog the other night might have caused Bill's heart attack, I mean it must have put a lot of strain on his heart. I shouldn't have let him do it.'

'I would have liked to have seen you try to stop him,' she said.

'Still, I can't help but feel like what happened to him is partly my fault. So I don't think I should speak at the funeral. I just don't think it would be right.'

Mary looked at me and shook her head.

'No, Dan, you have to,' she said. 'Bill was as strong as an ox the night he helped you with the dog. He was right until the moment the heart attack took him, nothing he did or didn't do would have made any difference. It was just his time.'

'I still don't think it's a good idea for me to speak,' I said. 'Alex seemed really angry at me, I wouldn't want to upset him.'

'Bill would want you to speak, he thought the world of you,' she said. 'As for Alex, he's not mad at you, he's mad at himself, he and Bill didn't get on so well for the last few years, they just seemed to clash all the time. Now there's nothing that can be done. It's too late for Alex to sort things out with his Dad, and he's looking for someone to blame. I will not let him blame you; you and Rachel have done so much for me. Please, for Bill, will you speak at the funeral?'

I sighed and then smiled.

'I'd be honoured to speak tomorrow.'

She smiled. We chatted for a little while about the arrangements for the next day and then I noticed the car coming down the crescent and pulling into my drive. It must be Jim. I said goodbye to Mary and headed back home.

CHAPTER TWENTY

As I crossed Mary's front lawn to my own, I was shocked to see Jim get out of the driver's side of the car. Though he had passed his test at seventeen, he had always been unable to drive due to his epilepsy.

Kelly got out of the passenger side; she smiled as she saw me, and gave me a big wave.

'Dan Martin,' she said. 'I swear to God, you do not ever age, what is your secret?'

'Good genes, I guess, Kelly,' I said, walking over and hugging her.

Jim walked over and threw his arms around me; he gave me a bear hug. Jim was a good few inches taller than me, and a lot broader. He was what people often described as barrel-chested.

'Good to see you, mate,' he said, finally letting go so that I could breathe again.

'You, too,' I said. 'Thanks for coming so quickly. It means a lot.'

'No worries,' Jim said. 'Let's see if we can figure out your little problem.'

Rachel came out and greeted them. Then she led Kelly indoors to see the kids. Jim and I stayed outside. Jim went to the boot of his car and pulled out a large metal flight case.

'In here are the best pieces of equipment money can buy for ghost hunting. I'm not talking about the cheap shit you find on Ebay; those things couldn't detect a fart in a bath.'

He opened the case and waved his hands over the array of meters and machines within.

'If there is something to detect in your house, Dan, one of these will find it.' He picked up something that to me looked a little like a hairbrush, with a screen where the bristles should be. 'This is a FLIR i3 thermal imaging camera. It has a sensitivity of less than 0.15 degrees Celsius. It takes thousands of calibrated temperature readings in every shot. This thing shows any hot or cold spot before you even feel them.'

I nodded, showing him I was impressed. Next, he held up a small box like meter, it looked a lot like an amp meter. I had one of those myself somewhere in the house.

'This is a trifield EMF meter. This will measure even the slightest change in the non-ionizing electromagnetic spectrum. It covers all bases; magnetic, electric and radio slash microwaves.'

'That tells you there's a ghost around?' I asked.

'Well, so people say,' he said. 'It makes sense, though. I mean, ghosts must use some form of energy to manifest. As it's an energy you can't always see or feel, it is more than likely electromagnetic. Although some people believe that it could be anomalies in the natural electromagnetic field that affect the human brain, causing people to have these paranormal experiences.'

'So they're not real?' I asked, 'Just hallucinations?'

'It's just one theory,' he said. 'There is some evidence, though, that stimulating the brain with electromagnetic energy does bring on paranoia and the feeling you're not alone, but these experiments have been done in labs, with amounts of energy that you don't generally find in people's homes. It might explain away a few cases, but nowhere near all of them.'

He pulled out a digital camera.

'I take it you know what this is?' he said with a smile.

'Yes, I'm aware of cameras,' I replied.

'Sometimes just snapping away with one of these things you can pick some stuff up, most common thing is orbs, they look like little balls of light. I'm not sure myself whether they're just dust particles near the lens, but some people believe they're the first sign of a spirit trying to manifest.'

He took out what looked to me like a fancy Dictaphone. I'd had one of those at university to help me take notes; it took tiny cassettes. This one, however, had no cassettes. I could see the USB port on the side, this too was digital.

'Digital voice recorder,' he said. 'This can be used to pick up E.V.P.'

'What?'

'It's a way of picking up spirit voices, but they use electric signal in the air to affect the recorder. Sometimes you get a clear voice, sometimes you get what sounds like a drunk, asthmatic fax machine. I've heard some really convincing evidence from them, but I've also heard a lot of nonsense. People get a slight sound on it and then they start trying to decipher it. I often think they're hearing what they want to hear, not what they actually recorded.'

I looked at him quizzically.

'Do you believe in ghosts, Jim?' I asked. 'I mean you don't seem very complimentary or certain about most of these ghost hunting techniques.'

'I believe in ghosts,' he said, nodding. 'I saw one when I was a kid, remember? I don't know what they are though; I don't know if they're the souls of dead people. I'm not sure as I scientist if I could bring myself to believe that. What they are, though, is something that has been reported in every culture since the dawn of man. I just think that a lot of the theories are more about wish fulfillment than any real science, but these techniques, with the equipment I've brought today, do get results.'

'So how do we do this?' I asked.

'One room at a time,' he said.

I nodded and led him into the house.

When we got inside the house, Jim hugged Rachel, and told her how she gets more beautiful every time he sees her. Rachel laughed off his flattery with her usual modesty. He then scooped each of the girls up into his arms in turn and gave them each a big kiss. They laughed wildly, even Anna who would normally consider herself to be far too old for that kind of show of affection from an adult, then she had always had a soft spot for Uncle Jim. He was Godfather to both of them and always lavished them with attention and gifts whenever he saw them. Today was no exception; after he had put Anna down, he fished his wallet out of his pocket and pulled out a twenty pound note for each of them.

'Here you go,' he said, handing the money over to the beaming girls. 'Why don't Mum and Aunty Kelly take you girls into town to buy whatever you want?'

He winked at me. As much as he enjoyed spoiling Anna and Izzy, this was also a rouse to get them out of the house while we went about the business of investigating the supernatural phenomena that was occurring.

'That's a great idea,' I said.

'Your wish is our command,' Kelly said, smiling.

Rachel nodded.

'Okay, get your things together, ladies,' Jim said. The girls ran upstairs to sort themselves out.

'They're keen,' Kelly said.

Rachel looked at me and then Jim.

'Is it safe?' she asked, concerned. 'What you're going to be doing?'

Jim smiled and took her hands.

'I wouldn't be here doing this for you if it wasn't. Hopefully we can get you some answers; it sounds like the whole thing has got all of you spooked.'

'It has,' Rachel said.

'Well, hopefully, once we have more information we can figure out what to do to sort the problem out.'

Rachel hugged him, and thanked him for his help. He told her not to be silly.

Our two wives and the girls left soon after this. The house fell quiet as Jim started to take his equipment out of the case. He handed me the thermal imaging camera.

'Why don't you take this? It's fairly easy to use. Just point it around and if you see anything going green it means you've found a cold spot.'

I slowly turned around on the spot, panning the camera as I went. I saw my living room illuminated on the small screen in a plethora of shades of blue.

'What does blue mean?' I asked Jim.

'On a day like today, with the temperature being what it is, that's normal. Just look for anything that goes green to black, that signifies a major drop. Also anything going red, orange, yellow or white means something that is hot. It's far more unusual to get warm spots with a haunting, but it can happen.'

I saw what he meant as I spun the camera round to him. The shape of his body was illuminated in hues of orange and yellow.

'Has anything ever happened in here?' he said.

'No,' I replied. 'Anna thought she heard someone come in through the front door the other day, but no, nothing in this room.'

'Good,' Jim said. 'I'll use this room to take baseline readings.'

Jim continued to spend the next ten minutes taking readings all around the room with the trifield meter. He swept it slowly around the edges of the room, making notes on a little pad. Then he checked around all the power sockets on the walls, then at various heights in the centre of the room.

Next, he took readings around the room with a laser thermometer. He checked the ambient temperature in the room in several places, then took more specific readings from places like around the windows and doors.

'Okay, let's move on,' he said, putting the pad back in his pocket.

'Everything okay?' I asked.

'Yeah,' he said smiling. 'The readings in here were exactly what they should be.'

Next we quickly checked the kitchen, there was nothing of interest in their either. We moved upstairs; I led him down the hall to Anna's room. This was the room I was dreading. Of all the activity that had happened in the house, this had been the worst, the most unexplainable in any rational terms.

We stepped into the room. Jim instantly walked over to the message on the wall. The neatly carved Latin phrase still gave me a chill when I looked at it.

'So you saw this appear?' Jim asked.

'No, not as such,' I said. 'There was a poster over that part of the wall, but me, Rachel and Anna all heard it being carved, then when I took the poster down there it was.'

'Any idea what it means yet?' he asked.

I shook my head.

'I meant to look it up online, but with everything that's been going on around here, I keep forgetting.'

'Understandable,' he said. He took his finger and traced along the letters. 'This is amazing. It would be even more amazing if you'd seen it appear, but still.'

Jim took the E.M.F. meter out and began to scan the wall where the writing was.

'Nothing,' he said, a little disappointed. 'Let me try something else.'

He left the room and I heard him go down the stairs. I stayed in the room staring at the words carved onto my daughter's wall; again, anger and fear took hold. I had promised both Anna and Rachel that I would not let anything bad happen to them, but was Rachel right to worry? After all, if this thing could carve these letters so deeply into the plasterboard of the wall, what could it do to flesh? Were we all in real danger?

Jim returned, holding another box like instrument. This one seemed to have a sensor on the front and a digital display.

'What's that?' I asked.

'Geiger counter,' he said.

'Radiation? Really?' I said, concerned.

'Just a precaution,' Jim said reassuringly. 'Sometimes when there is this type of physical manifestation it leaves behind a low level amount of radiation. Nothing harmful, but detectable with one of these.'

He scanned the carving slowly with the Geiger counter. He watched the display screen intently, then sighed.

'Not a thing,' he said. 'I don't know what to say, mate, but there is no evidence of supernatural activity in this room.'

'That's not possible,' I said. 'We're not making this up you know, Jim?'

'I believe you,' he said. 'I'm just saying that as far as the usual physical evidence goes, I'm not getting anything.'

The same was true of the rest of the house; we detected nothing in any room in the house. No electromagnetic readings, no radiation, and not a single cold spot. I was disheartened to say the least. Though in the last few days I had been forced to change my mind on the existence of the paranormal, I still had faith that science would provide us with some answers. I sat down on the sofa heavily. Jim came and sat opposite me.

'Not what you were hoping for?' he said.

I put my head in my hands and rubbed my face.

'No, not really,' I said. 'I hoped that you'd be able to tell me something. Something concrete about what we're experiencing here.'

'Sorry, Dan,' he said. 'I wish I could have been of more help, but you know this isn't an exact science?'

'I know,' I said. 'I feel bad for wasting your time.'

'Hey, that's not true,' he said with a smile. 'It gave me a great excuse to come and see you. Plus the fact that there wasn't a single unusual reading in the whole of the house was interesting in its own way. I've never known of a place that has had the kind of activity you've described to me that hasn't produced a single reading.'

I smiled.

'How about you show me this monastery basement you found?' he said. 'Maybe there are some readings down there. After all, a lot of the times hauntings start after something old is disturbed in someway.'

I nodded in agreement.

CHAPTER TWENTY-ONE

As we climbed down the scaffolding that the archeology students had erected to make access to the undercroft easier, I noticed that the lights were not on down there. Paul, Rick, and their fellow students had obviously not started their work down there yet today. I knew that the switch for the lights was to the left of the bottom of the scaffold. So once I felt stone under my feet, I put my left arm out a switched the lights on. The whole room was illuminated.

Jim looked around, open-mouthed. He was obviously in awe of the sheer size of the under ground chamber.

'Wow,' he eventually managed to say.

'I know,' I said.

'You found this?' he said.

'Actually it was the dog, really, but I was the first person down here.'

Jim walked over to the wall; he ran his hands along the stone.

'It's amazing,' he said. 'How old did you say it was?'

'The archeologists think it's nearly nine hundred years old.'

'Unbelievable, you said something about it having a dark past?'

I explained to him what Rick had discovered about the evil Benedictine monks of St Martins—the criminal activity, the rapes, the torture and the murder. As I recounted the story to Jim, it seemed that the temperature in the undercroft began to drop. I did not know if this was true or whether it was in my mind.

After all, the atrocities I was describing had taken place in this very spot where we stood.

I continued on to the end of the tale, telling Jim how Henry VIII himself had overseen the destruction of this monastery. I could feel the goosebumps on my arms; if the temperature change was not real, then my mind was creating such a vivid illusion that my body was reacting.

'Fuck me,' Jim said, his eyes expressing his shock at the tale of St Martins.

'Hard to believe it all happened right here,' I said.

'Well, if there was ever a really good candidate for a haunted location, this is it. All of those horrific things happening here must have left some energy behind.'

'Is it just me, or has it got colder since we got down here?' I asked rubbing my arms.

'I thought that,' he said. 'I didn't take a temperature reading when we first got down here so there's no way to know for sure, but it certainly feels colder.'

I lifted up the thermal imaging camera and saw the shades of blue down in the undercroft were considerably darker than they had been back in the house. It was perfectly natural for an underground chamber made of old stone to be cooler than a modern house on a hot summer day. As I scanned around the room, I saw the blues getting darker, turning to green the further I went. At the far end of the room stood the well. On the monitor screen of the camera, it showed up as black. It was ice cold; tendrils of black were spewing out of it into the air.

'The well is really cold,' I said.

'Must be cold air coming from below,' he said, taking the camera from me and looking at it. 'It shouldn't be black though, that suggests that it's below freezing. That air coming out of it looks really creepy on here doesn't it?'

I nodded. Jim handed the thermal imaging camera back to me. He took out his digital camera and began to snap shots of the well. The flash lit the room up like there was a lightening storm in the chamber around us. The air felt as heavy and charged as it would in a storm.

Jim began to scan through the images he had taken on the camera. Though it was a small screen, the detail of the image was superb. The first few were all normal, then he came to one in which there appeared to be a white vaporous shape above the well. It was not distinct, but it had a vaguely human form. I looked at Jim.

'Is that a ghost?' I asked.

'It could be,' he said, looking at the image. 'But there are hundreds of possibilities of what it could be. A photo alone doesn't prove anything. I need to get some readings.'

He handed me the Geiger counter.

'I don't know how to use this,' I said. I had handled one once at university, many years ago, but it was more of a tool for physicists and geologists than for a biochemist, and certainly a secondary school chemistry teacher.

'Just hold it up and watch the display. If it starts to go up let me know,' he said, switching on his trifield meter. 'Ready?'

I wasn't. It dawned on me at that moment how utterly not ready I was. How had this happened? How in such a short space of time had I gone from a man who didn't believe in anything supernatural to a man stood in an underground chamber holding ghost hunting equipment, looking to prove that my home was haunted.

'Dan? Are you ready?' Jim repeated himself.

'As I'll ever be,' I said.

The two of us walked side-by-side slowly towards the well. The air felt heavier the closer we got. I could feel that inexplicable feeling of dread building in the pit of my stomach again.

Jim kept glancing over at the Geiger counter I was holding out in front of me. So far, the number on the LCD display had not changed, nor had I noticed the needle on his trifield meter so much as flutter.

'Looks like the readings down here are as negative as they were up in the house,' Jim said.

At that moment, the little LED lights on his meter flickered to life and the needle began to rise up the scale.

'Here we go,' Jim said, stopping in his tracks.

There was a sudden beep from the device in my hand; the sound reverberated around the chamber. I have to admit that I felt my heart stop beating briefly at the sound and then come back in much faster than before. The numbers on the LED screen began to rise.

'Is it dangerous?' I said, concerned.

'No,' Jim said. 'It would have to get up a lot higher than that to be of any concern.'

We continued to walk towards the well. The needle on the trifield meter kept rising, the Geiger counter kept beeping. The tempo of the beeps seemed to increase the closer we got to the well. The number on the display seemed to go up with every step I took. So, too, did my heart rate. I began to feel the same fear I had felt the first time I had come down here.

'These are some serious readings!' Jim exclaimed, delighted. He obviously was not experiencing the same dark feelings of apprehension that I was.

'Does it prove there's a ghost?' I asked.

'Not conclusively, Dan,' he said. 'Readings like this are very unusual, though.'

Both the meters continued to rise the nearer we got to the well. Though I knew well enough that the levels of radiation were nowhere near a harmful level, I still could not help but feel frightened as the counter rose and rose. What if it never stopped climbing? What if it never stopped? What if the level of radiation down here was so high that it peaked the Geiger counter? Then perhaps it would be a dangerous level. What if I had exposed myself, my friend and those poor archeology students to fatal levels of radiation? Was it already destroying my cells? Would I soon start to feel the effects of radiation sickness?

We reached the well. The air coming up from beneath hit me in the face hard, like a snowball thrown with great force. It took my breath from me, like stepping into a northerly wind in winter. I looked at Jim and could see from his face that it had the same effect on him.

'That air is far too cold,' he said. 'It's like an Arctic breeze. Point the thermal imager down there.'

I had almost forgotten that I was holding the thermal imaging camera; the Geiger counter had been taking so much of my attention. I raised the special camera and aimed it down into the well. The screen was as black as the darkest night. The air coming up from below was so cold that there was nothing visible on the screen. I showed it to Jim. He shook his head in disbelief.

'It must be faulty; it's not possible that it's that cold down there,' he said. He began to fumble through his pockets.

'What do you mean not possible?' I said. 'You can feel how cold it is.'

'Yes, but to show up as completely black, the temperature down there must be about twenty degrees below freezing.'

He finally found what he had been searching for in his pocket.

'Laser thermometer!' he exclaimed. He pointed it down the well and pressed a small button on the side. I saw disbelief on his face.

'What?' I said.

'According to this the air down there is thirty below freezing. That's not possible. If it were that cold we'd be freezing to death right now. I know it's cold but...'

He was cut off by the sound of the Geiger counter beeping constantly. I held it up.

'What's wrong with it?' I yelled at Jim.

'I don't know,' he said, then looked at his trifield meter. 'This one is going mental as well.' He held it up to me. I could see the needle swinging back and forth from the lowest position to the highest; the LED's on it were blinking rapidly.

I knew we had to get out of there. In my mind, I knew that was what we had to do. We had been daring the entities to give us sign of their existence, pushing them to give us some proof. Perhaps we should have left well alone, as now they were giving us what we had been looking for in the most extreme way and I, for one, was terrified.

I wanted to scream at Jim that we had to leave, but the words would not form in my mouth. I tried to move, to motion to him that we should go, but I was glued to the spot. I was no longer in control of my own body; something was holding me in place. It wanted me to witness its power.

Then it was over. The cold air was gone, the meters stopped their madness and all was still in the undercroft. I stared down the well. The air coming up from beneath was now only a few degrees lower than the ambient temperature of the room. I ran my hands through my hair, which still felt cold to the touch, and realised that the strange paralysis was gone too.

'What just happened, Jim?' I asked, able to speak again.

There was no answer.

I turned to Jim and at first could not see him, then I saw him seizing on the floor, I dropped to his side and began to help him. This was not the first time I had seen Jim have a seizure. I had looked after him several times over the years, but never in a place like this.

CHAPTER TWENTY-TWO

It had taken about five minutes for Jim's seizure to finally stop. During that time I had gotten him into the recovery position and rested his head on my knee. There is a myth that you should try to stick something into the mouth of an epileptic having a seizure to stop them from swallowing, or biting off, their own tongue. This might have been true in the past, but Jim had always told me not to do this as the chance of him swallowing, or biting off, his tongue was far lower than the chance of him breaking his teeth on whatever was shoved in his mouth, or for that matter biting off my fingers.

Instead, you just get them into the recovery position to stop them choking and protect their heads from hitting anything as much as you can. Other than that you just wait and time the seizure.

As always, when it was over Jim was completely disorientated, like someone who has woken from a deep sleep suddenly. Under normal circumstances I would have waited at least fifteen minutes to try to move him, but after what had just happened I was not prepared to wait in the undercroft a moment longer.

'We have to get back up to the house, Jim,' I said, trying to lift him.

'Huh?' he said.

'We have to get out of here. Can you stand if I help you up?'

He tried to get his feet under him and push himself up, while I held him up. Jim managed a few tentative steps before his legs buckled under him; he went back to the floor, pulling me with him.

'What? Err nmn make irt,' he mumbled incoherently.

'Come on Jim,' I said. 'We have to try again.'

I started to pull him, at first he was dead weight, too much for me to lift, then slowly he began to push himself up to his feet. Once upright, we stood there for a few seconds allowing him to try to get some semblance of balance.

'You okay to walk now?' I asked.

'Yeah,' he managed.

Steadily we made our way back to the scaffold. I propped him up against it for a moment while I tried to figure out how I was going to get him up there. Jim was a lot bigger than me. If he was helping, it was possible that I would be able to assist him up the climb. If not, or if he stopped supporting himself, then he could end up falling. I was contemplating leaving him in the undercroft while I went to get some help.

I looked over to Jim and saw that he was standing unsupported; he was no longer propped up against the scaffold. His eyes seemed a lot clearer; the haze that was always left in the wake of the seizure seemed to have passed. He would be weak, but should manage the climb with my guidance.

'What happened?' he said. I suspected that he knew full well what had happened. He had been through it so many times that he must be used to it by now. I figured he was just hoping he was mistaken. He'd told me earlier that he'd gone a long time without a seizure. Now he would have to give up his driving license again.

'You had a seizure,' I said. 'At the well.'

'Well?' he said, sounding confused.

I pointed over to the well at the other side of the room. It was common for Jim to lose some memory around a seizure. I had been hoping this was not the case this time. I knew now, though, that he did not remember what had happened, the low temperatures, the meters going insane and how it had all suddenly ended. This meant that only I was witness to it, and as I stood across the room from the well, I could feel the memory of it slipping away myself. I began to think that maybe it had not been as bad as I remembered, maybe the fear I was experiencing had made me interpret the situation far worse than it was.

This, of course, was the power of the well. I know that now as I sit in this little room. As I write this record of the events that occurred in that place, with that thing sat there grinning at me, I know that the well makes you forget. It did it to me several times, and it did it to poor Thom. You feel its true horror when you are near it, but when you are away the fear dissipates and the memory distorts.

Back on that day with Jim, I was still a victim of its power. I knew that something had happened, but as we stood by the scaffold, it was suddenly seeming less and less extreme in my memory.

By the time Jim and I had slowly ascended to the surface, it felt as though we had just got some unusual readings and then Jim had suffered his seizure. We went inside and I made him a sugary tea and we sat in the garden and waited for the ladies to return.

Rachel and Kelly came back with the girls about half an hour later, the second they walked out into the garden both women knew what had happened. Like me,

199

they had seen the seizures, and their aftermath, many times. Kelly rushed over to Jim and threw her arms around him.

'Are you okay?' she said, kissing his forehead.

'Yeah,' He said with a tired smile. 'Just feel a little beat up, you know how good Dan is at dealing with my fits.'

Kelly looked to me and took my hand.

'Thanks, Dan,' she said.

'Not a problem,' I said.

Kelly nodded and returned to hugging her husband. Rachel put her arm around me. I kissed her hand.

Kelly drove when they left an hour later. Jim sat in the passenger seat. I knew that probably by the time they reached the end of the road that he would be asleep. When we shared a house at university, he had always slept for hours on end, sometimes days, after a seizure. I was disappointed that we had not found more evidence to prove that the house was haunted.

'So there was nothing unusual at all?' Rachel asked in disbelief.

'No, just a few weird readings down in the undercroft,' I explained. 'But as Jim said, there could be numerous natural reasons for that.'

'So what do we do now?' she asked.

'I don't know,' I said. 'We'll figure something out.

We ate lunch. As we did, Paul and Rick arrived with a small group of students. Paul knocked on the kitchen door as Rick led the others down into the undercroft.

'Hi, all,' he said cheerfully as he entered. 'Just to let you know we're going to start work now.'

'Okay,' I said. 'What's the plan for today?'

'Not much,' he replied. 'Just do as detailed a survey of the site as we can.'

'Well, if you need anything you know where we are.'

He thanked me and headed off to join his colleagues in the undercroft. Rachel and I laughed at the way he seemed like a kid on Christmas morning; the excitement was evident in everything from the glint in his eyes and smile on his face, to the tone of his voice and the spring in his step.

After lunch, Rachel decided to take Izzy to the park to have a run around. She asked Anna if she wanted to go, but she declined, saying she was tired from the shopping trip.

After Rachel and Izzy left, Anna sat watching a DVD in the living room. She was still refusing to enter her room. I would have to move her bed out later. She had slept on the floor of Izzy's room last night as I had forgotten to move her bed down the hall.

I sat at the computer. I searched Google for translation sites. After checking a few out, I finally found one that claimed to be able to translate Latin. I was not holding out much hope of it working. Jeff Weston had told me that most of these sites were very poor and would not produce great results. I had to try, though. I typed the phrase 'OCCIDERE MERETRICES' into the first box marked FROM. I clicked on the pull down menu and selected Latin from the numerous languages. Then on the second box, marked TO, I selected English as the language to translate into. I clicked the translate button and waited a few moments. The phrase that appeared in the English box, though a little disturbing, made no sense whatsoever. It read, 'MURDER WOMEN FOR SALE.' What was that supposed to mean?

I clicked off the website in annoyance. I went and joined Anna on the sofa. I don't know what the film was that she was watching, but I suspected from the pale, pretty boy who couldn't act and the sombre tone that it was one of the *Twilight* films.

'How you doing, kiddo?' I said, putting my arm around her.

'Ok I guess,' she said.

'Still feeling a little spooked?' I asked.

'I don't want to talk about it,' she said.

'Why not?' I asked

'Because I think the ghost can hear us talking,' she said. 'It wants us to be scared. It wants us to talk about it. So I'm just trying to ignore it, then maybe it'll go away.'

I thought about what she said. Somehow it made sense. It seemed that since the first time we had experienced anything in the house, it had become all that we all spoke and thought about. Apart from Izzy, who luckily seemed unaware of the happenings. The rest of us, though, it was constantly on our minds, and with each day of us thinking about it and talking about it, the activity seemed to be getting progressively worse. Perhaps Anna was right? Perhaps we were giving it power? Maybe if we ignored it the activity would decrease and eventually stop entirely.

We both jumped as there was a loud bang on the window behind us. Anna clung to me for dear life. I spun my head around to see Paul stood on the patio waving at me frantically. I waved for him to come in and he disappeared. I heard the back door open and Paul came almost running into the room. He was panting a little.

'You scared the shit out of us,' I said.

'Sorry. I just had to come and get you. You need to see this,' he turned as though headed for the kitchen door again. He was obviously expecting me to follow.

'Wait!' I yelled making him stop in his tracks. 'What do I have to see?'

'Graffiti,' he said with a look of excitement. 'Medieval graffiti.'

It sparked my interest. However, I did not want to leave Anna alone in the house in the fragile state she was in, nor did I want to take her down into the undercroft. I didn't think she could handle that right now. I turned to her.

'Why don't you walk down to the park and meet up with Mum and Izzy? Take Mojo with you,' I said. She did not look keen on the idea. 'You can tell them about how I'm putting your bed in her room and you're going to be sleeping in there for a while.'

'Okay,' she said in the begrudging tone that only a teenage girl can truly achieve. She got up and called the dog, who came running, then she headed for the front door. As she opened it, a thought occurred to me.

'But Anna,' I said, making her turn back to me. 'Don't tell Izzy why, it'll just scare her. Say it's because we're worried about her sleepwalking with the hole in the garden.'

She nodded. She was a teenage girl, and enjoyed winding her little sister up, but she also felt very protective of her and would not do anything to genuinely scare the younger girl. After she had gone out I turned back to Paul. He wore a curious expression.

'What?' I asked.

'Oh sorry, I was just wondering what the real reason she was going into her little sister's bedroom was.' He looked embarrassed after saying this, realising that maybe it was too personal a question.

'Oh nothing, really. Just Anna isn't comfortable sleeping on her own after Bill dying and with what happened at the Taylor's place.'

'Oh God, yeah,' he said, shaking his head. 'I can't believe that. Mikkala always seemed such a lovely girl.'

I found him referring to Mikkala as a girl funny, she could have only been a year or two younger than he was. As I knew only too well, academics always see them selves as older and more mature than anyone who didn't go to university. It is one of their most pretentious traits. It was a trait that I knew I had possessed in my youth.

'Let's take a look at this graffiti then,' I said.

Paul nodded and led us out of the house.

The first thing that struck me when I got down into the undercroft was how light it was, since I had last been down there the guys had erected a lot more lights. It looked almost cheery down there, except where the dark shadows clung on. It was only in these places that the true eeriness of the place lingered. Paul and Rick had invited a few of their fellow archaeology students to help with the work. They were younger, most likely undergraduates who had jumped at the chance to get out in the field and study something real. There were three of them, two young men and a young bookish looking girl. The two men were measuring out the exact dimensions of the crypt, one using a laser tape measure and the other jotting down the measurements on a well-drawn floor plan of the room. Paul and Rick had already done a rushed job of this on their first visit down here, but if they wanted to get their work published, they needed more accurate measurements and diagrams.

The girl stood on her own in one of the shadows; she kept looking at the walls and then making notes on a A4 pad she was holding. It was over to this girl that Paul led me.

'Sarah? This is Mr Martin. He owns the house and land above us.' The girl placed the pad on the floor next to her and then shook my hand.

Paul turned to me.

'Sarah here is one of the best undergraduate students the university has, definitely headed for a first.'

I could tell from his tone that Paul had a crush on the girl, now I could see her properly I could understand why. Despite her baggy and plain clothes, she had almost perfect features. She wore no makeup and it was clear that she did not need to. She smiled at the praise from Paul, but I could not tell if this was a sign that she was equally attracted to him

'Pleased to meet you, Mr Martin,' she said with a smile. 'It's such an honour to be part of the first group to examine this site.'

'You're welcome, I guess,' I shrugged.

'Sarah was the one who found the graffiti,' Paul said.

'Carvings!' Sarah corrected him. 'Though I'm sure their purpose was no different to anyone writing on a wall nowadays.'

'When were they done?' I asked.

'I think they're from the time the place was in use,' Paul said.

'Yes, they're written in Latin, and the style of the lettering seems to indicate that it's monastic. They range in age from the building of the abbey to its destruction. Luckily for us the monks dated most of their carvings,' Sarah explained.

'At the time this monastery existed monks were about the only people in the country who could write. There wasn't much room for individuality in handwriting styles. They were all taught to write in a specific way. The carvings seem to fit that.'

'They're in Latin?' I asked, suddenly remembering the writing on Anna's Bedroom wall.

'Yes,' Paul answered, 'though there was the Anglo Saxon form of the English language at the time. It was mainly a spoken language, for writing the church was still using Latin, even over here.'

'You read Latin?' I asked

Paul shrugged.

'I can read some very basic stuff,' he said, and I felt a little disappointed. 'But Sarah here is almost fluent.'

I searched my pockets; the piece of paper with the phrase on it was no longer there. I must have left it at school. I was going to have to go u stairs and copy it down again and show it to this young woman.

'So what is written on the walls down here?' I asked.

'Most of it is the sort of thing you would expect,' Sarah said. She led met to a place on the wall where there was a phrase carved. As I looked at it, I felt chilled to my core. The style of the writing was exactly the same as that of the message on Anna's bedroom wall. The phrase down here read 'Laudatate Deo.'

'What does it say?' I asked.

'Praise be to God,' Sarah translated. 'The sort of thing you'd expect. It's dated as 1099 AD, so not long after the abbey was built. That one over there is a little more like modern graffiti.'

I followed her over to another carving. It read 'Frater Simon Futuit Porcos.'

Sarah chuckled as she looked at it again.

'It says, "Brother Simon fucks pigs."' She said, laughing. I smiled myself, but could not shake off the feeling of dread. Sarah led us further down the room.

'Things get a little darker here. Also they're dated later, from about 1200 AD onwards,' she said, pointing at a carving that read 'Infernum Expectat Omnes.'

'Infernum?' I said. 'Does that mean fire? Like inferno?'

'No. It's where the word originates, but it's more like infernal. The message says, "Hell awaits us all."'

'Cheery,' I said.

'Oh it gets worse.' She led us to another carving. This one read 'Domini habitat infra.'

'This one is kind of creepy,' Sarah said. 'It says, "Our lord dwells below."'

I was shocked at these words. Even though I knew that the monks who lived here were corrupt, this sounded so wrong.

'Were they devil worshippers?' I asked. Again, I was reminded of the urban legends about mad Dr Richards.

'We don't know,' Paul answered. 'That certainly sounds ominous. Tell him about this one.'

He pointed to a carving that read 'Homicidium et Irrumabo, Homicidium et Irrumabo, in Antiqua Vult Ad, Homicidium et Irrumabo.' I knew enough to recognise the word was the origin of homicide.

'What does it say?' I asked.

'Murder and fuck, murder and fuck, the ancient one wants us to murder and fuck.'

My fear was rising. The nature of these messages was making me worry what was written on my daughter's wall. Was it something as evil as this? I had to know. There was no time to go and copy the message. I had to show them.

'There's something in the house I need you to translate,' I blurted at Sarah. 'A Latin phrase.'

She looked confused but then smiled.

'Okay,' She said. 'There's one more I think you should see.'

She headed across the crypt, towards the well. When I realised where she was heading, I hesitated. The awful feeling I had experienced the first time I saw it still lingered in my mind, but I also had to know what she wanted to show me. She knelt down in front of the well and pointed to the stones that made it. I knelt beside her and shuddered, I had not seen the phrase last time. There had not been enough light. It was spread across several of the larger stones and read 'Furor et Salutem Exspecto Sub.'

'Madness and salvation await beneath,' she said quietly.

CHAPTER TWENTY-THREE

Sarah stood looking at the carving on the bedroom wall with her mouth open in shock. Paul looked at me, confused.

'Who wrote this?' Sarah finally managed to ask.

I shrugged. Paul came over and examined it.

'It's carved in exactly the same style as the ones down in the undercroft,' he said, running his fingers over the words. 'Even the depth looks the same. Your daughter did this?' he asked me.

I shook my head.

'No,' I said. 'We didn't see who did it, we just heard it happen'

'What?' Paul looked even more confused

'Me, my wife and Anna all heard scratching going on at this wall. There was a poster over this spot. When I took it down these words had appeared. They weren't there when we moved in.'

Paul shook his head.

'That doesn't make any sense,' he said. 'You're trying to say these words just appeared on the wall out of thin air?'

I nodded.

'You think the house is haunted?' Sarah asked.

I nodded solemnly.

'I don't believe in ghosts,' Paul said.

'Neither did I,' I said, becoming annoyed at defending myself in my own home. 'But with this and other things that have been happening, I can't think of another answer.'

Paul looked at me; he was trying to read if this was some kind of trick. He saw that I was genuine.

'How?' he asked.

'I don't know,' I said. 'But I need to know what that means.' I pointed at the carving on the wall.

'It says, "Kill the whores."' Sarah said softly.

'I think my family is in danger,' I said.

'Look, I know someone who might be able to help you get some answers,' Sarah said, putting a reassuring hand on my arm. 'Just let me make a quick call.'

She took her phone from her pocket and left the room. Paul was still staring in disbelief at the carving.

'I swear to you I'm not making this up,' I said.

'I believe you,' he said, once again tracing his hands over the words on the wall. 'I just don't know how this can be happening.'

'There must be something somewhere about this place,' I said. 'I mean look at all the terrible things that have happened here over the years. Surely there must be something written down somewhere that could help clear all of this up.'

He nodded. This he could process, this he could handle. He was an academic after all.

'I'll leave Rick and the others handling things down there,' he said. 'I'll head over to the university and do some research, see if there's anything that can help.'

'Thank you, Paul,' I said. I felt a sudden and overwhelming affection for him. Like myself, everything he believed in had just been called into question. It would have been so easy for him to assume I was lying, or mad, and having nothing more to do with me. He didn't, though, he believed me; moreover, he was willing to help me.

Paul went and told Rick he had to leave. Sarah returned from her phone call.

'My mum is a medium,' she said. 'She helps a lot of people with hauntings. I called her and if you want her to she will come over and have a look at the house.'

I remembered how I had scoffed at the idea of a psychic, but the nature of the words on my little girl's wall had filled me with a fear that far out weighed my scepticism.

'Really?' I asked. 'When can she come?'

'She can make it tonight.'

I nodded, desperate for answers.

Sarah smiled and nodded back at me.

Paul left for the university, promising to call me should he discover anything. Sarah left to talk to her mother, the medium, and suddenly I was alone in the house. Alone with my fear. At that time, I did not fear the entity itself. I was scared for the safety of my wife and daughters, women had not fared well here throughout history.

My fear turned to anger. I had never been what you would call a man's man. I didn't like football and had never been in a fistfight in my whole life. When it came to protecting my family, though, I was prepared to do anything. I wandered back into Anna's room.

'What do you want?' I shouted at what I could not see, but was sure was present.

I was suddenly aware of how quiet and still it was in the house. There was no sound at all, like I was sealed in some kind of vacuum, cut off from the rest of the world, perhaps even cut off from time.

'You want us to leave?' I yelled again. There was still that deafening silence. My sense of dread and my anger rose simultaneously.

'This is my house!' I shouted. 'I'm not going anywhere!'

The temperature in the room dropped noticeably. I felt the hairs on my arms stand up on end like there was a static charge in the room.

'What do you want?' I screamed now. 'You want to scare us?'

The temperature dropped even more. I felt the goose pimples rising now. Whatever it was that was haunting us was in that room with me. I was sure of that. I could feel it. Still I had that sense of being isolated from the real world.

'You want to hurt us?' I asked.

The electric charge in the air increased, I felt the hairs on my head moving as if I had just rubbed a balloon and then moved my hands over my head. It was gaining energy. It was gaining strength.

'What do you want, you bastard?' I screamed at the top of my voice. 'You want us dead?'

Then I heard the scraping sound behind me. I turned slowly. I looked at where the message was written, just below it I could see something being etched into the wall by an unseen hand. First a Y, then slowly it formed an E, and finally it scratched an S on the wall. One word, one answer, in English, so that I could understand its intent. YES. This thing wanted me and my family dead. I screamed at it, a guttural and incomprehensible cry of fear and anger. I went to the spare room where I knew I had a toolbox. Inside it, I found my claw hammer, which I took back to Anna's room. There I used it to furiously scrape the words away, all of them. I was so rough that I took away chunks of the plasterboard, exposing the wooden frame of the wall in places. When I was finished, there was no trace of either the Latin message or the word YES. I threw the hammer to the floor, and dropped to my knees, physically and mentally exhausted.

The house was still silent, apart from one brief noise, a deep and malicious laugh that seemed to come from everywhere and nowhere all at once. I screamed again then curled up on the floor and began to sob.

CHAPTER TWENTY-FOUR

At some point, I must have fallen asleep there on the floor of Anna's room. I was woken by the sound of Rachel and the girls returning from the park. I heard Izzy giggling and screeching as she ran into the house. Then I could hear Rachel telling her to calm down.

I forced my self to my feet, not wanting them to find me passed out on the floor. I felt a little lightheaded as I first rose to a crouching position. I couldn't muster the energy to continue standing.

I heard Izzy switch on the television in the living room; the volume was high and I could hear the theme tune to *Peppa Pig* blaring out.

I struggled to my feet, using the wall to support myself. As I did this, I caught sight of myself in the mirror on Anna's dressing table. I was a state; my hair was damp with sweat, as was my shirt. I looked pale and exhausted. If I let them see me like this, I knew that Rachel would panic. I quickly taped back up the poster to cover the mess I had made of the wall, though the evidence was still all over the floor.

As quietly as I could manage, I began to drag Anna's bed out of the room. I hoped that the volume at which Izzy was watching the television would cover the sound. My plan was to get it to the door of the younger girl's room and then make as much noise and sound of effort as I could. Then they would think that I had been struggling with it for some time and that would explain my appearance.

I got the bed down the landing almost soundlessly. It was a divan style single bed with castors on the base; this made it fairly easy to move. The only problem arrived when I reached the other end of the landing and found that the hallway was not quite wide enough for me to spin the bed round to wheel it straight into the room. I had to lift one end and tilt it slightly. This enabled me to get it halfway through the door. It was at this point I decided to announce my presence in the house by dropping the bed to the floor; it thumped loudly. As I heard Anna scream downstairs, I instantly regretted this. Given the fragile state of us all at this time, I should have known that a sudden loud bang from above would instantly be attributed to our spectral inhabitants.

'Sorry!' I yelled down the stairs. 'It's just me.'

Rachel came up the stairs with Anna hanging behind her. Izzy, it was clear, could not be shifted from *Peppa Pig* by any form of interruption, natural or supernatural.

Rachel looked at me and laughed nervously, holding her hand to her chest.

'Jesus, Dan, you scared the shit out of us,' she said. 'I thought you were still down the hole.'

'No,' I said. 'I came in earlier and have been up here trying to shift this bed ever since,' I lied.

Rachel came closer and I could see from the look of her face that she was concerned.

'It must have been hard work,' she said. 'You're soaked in sweat and you look shattered.'

'I am,' I said. 'I'm not as fit as I used to be,' I said.

'Want a hand?' she asked.

I nodded.

Rachel and Anna helped me get the bed the rest of the way into the room and then position it where was best. After that, we went downstairs and Rachel made me a cup of tea which I took out to the patio table and drank while smoking a cigarette.

Rachel made the girls a quick sandwich, which they ate whilst arguing over what to watch, then joined me outside.

'So what's going on?' she said.

I should have known better than to try to get anything past her, she had always been able to see straight through me.

'Down there,' I said, pointing at the hole. 'Down there, carved into the wall are Latin phrases.'

'Like the one on Anna's wall.'

'Exactly the same,' I said. 'The lettering style, the depth of the carving, they could have been done by the same person.'

'What do they say?' she asked me.

I went through what I could remember from what Sarah had told me. How they ranged from the normal religious things you would expect from monks to the humorous statement about brother Simon and his affections for swine. This made her laugh. Then I told her how they became much darker, talking about Hell and lords below. I saw her begin to tense. I realised that it was how I must have looked when Sarah was translating them for me. I finally told her about the words scratched into the well itself, they stuck with me clearly. 'Madness and salvation await beneath.'

'My God, Dan!' Rachel said. 'What happened down there?'

I then explained that Paul had gone over to the university to try and discover exactly that, I also told her about Sarah and her mother the medium.

I looked at my watch and realised that they would be here soon.

'What did the message on Anna's wall say?' Rachel asked.

I didn't know what to say. The truth was too horrendous to tell her, but I couldn't lie to her. She knew that Paul and Sarah had seen it, and that the girl had translated it for me.

'Once this is all sorted I'll tell you,' I said. 'Right now I don't even want to think about it. I scraped it off the wall. It's gone.' I took her hand. She stroked mine. I could see in her eyes that she wanted to know, but I could also see that she wasn't going to push it. I didn't tell her about the other word I had seen appear on the wall with my own eyes, the simple YES in answer to my question about whether it wanted us dead. I left that out, because despite the energy I had felt in the room and even though I had heard that menacing laugh, I still believed that this thing could not hurt us. It could scare us yes. Over time I was sure it could drive us mad. To physically harm us though, it just didn't seem possible. If only I had known the truth.

CHAPTER TWENTY-FIVE

Inside the living room, we found that the girls had stopped arguing and agreed on watching *Toy Story 3* on DVD. It was great to see Anna looking more relaxed. Rachel had agreed to take the girls out for tea this evening; we felt that it would be a bad idea to have them in the house while the medium was here.

When she told them, we had usual arguments. Izzy wanted to go to Pizza Hut and Anna wanted to go to Nandos. After much disagreement the decision was finally made that they would drive over to Peterborough and go to Frankie and Benny's. The Italian/American style restaurant was a favourite of ours when we had been to the cinema over there.

The girls changed quickly and were just coming down the stairs as there was a knock on the door. I went and opened it. There stood Sarah and her mother. In my mind, I had been expecting a short woman with oversized glasses and a strange voice. I guess I had seen the film Poltergeist one too many times. Instead, Sarah's mother was a tall, slim woman in her late forties. It was evident where Sarah had got her looks from, she was dressed in a pair of jeans and a tailored shirt. I had been expecting tie-dyed dresses and crystals.

'Hello again, Mr Martin,' Sarah said warmly. 'This is my Mum, Jean.'

I shook hands with Jean.

'Please call me Dan,' I said. Then I stepped outside and pulled the door to behind me. I lowered my voice before continuing. 'Look, can we just keep it quiet until the kids have left? I don't want to scare them anymore than they already are.'

'Of course,' Jean said.

Sarah nodded in agreement.

I reopened the door and ushered them inside. Izzy was running around the room like a lunatic whilst waiting for Rachel to take them out. Anna sat on the sofa and regarded the visitors quizzically.

'Hey, girls?' I said, stopping Izzy in her tracks. 'This is Sarah and her mother Jean. Sarah is a friend of Paul and Rick's. They've come to have a look at the room under the garden.'

'Pleased to meet you,' Izzy said, offering a little curtsy. This was her new thing and it was very cute.

'Hello,' Anna said before turning her attention to the television.

'Can I get you a drink before we head out?' I asked. 'Tea? Coffee?'

They both wanted coffee. They sat on the sofa next to Anna while I made the coffee. I heard them asking the girls about school and what they had planned for the upcoming summer holiday. As would usually happen, it was Izzy that was doing most of the talking.

I heard Rachel come down and introduce herself before coming into the kitchen to join me.

'You didn't mention how pretty she was,' she said with a knowing smile.

'Who?' I asked

'Oh please,' she said, slapping my arm. 'That Sarah is one very attractive girl.'

'I think Paul has a thing for her,' I said.

'I'm not surprised.' She came up and kissed me. 'I'll call you when we're done eating to see if I have to keep them out any longer.'

'Okay,' I said. 'Hopefully this won't take too long.'

I took the coffees into the living room. It was very quiet. Sarah was sat reading a magazine that Anna had left on the coffee table and Jean was sat with her eyes closed.

'Is everything okay?' I asked.

Jean opened her eyes and smiled. She took the coffee off me.

'Yes,' she said. 'It's just part of the process. I have to relax myself in order to open up to the spirit world.'

'Okay,' I said and handed Sarah her coffee. 'Do you need quiet?'

'It helps,' Jean said, smiling.

'In that case I'll just take my coffee on the patio and have a smoke,' I said, not wanting to interrupt.

'I'll join you,' Sarah said. Pulling a packet of cigarettes from her coat pocket, she opened the packet and offered me one. I took it.

'Thanks,' I said

'It should only take a few minutes,' Jean said.

I smiled and nodded, Sarah and I headed outside to the patio. We sat down with our coffees. It was late afternoon and the sun was just starting to give everything an orange tinge. We lit our cigarettes.

'How long has your mum been doing this?' I asked.

'As long as I can remember,' she said with a smile.

'Do you believe in it?'

'When I was young I did without question,' she said. 'As I got older I did start to think maybe it was a hoax, but Mum swears she's never made anything up, and sometimes she is really accurate. I guess now I'd rather believe there was some truth to it than believe my mum is a crazy old bat!'

I laughed.

'Yeah, I guess I'd take that choice as well,' I said. 'You ever have any experiences yourself? They say that these sort of gifts run in families, don't they?'

She smiled.

'Maybe.' Then she shrugged. 'I don't know. When I was little I used to have some imaginary friends who seemed very real to me, but as I got older and I learnt more, I guess if I ever had the gift I shut it off.'

We talked a little about the undercroft, about what an amazing discovery it was. She couldn't believe that she had got the chance to be part of the team who first examined it.

'I mean there's a very good chance that no one has been down there in seventeen or eighteen hundred years, and it's perfectly preserved,' she said. Her eyes brightened as she talked. It was clear how passionate she was about the subject. 'It's like you found a giant time capsule.'

'Well, actually it was him that found it,' I said, pointing to Mojo who was laying on the grass, never taking his eyes off the hole, but not daring to venture any nearer.

'Whoever it was, it was a hell of a discovery.' She smiled.

I drank the last of my coffee and then reached in my pocket to retrieve my own cigarettes. I lit one and then offered the pack to Sarah. She held up a hand.

'I'm trying to cut down,' she said.

'Me too,' I said, taking a long draw on it.

Sarah laughed.

'You have lovely children,' she said.

'Thanks,' I said. 'But you don't have to live with them. No, I'm kidding, they're great; they're the reason I'm doing this. If it was just me in the house there would be no way I'd call in a psychic, no offence to your mother, it's just I don't believe it can hurt us.'

'But because of your daughters, you're not willing to put that theory to the test,' she said.

'No,' I admitted. 'I have to be sure, for their sakes.'

As I finished my second cigarette, Jean opened the kitchen door.

'I'm ready,' she said. 'Shall we begin?'

I nodded. I stood up and followed Sarah back into the house. Suddenly I felt a sense of enormous foreboding. I looked towards the horizon. As if nature wanted to mirror my own mood, there were dark and unsettling clouds gathering in the suddenly darkening east, a storm was coming. Of that, I was certain. Except it turned out to be a very different kind of storm.

CHAPTER TWENTY-SIX

I wasn't sure what to expect from having a medium in my home. I have to admit that before that night my only knowledge of mediums had come from horror films and bad ghost hunting TV shows, the validity of which I was highly sceptical about. After all, why were all spirits called John, and why did they all have scouse accents?

I was surprised by the matter of fact nature of Jean's process. She walked slowly around the house, from room to room, lingering in each a little while before moving on to the next, all the time saying nothing. Sarah and I followed her in silence.

Eventually she led us back to the living room and sat down. Sarah took the seat next to her and I sat opposite.

'I'm not sure what to tell you, Dan,' she said calmly.

'Is it bad?' I asked, feeling the dread start to creep inside me again.

'No,' she said. 'Far from it. I sensed absolutely nothing in the whole house.'

I was astonished. After everything I had experienced in the last few days, the events that had turned me from a nonbeliever. I could not see how a so-called medium could come into this house and not sense anything.

'That's impossible,' I said. 'I know that there is something here.'

'I believe you,' she said. 'Sarah told me about the message on the wall. All I am saying is that whatever it is, it is not here now.'

'Where is it then?' I asked, trying to make sense of it all.

'Wherever it resides,' she said. 'This thing does not haunt your home. It is not bound here, it is merely visiting.'

I shook my head.

'No, it was here no more than two hours ago,' I said. 'I saw it write on the wall again. I heard the bloody thing laugh at me.'

'Perhaps it sensed my presence and left?' she said. 'Perhaps it doesn't want me to find things out about it? Perhaps it doesn't want me to help you? Perhaps it doesn't want to cross over to the other side?'

I put my head in my hands; I felt all hope slipping away from me. I had been so sure that this would turn up some answers, but it didn't. The thing was toying with me, with my family.

'Is my family safe?' I asked.

Jean looked at me. From her expression, I could see that she was struggling to find something reassuring to tell me.

'Ghosts cannot hurt the living, Dan,' she said finally.

I sighed with relief.

'But there are other things out there that can,' she said. I looked at her.

'Like what?' I asked confused.

'Some call them demons, some call them elementals, some even call them divas,' she said. 'Whatever their true name, and origin, they are spiritual entities that were never human. They are not the souls of the departed; they are something else, something older. At best, they are indifferent to us living people. At worst, they are hateful towards us.'

I was hearing the words she was saying. At the back of my mind, locked away, was the voice of the old, rational Dan Martin. He was screaming that this was nothing more than superstitious mumbo jumbo. For some reason I wasn't listening to him. I believed every word that Jean spoke. The irrational voice that had woken last night was now completely in control of my belief system.

'What can they do?' I asked.

She shrugged.

'People believe different things,' she said. 'Personally I've only encountered a few, but I've seen people clawed and bitten by them.'

'I see,' I said.

'But I've heard stories of them causing deaths, setting fires and all sorts of horrific things. Maybe they are just stories.'

'How do I know if it's one of these things?' I asked.

'If it was here now I would be able to tell you,' she said.

I sat in thought for a few minutes. Then it came to me.

'Earlier,' I said. 'I think I might have called it here. I was angry and yelling at it. I could feel the energy in the air as it got stronger. What if I was to call it now?'

Jean shook her head.

'If this thing is some form of demon, I think that summoning it would be a very bad idea.'

'I need to know what I'm dealing with, Jean,' I said.

She looked concerned but nodded slowly.

I led Jean and Sarah upstairs to Anna's bedroom. We agreed as that was the place that it had made it's most physical of appearances it would be the best place to try to call it out. We entered the room. I went to switch on the light and Jean grabbed my hand to stop me.

'These things usually work better in low light,' she said. She reached into her handbag and pulled out a tea light candle, she placed it on the top of Anna's dressing table. She looked at Sarah who took the hint and handed her mother her lighter. Jean lit the candle and its dim glow flickered around the room.

Jean ushered us into a rough circle in the centre of the room. She said a little prayer of protection. This was a precaution she always took before attempting this sort of thing.

'Normally I would suggest that a medium was the one to try calling out,' she said, 'but given that you had this experience earlier, Dan, I think it should be you.'

I nodded and took a deep breath.

After a long pause, I realised something.

'I have no idea what to say,' I confessed.

'You said that earlier you were shouting at it. Getting angry and trying to get a rise out of it,' Jean said. 'Perhaps you should try something like that again.'

'Okay. I can do that,' I said. I paused again. I pictured Rachel and the girls. I thought about how much I loved them, and how much I would do to protect them. I thought about how I would feel if anyone, or anything, tried to harm them. I felt my anger rising. I thought about how scared Anna had been last night, how this thing had frightened my wife and my daughter. I thought about the foul message it had scratched into the wall.

'You see what I did?' I said loudly. 'You see what I did to your carving? I scratched that fucking thing right off the wall. Right off my wall!'

I could feel the adrenaline pumping through my system.

'Did it just get colder?' Sarah asked in a hushed voice.

I hadn't noticed it myself.

'I think so,' Jean said. 'Keep going, I can sense something is trying to manifest.'

I held onto the anger that was seething in the pit of my stomach.

'You think you can come into my house and threaten my family?' I yelled out. 'You know what I think? You can't do a fucking thing to hurt us. All you can do is write on a fucking wall. So what? I teach twelve-year-olds who can do that. I'm no more scared of you than I am of them.'

This time I felt it, the room was much cooler than it had been, much cooler than it should have been given the temperature outside. Not only that but there was that charge in the air again, that strange sense of being inside a vacuum. Jean closed her eyes. I guessed that she was trying to sense what was causing the change in the atmosphere of the room. Sarah looked around nervously.

'Again, Dan,' Jean said.

'If you want to hurt me, now's your chance,' I said. 'Or can you just threaten my little girls? Is that all you can do? I want you to hurt me now! Prove you can do it. Or get the fuck out of my house!'

The charge in the room had built up now. I could see the way it was making stray hairs on the women's heads stand on end. I could feel that mine was doing the same. The candle began to flicker wildly, making thick black shadows dance across the walls. I could see the fear on Sarah's face. Jean however was still stood with her eyes closed.

Suddenly the candle blew out, throwing the room into darkness for a few seconds before my eyes adjusted to the dim last light of the setting sun coming in through a crack in the heavy curtains.

'Is that the best you can do?' I yelled. 'Blowing out a candle? Jesus, both my girls have managed that trick on their first birthday. You're just a...'

'Mum!' Sarah screamed, cutting me off. I looked to Jean. She was stood rigid. Her eyes shut tight. Her head was tilted to the left and she was foaming at the mouth.

'Stop it!' I shouted.

In that instant the energy in the air dispersed and the temperature seemed to return to normal. Jean fell to the floor. Sarah rushed to her side, and I quickly joined her, both of us down on our knees next to her.

'Mum? Mum, are you okay?' Sarah said in a panic.

Jean sat up wiping her mouth.

'I'm fine baby, I'm fine,' she said, hugging her daughter. 'But I could do with another coffee,' she said, turning around to me.

Ten minutes later I took the coffees out onto the patio where Sarah and Jean were sat. Sarah looked a little calmer. She was smoking; I could tell from the ashtray that she had already had two. She must be chain smoking. I set the drinks down in front of the women and then lit myself a cigarette and sat down opposite them.

'Are you sure you're all right?' I asked Jean. 'There's a doctor a few doors down the street, I could ask him to come and check you over.'

Jean smiled and sipped her coffee.

'I'm fine now,' she said. 'It was just too much energy for me to handle. I was trying to sense it, but it was fighting me. It didn't want me knowing what it wanted.'

'Well, it scared the shit out of me,' Sarah said.

'Me too,' I agreed. 'I'm sorry I got it so mad.'

'Don't be,' Jean said. 'You just did what I told you to do. I wasn't prepared for it to be so strong.'

I took a draw on my cigarette and blew the smoke out slowly. I considered the situation I was in. Less than a week ago, I would have not believed it if anyone had told me I would be sat in my back garden with a psychic after having a paranormal experience in my haunted house.

'What is it Jean?' I asked. 'What am I dealing with in there?'

'Honestly, I don't know,' she said, and I felt my heart sink.

'It was worth a shot I guess,' I said.

'I can tell you it's not a ghost,' she said. 'Your house is not haunted in that sense. The thing that came into that room has never been human, but it didn't feel like any demon I've ever come across.'

'So it's something else?'

'Yes, but I don't know what. It felt stronger than anything I've ever encountered before, and older, so much older. The way it blocked me from reading it, I've never had that before.'

'So what can I do about it?' I asked.

'I don't know. I have some friends who have more experience of the darker ones than me,' she said. 'One thing I can tell you is in my opinion, you need to get your family out this house. Don't spend another night in this house.'

CHAPTER TWENTY-SEVEN

After they left, I sat alone in the house. I listened intently for some sign of activity. There was none. The house was silent. Were we all just making a big deal out of something that was not that serious? I was willing to admit that there was definitely something strange happening in the house. Perhaps it was supernatural, but bar one slightly threatening message on the wall and a few sleepless nights, what real damage had the entity done? Nothing.

Could I have been right when I told Anna that it couldn't harm us? After all, it had not attacked anyone yet. Sure, there had been the incident with Jim down in the undercroft, but Jim was an epileptic. He hadn't had a seizure in years, but it was a time bomb ticking in his head every day. It was only a matter of time before it went off, it could have been nothing more than coincidence.

The things I had experienced in Anna's room earlier today could have been easily attributed to a panic attack, or a symptom of the stress I had been under.

As I reflected on these things, I felt as though a weight had been lifted off of my shoulders. My rational mind was again regaining its dominance over the irrational voice.

Just because I accepted there was a potential supernatural element to the things we had been experiencing, it did not mean that we had to assume that they were responsible for everything.

The things that had happened to Jean in Anna's room could easily have been either deliberately or, more likely, subconsciously. She so wants to believe the things she says that her body reacts accordingly. So what should I do about her warning? She told me to take my family and leave the house. It was an easy thing to say, but not to do. Where would we go? Would we be able to return? What about Bill's funeral tomorrow? There were far too many complications for us to be able to just leave because of such innocuous activity.

So I made the decision that for the time being we would stay. Rationality had to win. I decided that I would neglect to tell Rachel about the warning; I would tell her that Jean was going to contact some people who might be able to help us more.

I felt bad for lying, but I knew too well that if I passed the warning on to Rachel that she would want to leave tonight. There was no way we could do that.

This would turn out to be one of the worst decisions I could ever have made.

When they returned home, Rachel insisted that both of the girls had baths and washed their hair that night. This was not a tall order for Anna, who would do this most nights anyway, but Izzy had only had her hair washed the night before; she took some convincing. Then they had to sort out their outfits for the funeral the next day. I knew that Rachel would get my suit, shirt and tie out ready for me.

While the girls and Rachel were upstairs, I opened up the computer. I sat staring at a blank page. I should have written my speech for the funeral earlier, but I had not found the time. Now I could not think of what to say. I had only known Bill for a very short time, and though we had become very close, there was so much I didn't know about him. I began to wish that Mary had not asked me to speak. I was honoured that she thought Bill had regarded me so highly that he would want me to give a speech, but I had no idea what I could say. There would be people there who had known Bill for years. I felt like I had no right to tell these people about a man they had known infinitely longer than I had. I closed the computer down in frustration at my own inability to write the speech.

I went to the kitchen and poured myself a glass of water. My head was swimming with thoughts of Bill, how I had felt about him, the qualities I admired in him. Every thought, though, led me to replay his final moments over and over in my mind.

The doorbell rang, dragging me out of my memories. I walked to the door and opened it. Outside my door, once more in his long coat and hood, stood Alex Jenson.

'Hi, Alex,' I said, smiling, hoping that we had gotten over our initial meeting. 'What can I do for you?'

He made a quiet snort of derision; obviously he still bore me a grudge.

'Nothing for me,' he said. 'Mum asked me to ask you to pop over and see her.'

'Is she all right?' I asked.

'What do you think?' he said sarcastically. 'She wants to talk to you about the funeral.'

'Okay,' I said, stepping out of the door. I headed across the lawn towards Mary's place. Alex headed up my drive.

'Where you going?' I asked.

'Out,' he said, stomping off into the distance. I had been making allowances for his attitude towards me, due to his father's recent death and the circumstances of our first meeting. However, I felt angry at him for Mary and Maggie's sake now. It was the night before his father's funeral, a time when I'm sure his family needed him, and there he was going out. I shook my head and headed to Mary's door, I knocked and Maggie let me in.

'Hi, Dan,' she said. 'Mum's in there,' she pointed towards the living room.

I smiled and walked into the room. Mary was sat on the sofa. She smiled at my arrival, though I could see from her red eyes that she had recently been crying.

'Thanks for coming round, Dan,' she said, standing up and hugging me. 'I wasn't expecting you to come over so quickly.'

'I had a free spot in my schedule,' I said jokingly.

We sat down.

'I just wanted to thank you for agreeing to speak tomorrow,' she said.

I felt a twinge of guilt at my inability to write the speech.

'To be honest with you, Mary, I haven't got a clue what I'm going to say. I've been trying to write a speech, but I can't find the words.'

She smiled.

'Don't plan it,' she said. 'Let it come from your heart, say what you feel. That's what Bill always used to do when he had to give a speech, and I'm sure that's what he would want from you. Something true.'

'But what if I get up there and the words won't come?' I said. 'Everyone there would have known Bill better than I ever did.'

She shook her head and smiled.

'You're wrong about that,' she said. 'Bill knew many people in his life, but he never had many close friends. You were the first person in years he connected with. You'll know what to say. I'm sure of that.'

I was not so sure, but at least her request for me to wing the speech on the day got me out of the trauma of spending the whole night trying to write the damned thing.

We talked about the plans for the next day. We talked about Bill and how funny he would have found it to attend his own funeral. Mary said he would have howled with laughter to see everyone looking so sombre. She knew that he would want it to be a celebration of his life and not a mourning of his death.

The wake was going to be held at the upstairs of the cricket club in Darton. Bill had played for the team for a few years when he was younger, and had always kept up his membership.

I looked at my watch and saw that it was heading towards half eight. I had not told Rachel where I was going, though considering she and the girls were preening themselves and selecting outfits, she probably hadn't even noticed my absence. I made my apologies and got up to leave. Mary gave me another hug, and this time kissed me on the cheek.

'See you in the morning,' I said. 'And if you need anything, just ask.'

'Thank you, Dan,' she said.

I walked home and entered the house. The phone was ringing and Rachel was coming down the stairs.

'Where have you been?' she said, looking confused. Obviously, I was right. My absence had not been noticed.

'Next door,' I said. 'Mary wanted a quick chat.'

Rachel nodded and I answered the phone.

'Hello,' I said.

'Good evening.' The professional-sounding voice on the other end of the line replied. I did not recognise the voice. 'Is that Mr Martin?'

'Yes, I'm Dan Martin,' I said.

'Good. Mr Martin, this DCI Parker of Darton CID,' he said. Why is it that whenever you answer the door or phone to the police your stomach somersaults up into your throat?

'How can I help you?' I said.

'You live next door to Mrs Laura Taylor and her son Leo, don't you sir?' he asked, even though he was well aware that I did.

'That's right,' I said. 'What's wrong? Has something happened to Leo?'

'No, sir,' Parker said. 'He's still in critical condition but there's been no developments. I'm calling about Miss Parivnic.'

'Mikkala?' I said. 'I still can't believe she would do something like that. She loved that little boy so...'

'Yes, sir,' Parker said, cutting me off. 'Sometimes people do things that are completely out of character. We are trying our best to get to the bottom of the whole thing. At the moment, though, she is still our prime suspect. We have a problem, though, she's refusing to talk to anyone, she won't talk to us. She won't talk to the court appointed lawyer, she won't talk to anyone, except to tell them she wants to talk to you.'

'Me?' I said. I was shocked and confused. 'Why does she want to talk to me?'

'I don't know, sir,' Parker said. 'I was hoping that you might be able to shed some light on that. Were the two of you close?'

'Well, she lived next door,' I said. 'Leo and my youngest daughter used to play together, so we saw quite a lot of Mikkala. We'd chat when we saw each other.'

'Were you intimate with her?' he said bluntly.

'What?' I said, stunned. 'I'm married.'

'Yes, sir, but a pretty young girl like that living next door, alone in a foreign country, these things happen sometimes, sir, I'm not here to judge.'

'I'm happily married, Detective,' I said firmly. 'And I don't like the inference.'

'Sorry, sir,' Parker said, sounding friendly. 'I had to ask, though, sir. We're trying to think of reasons why she wants to speak to you.'

'Well, I'm as stumped as you are,' I said honestly. I could not for the life of me think of a single reason why Mikkala would want to speak to me. I know she was in a foreign country, but she had friends.

'We would really like to find out, Mr Martin,' Parker said. 'Would you be willing to come in and see her?'

I did not know how to answer this. I felt sorry for Mikkala locked up so far from home, on such a horrendous charge, but what if she was guilty? I did not know if I could, or wanted to, face her if she was capable of such a terrible act.

'Mr Martin?' Parker said after my long pause.

'I don't know,' I confessed. 'I mean if she's guilty, I don't ever want to see her again.'

'I can understand that, Mr Martin,' Parker said. 'But it will be difficult to get to the truth unless she talks to us. If you came in then maybe she would give you some information that will help us.'

How could I refuse? It was the least I could do if I could get some answers as to what had happened, I owed it to Laura and poor little Leo to try.

'All right,' I said. 'When?'

'Could you make it to the station now?' he asked.

'I suppose I can,' I said.

CHAPTER TWENTY-EIGHT

The police station in Darton was situated on the outskirts, on the Boston Road. This was the complete opposite end of town from Glenley, meaning that I had to negotiate two level crossings and the diabolical one way system through town to get there. Luckily at that time of the evening there was little traffic, just the young men with their body kits and subwoofers roaring through town sounding like their exhausts were about to drop off.

When I reached the station I reported to the front desk. The desk sergeant asked me to take a seat. I did not have to wait long for DCI Parker to come and meet me. He was younger than I had expected him to be from his voice. He looked as though he was only a few years older than me, but his thinning hair and the dark bags under his dull blue eyes told me that he had seen far more in this life than most people ever would.

He strolled over holding out his hand.

'Mr Martin,' he said, shaking my hand. 'Thank you for coming so quickly. I'm sure you can appreciate our need get moving on this case?'

'Of course,' I said. 'I'm just not sure what help I can be.'

He stopped and looked at me; I could tell that he was assessing me, trying to gauge what kind of a man I was, whether there was more of a connection between Mikkala and myself than I was letting on. I recognised the stare, as subtle as it was. It was one I had seen before; it seemed that all experienced police officers were capable of it. They tended to do it the first time they met you, even in a social context, sizing you up.

Even Bill had done it the first time we spoke over the fence the day we moved in. This ability to read people tended to make them a good judge of character.

Parker smiled. He had obviously made his decision that I was not hiding something from him.

'Anything you can find out could help us, Mr Martin,' he said. 'We're really struggling on this one, what evidence we have is purely circumstantial. We can't mount a real case unless we can find some kind of motive.'

'I see,' I said.

'We're holding her on a charge of attempted murder, but from what the doctors at the hospital are saying, it's only a matter of time until that charge gets upgraded to murder.'

I was shocked.

'Oh God,' I said. 'Poor Leo.'

We hadn't seen Laura since the day it happened, she had spent all her time at the hospital at her child's side. My heart broke for her, it was clear, to anyone that spent more than five minutes with her, that she had not yet got over the death of her husband. The only thing that kept her going was her son, now she stood precariously on the cusp of losing him too.

'You see now why any information you can get from her is so important to us,' Parker said.

'Yes,' I said, nodding, then after a pause, 'I still can't believe she would be capable of such a thing though. I mean we didn't know her that well, but she seemed so happy, and she loved Leo.'

'Mr Martin,' he said. 'I stopped being shocked a long time ago. You can never really know what another person is capable of, no matter how well you know them. The only thing I'm certain of anymore is that there is no end to the cruelty that people continue to inflict on each other.'

It was a shockingly cynical statement. Even in our darkest hours, most of us would like to believe in the overall good of mankind.

Parker led me through a series of corridors. The police station seemed much bigger than it looked on the outside, due to it's labyrinth of warren like passages. Eventually we reached a door marked *Interview Room 3.*

'She's waiting in there for you,' Parker said. 'She won't allow us to record the conversation, nor will she allow an officer to be present in the room while she speaks to you.'

'Okay,' I said, I was a little troubled by this. I still didn't believe that Mikkala was capable of the crime she was accused of, but if she was, what else was she capable of? Was I safe?

Parker obviously saw the concern on my face.

'Don't worry, though,' he said reassuringly. 'Me and two officers will be right outside the door, if you need us just shout.'

I nodded, then opened the door and stepped in.

The room was not at all as I had expected it to be, then my knowledge of police interview rooms was really limited to what I had seen on crime dramas on the television. I had been expecting a small room with a table with four chairs, a tape recorder and a two-way mirror on the opposite wall.

Instead, it was a large brightly lit room with two comfy looking sofas on either side of a coffee table. Two steaming coffee cups sat on the table. Mikkala was sat on the right hand sofa, her legs up under her. She was dressed in oversized jogging bottoms and a navy blue T-shirt that I assumed had been given to her here at the station. Her long dark hair was scraped back in a ponytail. She wore no makeup, not that she usually needed it. I had always thought that she was one of those naturally beautiful women who never needed to try. Now, though, I was shocked to see her, she looked exhausted and gaunt, like she had not slept or eaten since her arrest. There were dark rings under her eyes and her complexion seemed sallow.

I offered her a gentle smile and then took the seat opposite her. She returned the smile, although it looked weak and as though it took all of her effort to manage it.

For a while, we sat there without speaking. I didn't know what to say to her. She picked up her coffee and took a sip. I did the same. The mere act of drinking a cup of coffee seemed in someway to mask the weirdness and awkwardness of the situation.

It made me able to distance myself from the location and imagine that we were just two acquaintances catching up over a coffee.

'How are they treating you?' I finally asked to get the conversation going.

'Well enough,' she said, her voice sounded weak and distant, her eyes focused on the window and not on me. 'They are very kind really, all things considered.'

'DCI Parker said that you wouldn't speak in their interviews,' I said.

'I have nothing to tell them,' she said, her gaze still on the window, though now I realised that she was really focusing beyond the window, as though she could somehow see into the world beyond.

'He said that you wanted to speak to me,' I said. It was time to find out what this was all about.

She nodded slowly then turned to look me in the eyes, I saw great pain and fear in her eyes.

'Yes,' she said. 'I needed you to know.'

She put down her coffee and leant forward; she placed her head in her hands and sobbed.

I felt an urge to stroke her hair, offer her some small gesture of comfort, but then I remembered poor little Leo, lying in the hospital, slowly dying, and I refrained.

'Needed me to know what?' I asked.

She looked up at me and tears ran down her cheeks.

'I know that I'll pay for telling you,' she said, 'but I can't let it happen again.'

I had no idea what she was talking about.

'I did it,' she said in a near whisper.

'What did you say?' I asked.

'I did it,' she repeated. 'I poisoned Leo.'

I felt my heart sink and my anger rise. She had called me here to confess to me.

'Why are you telling me this?' I asked. 'Why not tell the police?'

Suddenly she rose to her feet. The abrupt movement gave me a jolt of fear and I felt my heart racing a little. She wandered over to the window. She again gazed out.

'Because they wouldn't understand,' she said without looking at me.

'And you think I will?' I said

I could see that she was shaking her head.

'No, I don't expect you to understand,' she said. 'Not yet, but you will.'

Now I stood up.

'Stop talking in riddles, Mikkala, or I'm going to leave.'

She spun around to face me, her eyes burning with anger.

'You think I called you here for my fucking benefit?' she virtually spat at me. 'You think I want your help? I'm trying to help you!'

She looked back out of the window. I stood there in shock for a few moments, then subconsciously inched my way closer to the door, closer to the safety of DCI Parker and the officers outside the room.

'Help me?' I said.

'Yes,' she said, her voice calm again. 'I did it, I poisoned him, but I had no choice, I wasn't in control. I knew what it would do if I didn't. It showed me things. Terrible things. What it would do if I didn't obey.'

She dropped to her knees sobbing. I could see now that the poor girl had completely lost her mind. I wanted to leave the room and tell Parker that she was mad, that she was in no way fit to stand trial, yet something stopped me. She had said that this was for my benefit. I needed to know what she meant, even if I was not sure what she was talking about.

'I don't understand,' I said.

She looked at me, her face a mask of grief and torment.

'I loved Leo!' she cried. 'I would have done anything to protect him. Yet it made me do that to him, can't you see what I'm saying?'

I shook my head.

'It makes you hurt the ones you love, it makes you do the most evil things. It didn't want us, though, it just saw an opportunity. It wants you, Dan! You and your family!'

'What does?' I shouted, her words spinning in my head, not making any sense.

'The fucking thing! The Devil. Whatever the fuck it is!' she screamed and charged at me.

Her outburst brought Parker and the officers crashing into the room. The two uniformed officers, a man and a woman, grabbed Mikkala before she could reach me. They tackled her to the floor. Parker grabbed me and pulled me out of the room. As we came out of the room, I saw more officers running to assist with restraining Mikkala.

'It will come for you, Dan!' she screamed. 'It will come.'

Parker dragged me down the hall and sat me down in another room. I sat there stunned at what had just happened. Parker left the room, I assumed to make sure that Mikkala was escorted safely back to her cell.

Had she lost her mind? Had I been listening to the delusional ravings of a madwoman? Something about her words chilled me to my core. She had spoken of a thing, a devil, that was coming for me and my family. Was this all inside her mind? Or was it connected to the activity in my home, or was she referring to the entity that the medium, Jean, had spoken of earlier that evening? She had said that the thing had never been human, she had warned me to get my family out of the house, but I had chosen to ignore her. Had I made a huge mistake? I couldn't let myself believe that. I made the decision that tomorrow, after the funeral, I would tell Rachel everything, and together we would decided whether to leave the house or not.

Parker returned.

'Are you all right, Mr Martin?' he asked, looking concerned.

'A little shaken up,' I confessed. 'But apart from that fine.'

'I'm sorry, Mr Martin,' Parker said. 'I had no idea she would go off like that. She's been so docile since she's been here. I just assumed she would stay that way.'

I nodded my head in acceptance of his apology.

'No real harm done,' I said.

'Mr Martin, I need to ask you if she said anything that could help us with the case against her?'

I thought about it, she had said a lot. How could I tell him that she had told me that a devil made her do it, but she could be right as my house was under attack from some supernatural entity? He would have put me in a cell next to her.

'She told me she did it,' I said. 'That something evil had made her do it. It seems like she's completely lost her mind.'

'Either that or preparing for an insanity plea,' Parker said with what I could see was his usual world-weary cynicism.

I shook my head.

'I knew her well enough to know that the person I just spoke to wasn't the Mikkala I knew.'

Parker nodded.

'Fair enough, Mr Martin,' he said. He walked over to his desk and pulled out a form. 'If you could just write down what she told you on this form and any observations you made about her state of mind and sign it, then you can head off home.'

I took the form from him. Well really it was less of a form and more of a blank sheet of paper with 'witness statement' written at the top and a box for a signature at the bottom. Parker handed me a pen.

'Please use my desk,' he said

There was a knock on the door and a uniformed officer walked in.

'Sir, could I have a word?' the officer said. 'Outside?

'Excuse me a moment, Mr Martin,' Parker said before stepping outside with the uniformed officer.

I sat there at Parker's desk and began to write down the things that Mikkala had said, or as many of them as I could make sense of. I was aware that Parker had not shut the door properly and I could hear them talking in hushed voices. Most of it I couldn't make out then Parker said something that sent fear shooting through me like an electric current.

'Blackfriars Crescent,' he said. 'You've got to be shitting me?'

'I wish I was,' the officer replied. 'The first unit there said it's a fucking mess.'

'Okay,' Parker said. 'Get a car. I'll meet you outside.'

Parker came back in. I tried my best to hide the fear on my face. I didn't want him to think I had been eavesdropping on a police matter.

'Something of an emergency has come up that needs my attention, Mr Martin,' he said. I hoped this was a good sign, surely if the problem was at my house he would have told me? Or would he?

'All right,' I said. 'I understand.'

'If you could finish filling in the form in the reception area and then hand it to the desk sergeant, I would appreciate it.'

'Of course,' I said, panic still bubbling under the surface.

'Thank you.'

Parker escorted me to reception. He did not say any more about the emergency that had come up. Instead, he just thanked me again for my help and said that he would be in touch if they needed any more information. Then he left the station. I watched him run to the waiting police car, which sped off down the Boston Road, heading towards Glenley.

I sat down and began to write as quickly as I could. I only wrote down the essentials. I wanted to get out of there as quickly as possible. My rational mind was still telling me that if the emergency had been at my house then Parker would have said something, surely he would have taken me there with him.

That other voice, though, the one that had been gaining too much power recently, was telling me that it was my home. My family. Mikkala was right, it had come for them while I wasn't there to defend them; they were dead. The reason that Parker hadn't said anything was that I was the number one suspect. Here I was already in the station; when I handed that form in at the front desk, they'd stop me leaving.

I did my best to push these thoughts to the back of my mind as I wrote furiously. When I had written all I felt that I needed to, I signed the paper and rushed up to the front desk. The sergeant wasn't there. I rang the buzzer. I waited.

After what felt like ages, the desk sergeant appeared, carrying a steaming coffee cup.

'Sorry,' he said with a smile. 'I was just getting a cuppa.'

'It's okay,' I said, smiling. I handed the form through the slot to him. 'Could you see that DCI Parker gets this when he gets back.'

'Certainly, sir,' he said, lifting it up.

'Thanks,' I said. I turned and started to head towards the door.

'You can't go yet, sir,' the desk sergeant called after me. I could almost hear the irrational voice in my mind laughing and saying, '*I told you so.*' I turned around.

'You need to fill in your address on the back,' he said, holding up the form. I sighed with relief and returned to the desk. He passed the form back through to me. I quickly scrawled my address and phone number on the back of the form, then slid it back through.

'Thanks, sir,' the sergeant said. 'Have a good evening.'

I said goodnight and headed back to my car, wondering what new horrors were awaiting me at Blackfriars Crescent.

CHAPTER TWENTY-NINE

As I came onto Blackfriars Crescent, I could see the flashing lights. People from all over the estate were huddled in groups at the side of the road, watching in morbid curiosity. At first, I could not tell where the emergency was. There were four police cars, a police van and two ambulances. I prayed that it was not my house, then I saw Rachel was stood on our lawn with Mary and Maggie.

A police officer was stood in the road, he motioned for me to stop then he walked over to my window.

'Sorry, sir, but there is no access at the moment,' he said. 'This is a crime scene.'

'I live just there,' I said, pointing to my house. 'That's my wife there.'

Rachel caught sight of the car at the right moment and waved over at me. The officer saw this and then turned back to me.

'All right, sir,' he said. 'Just take it slowly and pull onto your drive.'

'Thank you,' I said.

I crawled along at five miles per hour for the remainder of the distance. I pulled onto our driveway and then got out of the car. Rachel came running over and hugged me.

'What's going on?' I asked as we walked back over to Mary and Maggie.

'We're not sure,' Rachel said. There was a loud bang, like a gunshot. We came outside but couldn't tell where it had come from. Then a few minutes later, there was another. Then the police came screaming

251

down the road and bust their way into the Marklews' house.'

The Marklews, the good doctor and his harridan wife. We could only assume that the worst had happened from the sheer number of police here. It was then that I saw Parker walk out of the house.

'Hold on a minute,' I said to Rachel and the others. I headed across Mary's lawn and onto the street. I got fairly close to Parker before I was stopped by another uniformed officer.

'Excuse me, sir,' she said, 'but I need you to go back a little, this is a crime scene.'

'I understand,' I said. 'I just wanted to speak to DCI Parker.'

The uniformed officer looked at me for a few moments then turned to where Parker was stood.

'Excuse me, sir,' she almost yelled at him. Parker looked across. 'This gentleman would like to speak to you.'

Parker nodded and waved, motioning for her to let me through. She stepped aside and I walked over to Parker.

'Hello again, Mr Martin,' he said as I reached him. 'I'm sorry I had to rush off but as you can see I'm a little busy here.'

'Of course. I was just wondering what the hell was going on?' I asked.

'I'm not really at liberty to say at the moment,' he said.

'Oh come on,' I said. 'See there on my driveway, that's Bill Jenson's widow. I know you knew him. She's burying him tomorrow; she doesn't need more upset. We just want to know what's happened.'

Parker looked over at Mary and then back at me.

'Okay. For Mrs Jenson's sake,' he said. 'the gentleman who lived here...'

'Dr Marklew,' I said.

'Yes, Dr Marklew rang the station earlier to inform us that he had just shot his wife dead. Then he told us he was about to shoot himself. That's exactly what he did. They're both dead, single gunshot wounds to the head.'

I shook my head in disbelief.

At that moment, two paramedics stepped out of the Marklews' front door. They were respectively pushing and pulling a trolley on top of which laid the sheet covered corpse of one of the Marklews. The white sheet was soaking with deep red blood at the head. I wanted to turn away, to shield my eyes, and my mind, from the horror I was seeing. Yet for some reason I was unable to stop watching as the paramedics pushed the trolley up the driveway to the waiting ambulance.

'Why?' I said.

'We're still trying to figure that out. There was a suicide note but it was quite rambling.'

I watched as the paramedic loaded the corpse-laden trolley into the ambulance, then finally it was out of my line of sight and I turned back to Parker.

'Local gossip had it that she was cheating on him,' I said.

Parker nodded.

'That was in the note,' Parker said. 'Now please, Mr Martin, I have a lot to do. I will see you tomorrow at the funeral, if I can get there now, with all of this to deal with.'

'Thanks,' I said and wandered back home.

Once I had informed Mary and Maggie of what had happened we bid them goodnight and headed inside. Rachel looked tired. It felt like it had been a long time since we had a peaceful nights sleep.

'How are the girls?' I asked. 'Did they hear the bangs?'

She shook her head.

'I think they were both asleep, and you know our girls could both sleep through world war three.'

I laughed. It felt good to be reminded of something normal. Things had been so stressful and so strange for so long by that point. I took Rachel in my arms and held her.

'There's something wrong here, Dan,' she said. 'It's like the whole street has gone mad, death and sadness everywhere. Ever since Mojo found that fucking thing buried under our garden it's like some kind of emotional cancer has spread through the street.'

I nodded. It was the perfect analogy—a huge tumor, with tendrils spreading out across Blackfriars Crescent, its epicentre lurking beneath our garden, our home.

'It's not healthy for the girls, Dan,' she said.

'I know,' I agreed. 'After the funeral tomorrow, call your mother. See if they have room for us to all stay for a while, let things settle down here a little.'

'I don't know if I'll want to come back here,' she said. 'Not after everything that's happened.

'Neither do I,' I confessed. 'We'll get away for a while and then see how we feel.'

We continued to sit on the sofa cuddled up for a while. Neither of us spoke, we just enjoyed the comfort of each other.

Eventually we headed upstairs. We checked on the girls, who were thankfully both asleep. They had been spared the additional trauma of witnessing the events outside.

We left them and headed to our room. I was asleep almost as soon as my head hit the pillow.

I woke up with a start. There was a loud bang, it sounded like our front door had been kicked in. I looked to my side. There was no sign of Rachel; I was alone in the bed. My heart raced as I leapt to my feet, I ran out of the room and down to see if Rachel was with the girls. Their room was empty too.

'Rachel?' I called out as I sprinted down the hall towards the stairs. There was no answer. As I reached the top of the stairs, there was another thud on the front door. I ran down the stairs. I saw, through the frosted glass pane in the door, that there was a crowd of dark figures outside the door.

'The Monks!' the irrational voice told me.

I did not want to believe that, but I decided that leaving the door closed was a better option than facing whatever was trying to hammer it down. I ran into the living room. It, too, was deserted.

'Rachel?' I yelled again. There was no answer. I hurried into the kitchen as the pounding on the front door became almost deafening. The kitchen, too, was empty.

There was an almighty crash as the front door came off its hinges and whatever was responsible entered the house. I could hear countless hurried footsteps.

I saw that the door out to the garden was open. In fear of what was roaming the house, I ran outside. I headed for the far end of the garden, hoping to hide in the shadows. I looked back at the house and saw numerous dark figures at every window. I ran to the shadows, but tripped and fell to the ground. I looked to see what had impeded me, and to my horror knew instantly what it was.

There, arranged in a circle around the fence covering the hole, were three bodies of decreasing size. Each one was shrouded in a white sheet, bloodstained where the faces were. Without removing a single sheet, I knew instantly that it was Rachel and our daughters. I recognised them from the size and shape of their neatly wrapped bodies. Despite my fear of the things in the house, I could not help but let out a distraught cry of grief.

'He's outside,' I heard someone shout from the kitchen. I looked up and saw them running at me. They were not ghostly monks. They were not supernatural creatures of any form. They were armed police officers, their assault riffles trained directly on me.

Instinctively, I put my hands up. They stood there for a moment regarding me through their protective facemasks, and then they all began to fire.

I woke up screaming, throwing myself out of the bed and hitting the floor hard. Rachel screamed in reaction to my fall.

'Dan? What's wrong?' she said, looking terrified.

For a long time I couldn't answer. I just sobbed in her arms.

CHAPTER THIRTY

St Leonard's church was in the marketplace in the centre of Darton. It was fairly small in comparison to some of the churches I had seen in the area. St Botolph's church in Boston, for example, or 'The Stump' as it was more commonly known, was massive in comparison. Despite its more compact proportions, though, St Leonard's still managed to seem grand and ornate. Despite the summer heat outside, the air inside had a little chill to it, as always seemed to be the case in churches, which was a blessing in my suit and tie.

I had been to the church already that morning. Mary had asked me to drop off a flower arrangement and a large photo of Bill, as she and Maggie didn't have time. I had, of course, said yes. When I went to the church that morning, I had still been dressed in my cargo shorts and a light T-shirt. I had felt positively frozen.

Dressed in my suit and tie at the funeral, though, I had felt very comfortable. The church was nearly full. Mary had not been lying when she had said that Bill had known many people. There were quite a few police officers in uniform. I spotted DCI Parker among the crowd. He was dressed in uniform, something I supposed he did not do very often anymore. He saw me looking at him and nodded recognition.

Mary was sat near the front, flanked on either side by her children. Maggie was holding her hand. The two of them looked very dignified in their grief. Alex seemed to be just looking around the church. He was not paying any real attention to his mother or sister.

I was sat a few rows back with Rachel and the girls. Anna and Izzy were already crying, but they were quiet and gentle tears.

I looked at the pulpit; it was where I would be delivering my eulogy from. The site of it filled me with nerves. I still had no idea what I would say. Mary said that she had faith that I would find the right words, but as I looked at the pulpit, I feared more than ever that she was wrong to have such faith in me.

Rachel must have sensed my nerves as she squeezed my hand reassuringly and gave me a little sad smile.

The vicar began the proceedings by greeting everyone and then reading from the Bible. I have to admit that I didn't pay that much attention to the reading. Despite my recent change in opinion on the subject of the supernatural, my opinions on religion remained the same. It was not true, just a way that ancient people used to try to explain things that were well out of the realm of their understanding.

The vicar himself was a tall, slender man in his late fifties or early sixties. He had a thick shock of greying hair, that at a guess had been black in his youth. His most distinguishing features were his thick, bushy eyebrows and his Romanesque nose.

His voice was the same as every other vicar I had ever met, simultaneously soft and reassuring, but somehow dull and listless. As he droned on, his voice echoing around the church, I wondered what Bill would have made of it all. I knew that he put about as much faith in religion as I did. I imagined that if he had been sat there listening to this talk of Heaven and life eternal he would have rolled his eyes in boredom. The thought almost made me chuckle, but out of respect for Mary I held it back.

Soon the vicar was done with his readings and prayers and I heard him utter the words I had been dreading.

'Now we will have a eulogy from a good friend of William's, Mr Dan Martin.'

I stood up and walked down to the pulpit, my shoes echoing on the stone floor as I went. I passed Mary and she looked at me and gave me a small smile. I squeezed her shoulder and she patted my hand. I continued up to the pulpit.

I looked out at all the faces gathered there.

'When Mary asked me to speak here today I have to admit it was a shock,' I said. 'After all, I had only known Bill a few months before he passed away.'

I looked around at the gathered mourners. I think I was looking to see if any of them looked as though they thought I had no right to speak due to what I had just said. However, the only look of indignation in the room came from Alex. I had expected this.

'However, in those few months I had grown to consider him and Mary as my closest friends. That was because of the way Bill was. He was so welcoming to me and my family when we moved in next door to him. He was always willing to help with anything at anytime. He was always there to offer good advice. He made us feel like part of the family.

'I suppose in a way I saw Bill as a father figure. My relationship with my own father was never that good. Bill, though, exuded all the traits I believe a good father should, a sense of warmth and strength in equal measure. I can honestly say that I learnt more about how to be a good father from those few months with Bill than I ever learnt from my own dad. I like to think that I will be able to use those things he taught me in raising my own girls.'

I looked up and saw Rachel and the girls looking at me. They all offered me gentle, little smiles.

'I was with Bill in his last moments,' I said, switching my gaze to Mary. I guess I was seeking her permission to talk about this; she nodded as if telling me to go on. 'He was unconscious when I got to him. He came round long enough to say Mary's name, his last thoughts were of his wife. It was more evidence of the love they shared, a love that anyone who spent more than a few minutes with them could see. A love that I'm sure will carry on forever, it is surely stronger than death. I like to imagine that Bill is sat here at the back of the room listening to all of this. He'd probably be shaking his head at us all for making such a fuss on his account. He was modest like that. I'm sure, though, he would be happier to see us remembering his life with a smile on our faces rather than mourning him with tears in our eyes.'

The rest of the service went by in somewhat of a daze. It was more Bible readings, some prayers and hymns. Eventually the vicar concluded things.

'I have been told to inform everyone that the family are heading straight to the wake, and not attending the cremation in Grantham. They wish me to tell you that anyone who wishes to go over to the crematorium is more than welcome to.'

With a few more words of farewell, the vicar ended the service. People began to slowly file out of the church. Some went over to Mary and her children. Some came to me to tell me how moved they had been by my words. I graciously accepted the praise and then headed outside.

I pulled my cigarettes out of my pocket and shoved one into my mouth. I patted down my jacket and trouser pockets, only to realise I had forgotten to bring my lighter out with me.

'Need a light, Mr Martin?' Parker said, walking over to me. He was holding a Zippo. I nodded and took the lighter. I struck the wheel and lit my cigarette. I took a long deep draw on it before handing the lighter back to Parker.

'Thanks,' I said.

'No problem,' he said, lighting a cigarette of his own.

It was lunchtime and the marketplace outside the front of the church was bustling with shoppers and school kids on their breaks. Some of them I recognised. They offered me strange glances, the way schoolchildren always seemed to do when they saw a teacher outside of their usual environment; it was as if they thought that we lived within our classrooms, that we had no life outside of school, that our very existence in the outside world was some sort of infringement on their privacy.

'In the midst of life we are in death,' Parker said next to me. He, too, was regarding the people carrying on with their day-to-day lives unaware of our loss.

'Nice words in there,' Parker said. 'He meant a lot to you didn't he?'

I nodded.

'To the whole family,' I said. 'You look tired.'

Parker nodded.

'Very late night with everything that happened with your neighbours. Then there was the mess I came back to at the station.'

'What happened?' I asked

Parker looked around to make sure that no one was listening.

'I shouldn't really be telling you this,' he said in a hushed tone. 'But Miss Parnivc committed suicide after we left last night.'

I was beyond shocked. It was only hours since I had seen her.

'What? How?' I asked

'That's the strangest part,' he said. 'She drowned herself in the toilet of the cell.'

'You can't drown yourself,' I said. 'It's impossible, your body fights it.'

'That's what I thought,' Parker said, shaking his head. 'But it's clear as day on the CCTV footage of the cell. The officers returned her to her cell. She calmed down for a while, then seemed to get agitated again, as though she was arguing with someone. Then it was like she was fighting someone and they forced her head into the toilet and she drowned. The only thing is, there was no one else in the cell, it was just her. I guess when you're that far gone that you're seeing imaginary people the rules about what your body can and can't do go out of the window.'

I didn't know how to take it. Her words came back to me, the way she had spoken of devils. Had she believed so resolutely that this thing was after her that she had managed to override the body's natural instinct for self-preservation? Had she been right all along?

Had that thing come fore her? In the last week, I had come to realise that just because you couldn't see something did not mean that it didn't exist.

She had said that it was coming for me and my family. Suddenly in panic I looked around searching for Rachel and the girls. I spotted them exiting the church with Mary and Maggie. I sighed with relief.

'I suppose it saves the cost of a murder trial though,' Parker said.

'I thought she was charged with attempted murder,' I said, confused.

'Oh, I'm sorry, Mr Martin, I assumed you knew,' Parker said. 'Leo Taylor died last night. His poor little body couldn't cope with the damage the poisoning had done.'

I put my head in my hand and felt the tears rising to my eyes. That poor little child, he had been such a happy boy, despite all the tragedy that had already befallen his family. He was an innocent, taken away in such a horrendous manner. There was proof in his death that there really was evil in this world and none of us was safe from it. My heart broke for Laura. She had tried so hard to carry on for Leo's sake. Now it must seem that she had no reason to live at all.

'Oh dear God,' I said, looking at Parker. 'How is Laura?'

He closed his eyes for a moment.

'I really am the bearer of bad news today,' he said. 'I'm so sorry, but she took her own life just after the boy died.'

I felt my legs turning to jelly. It seemed like the light of the world was slipping away from me; I was about to pass out. I felt Parker grab me with a strong arm and hold me up.

'Mr Martin?' he said. 'Are you all right?'

'Need to sit down,' I managed to say. Parker led me over to the small wall that separated the churchyard from the marketplace. He lowered me onto the wall. A group of kids was walking past us. Parker called one of them over.

'Give me that bottle of water,' he said. The child, on seeing his uniform, didn't argue, merely handed the bottle over and ran off.

Parker handed me the bottle.

'Drink some of this,' he said.

I took a few gulps from the bottle and felt my stomach violently revolt. I threw up in between my own feet. Parker patted my back then handed me the bottle again.

'Try again,' he said. 'A little slower this time.'

I took a few delicate sips from the bottle, and this time the water stayed down. I felt the fogginess in my head begin to clear. I looked up and saw Parker looking down at me.

'Better?' he asked concerned.

'Getting there,' I said, then took a few more sips from the bottle of water.

My mind returned to the image of the evil spreading like a tumor from the undercroft, stretching out across Blackfriars Crescent. Its foul cancer had already taken six lives. How many more did it want?

'How can this all be happening in one street?' I asked, more to myself, but Parker chose to answer.

'You do hear of cases like this. Where you get a series of murder/suicides in a small area, they call them clusters. It's far more common in the U.S., but there have been a few examples in this country.'

'You think it's like a suicide pact?' I asked. This seemed preposterous to me.

'No,' Parker said. 'It's more complicated than that. It's like a mass hysteria, often brought on by a tragedy.'

There was no denying that there had been plenty of tragedy on Blackfriars Crescent in the last few days, but could anyone really pinpoint the beginning? Had it been Bill's death? As much as this had affected me and my family, I got the impression that none of the other neighbours had been as close to him as we had. Was it what had happened with Leo? That seemed more plausible, the shock of something so horrific, happening to someone so young, would shake anyone up.

'It was you finding that fucking undercroft!' the irrational voice screamed in my head.

For once, I chose not to argue. It was the undercroft, and that well. I had to get my family away from that house, but I also had to know what was down there. I needed to know what I was running from.

Rachel came wandering over to where I was sat. She looked concerned.

'Dan? Are you alright?' she asked.

I explained that I was fine; I had just gotten a little over-emotional. I introduced her to Parker. He shook her hand and said that he wished that he could have met her under happier circumstances. Thankfully, he did not inform her of what had happened, that Mikkala, Leo and Laura were all now dead. I would tell her myself in due course, but we needed to get through the rest of the day being strong for Mary.

'Well, I'll be in touch, Mr Martin,' Parker said. 'I'm sorry to have to leave but as you can imagine I have a lot of work to do.'

I shook his hand and thanked him for looking after me, and he left us alone. Rachel regarded me suspiciously. I have mentioned before how I was incapable of hiding things from her.

'What's happened?' she said.

I looked at her, trying to think of the right thing to say.

I couldn't.

'I'll tell you later,' I said. 'For now, let's just get on with this.'

I made to stand up, but Rachel put a firm hand on my knee to tell me to stay seated.

'No,' she said. 'Enough of that. Tell me now.'

I looked at her, about to tell her everything, when Izzy came running over.

'Mummy, Daddy!' she yelled. 'Auntie Mary says I can go in the big car with her. Is that okay?'

Saved by the bell.

CHAPTER THIRTY-ONE

I tried my hardest to put the news that Parker had given me to the back of my mind at the wake. Most of the people who were at the funeral had made it to the cricket club, so the function room and bar area were busy. Groups of police officers sat together exchanging their favourite stories about big Bill Jenson.

It was clear from the smiles and laughter that there was much love for him among his colleagues. Periodically they would pull me into their groups to thank me for the speech. They would then proceed to tell me what a great copper he had been, how due to his size he had terrified the living shit out of many a suspect.

There was much merriment in the room. It felt like this was truly a celebration of Bill's life, rather than a sombre mourning of his passing. When I sat with them, even Mary and Maggie were laughing and smiling, enjoying fond memories of the man they had lost.

Everyone seemed in good spirits, everyone except for Alex that was. I had been watching him since we arrived; he kept that same stony look on his face. He grunted at anyone who deemed to speak to him.

He just stood there at the bar sinking pint after pint of cider. I needed another drink so I went and stood by him at the bar.

'Rough day,' I said, trying to engage him.

'Uh huh,' he muttered without looking at me. I could sense the anger inside him. He had every right to be angry; he had just lost his father. Today, though, his mother needed him.

'I know you're having a tough time,' I said gently. 'But look around, people are smiling, this is a time to remember the good things. Go and sit with your mum and sister. They need you.'

He turned round and looked at me, his eyes cold and bitter.

'Why don't you mind your own fucking business?' he said, then turned away.

On any other day, I would have swung him back round to face me and told him how his mother and father were my friends so him acting like a little shit when she needed him was my business. For Mary's sake, though, I didn't want to make a scene.

'Grow up, Alex,' I said as I walked away.

'Fuck you, Dan,' he replied.

Seething, I returned to the table and sat down next to Rachel. She and Mary were discussing how Bill had always made a big deal out of Christmas for the kids.

'He used to hire out a Father Christmas suit every year and walk around the garden after they'd gone to bed, making so much noise they would look and see him. Then he'd wave and then look at his watch and shake his head. They used to jump back into bed quick as a flash.'

A little tear ran down her smiling face, the power of a happy memory at a sad time. Maggie came back over, having heard her mother's story.

'You know for years I was convinced that Santa was a clumsy great twat,' she said, laughing. 'He was always knocking over plant pots in our garden.'

Mary laughed.

'One of many accurate descriptions of your father, clumsy great twat,' she said.

We all laughed.

As the afternoon progressed, we heard many more stories about Bill the great bloke, Bill the wonderful husband, Bill the loving father and Bill the excellent copper. There was a large buffet and people kept eating and drinking and remembering Bill Jenson.

Every now and again, I would glance over to Alex. He was still at the bar and even more drunk. People were giving him pitying looks and keeping a wide berth of him.

I watched the pain on Mary's face when she saw him. I could feel myself getting angrier with him by the second. It was only Mary that was stopping me from confronting him. Maggie saw me looking over at him.

She sat down next to me.

'You know he is really pissing me off,' she said.

'It's not just me then?' I replied.

She shook her head.

'He's barely spoken two words to Mum all day, and it's breaking her heart,' she said. 'It's like always. It's all about him.'

Seeing how it was upsetting Mary and Maggie was making my blood boil.

At that moment, we were interrupted by the familiar sound of a spoon being tapped loudly on a glass, the universal signal in gatherings such as this that someone wanted to make a speech. The room fell silent as we looked around to see who it was. To my horror I saw that it was Alex, he was stood up on the bar, still tapping the glass long after the room had quietened.

Maggie looked distraught and Mary wore a concerned expression.

'Ladies and Gentlemen,' he slurred loudly. 'I would like to make a speech.'

Instinctually I got to my feet. I wanted to be ready if this went sour.

'For those of you that don't know me, I'm Alex Jenson,' he continued. 'I'm Big Bill's son.'

He laughed and looked down at himself.

'I know it's hard to believe that a weedy little guy like me came from Bill's stock, but there you go.'

There was a murmur of uncomfortable laughter around the room; it was as though even those that didn't know him could sense Alex's anger.

'I've overheard many you talking about what a great man my father was today,' Alex continued to slur. 'I thank all of you for your kind words. It makes me happy to hear what a wonderful colleague and friend he was to you all.'

There was now a stilted round of applause.

'No,' Alex said loudly. 'I'm not done yet, let me tell you all what an awful fucking father he was.'

I saw Mary begin to cry. Maggie leapt to her feet and stormed over to the bar. I followed at a distance.

'Get down and shut up, Alex,' she yelled at him.

'Well, hello, sis,' he said with a malicious grin. 'Hey everyone let me introduce to my dear big sister Maggie, or as I know her the favourite child.'

'That's enough Alex,' she said.

'No it's not!' he yelled. 'It's nowhere near enough. Do you have any idea to know what it's like to feel like a total fucking disappointment your whole life. Oh wait, of course you don't, he worshipped the ground you walked on. Nothing I ever did was enough for him.'

I looked around the room. Everyone was staring at the domestic scene unfolding, everyone except for Mary who was sobbing wildly into Rachel's shoulder.

I took a few steps forward and gently got hold of his arm, hoping to guide him down from the bar.

'Come on, mate, let's talk about this somewhere else,' I said reassuringly.

He pulled his arm away from my grip.

'You can fuck off as well,' he screamed at me. 'You and your speech about how he was like a father to you, you barely fucking knew him, how dare you. I was his son, yet he seemed to give more of a shit about you than he did me. Do you know what that feels like?'

I wanted to scream at him that he had no idea what a bad father was like. He may have felt like a disappointment to Bill, but at least Bill cared enough about him to be disappointed. My own father probably couldn't pick me out of a police line up.

'This isn't the time for this,' I said more firmly.

'Why, because no one can say a bad thing about Saint Bill today?' he yelled.

'Alex, stop. Look what you're doing to Mum!' Maggie shouted at him.

'She let him get away with treating me like I was a failure, she never defended me. He was never proud of anything I did. When I got good grades in maths and science he'd just go on about how badly I'd done in English. He never took an interest in me learning to play guitar, just wanted to know why I didn't want to play sports like a real man. He once told me that he was disappointed that I wasn't gay, at least then it would have explained why I couldn't kick a ball to save my life, apparently.'

'Alex, shut the fuck up!' Maggie said, grabbing his leg and yanking it hard. He came tumbling off of the bar, crashing to the ground with a thud. If he had been sober, it would have hurt like hell. In his state, though, he barely flinched. He was on his feet in seconds and squaring up to his sister.

'You bitch,' he said, bringing his fist back.

At that point, I stepped in. I grabbed the raised arm and tucked it up behind his back. I knew it was hurting but I didn't care.

'Let me go, you fucker!' he screamed. 'He's assaulting me, officers!' he screamed.

A couple of the younger police officers leapt up. At first I thought they were taking his complaint against me seriously, and that I was about to find myself arrested.

Instead, though, one joined me in restraining him, the other stood between him and Maggie.

'Time to go, sunshine,' the one stood in front of him said.

'Ready?' the other one said to me.

I nodded and together we started to move him, kicking and screaming, towards the door. I turned back to see Maggie rushing to her mother, who was by that point near hysterical.

The policeman in front of us barged open the double doors and we moved him down the corridor towards the main entrance.

'I'll sue you. All of you,' Alex cried out

'Good luck finding witnesses in a room full of coppers mate,' said the policeman in front as he barged open the main door.

The other policeman and I led him out of the building, I was getting ready to let him go.

'Put him on the street,' the policeman next to me said, so I kept up my grip as we led him across the car park and out of the entrance. Then we let him go.

He straightened up his jacket then looked as though he was going to try to take us all on. After weighing up his chances, he sheepishly tried to head back onto the grounds.

The policeman who had assisted me with restraining him put his hand up in front of Alex's face.

'Don't even think about it,' he said. 'You set foot back in there today and you'll be nicked for drunk and disorderly.'

'But it's my dad's funeral,' Alex protested.

'Then perhaps you should have kept your stupid mouth shut,' he said.

'Alex,' I said calmly. 'It's an emotional day, just go and sleep it off. I'm sure everyone will forget about it tomorrow.'

'Fuck you, Dan,' he said. 'I'll get you for this.' With that, he stormed off towards the town centre. I headed back inside to see what devastation Alex had left in his wake.

CHAPTER THIRTY-TWO

It took ages for Maggie and Rachel to calm Mary down. I was nervous on my return how she would react to me. After all I had just physically manhandled her son out of the building.

I needn't have worrie. Upon my return she threw her arms around me.

'Thank you, Dan,' she sobbed into my ear. 'I'm sorry you had to do that.'

I reassured her that it was fine.

'No, it's not. He shouldn't have behaved like that. I'm so ashamed.'

'Don't be too hard on him,' I said. 'People deal with things in different ways. He's having a hard time.'

'You're too kind, Dan,' she said. 'I just wish he knew how much Bill loved him.'

'I'm sure he'll figure it out one day,' I said.

'Bill was sometimes too hard on him. I know that, but it was only out of love. He worried about Alex far more than he ever worried about Maggie. She was so much like him; he knew she'd be okay. Alex always seemed so fragile. You know Bill, he was a big, strong man. He wanted Alex to toughen up, maybe sometimes that came across to the boy as him not loving him. That just wasn't true though.'

'Sometimes,' I said, 'it's as hard to be a son, as it is to be a father.'

The scene that Alex had created had left an uncomfortable silence hanging in the air. Soon after my return, people began coming over to Mary and giving her their condolences once more and then leaving.

It took about half an hour for the room to empty. That was when the real sadness of the occasion seemed to hit us. The room was now devoid of the warmth of bodies, of laughter, of even conversation. The tables still bore empty glasses, like memories of good times now gone. The buffet table still held food, but it was all past its best. The sandwiches were drying out as the salad began to wilt. It's strange how a buffet is such a perfect metaphor for life; when it begins it is a beautiful, wonderous thing, full of the promise of satisfaction, but over time people use up all that is good, leaving nothing behind but the worst parts, which quickly decay and become useless, until eventually it is all thrown out to rot.

We stayed until Mary had paid the caterers, and the bar, then we all headed back home. Rachel took the girls home on the train, whilst I gave Mary and Maggie a lift.

The ten-minute journey back to Glenley was a silent one. Mary sat in the back, staring vacantly out of the window. I guessed that she was remembering her life with Bill, and wondering what life would hold for her now without him.

Maggie sat next to me. She kept her eyes down. I could not tell if she was not talking out of grief about her father's death, concern about her mother or embarrassment over her brother's behaviour.

I, myself, was wondering if I would have to face another round with Alex when we got back to Blackfriars crescent. He had been heading towards town when I saw him last, but he could equally have been heading to the train station. If he had gone back home, would he have calmed down, or would he be more enraged than before?

I hoped, for my sake and no one else's, that he had crawled into a bottle in one of the pubs in town, and that neither his family nor I would have to see him until he had calmed down and sobered up. This was selfish I know, after all I'm sure his mother would have felt better knowing he was home and safe, than wandering the streets of Darton in an alcohol fueled rage. I, though, had had more than enough stress and conflict for a lifetime. Rachel and I had to sort out getting away from the house, though after a day like that it felt like a chore. I was drained, physically and emotionally.

As we pulled into Blackfriars Crescent I saw Paul, Rick and Thom, stood on their drive. They offered sombre nods of recognition. I returned a tired wave.

'You can't leave yet.' a voice said in my head, not the irrational voice that had been so vocal of late. This was a voice I was much more familiar with. This was the inquisitive voice of the scientist I had always been.

'You need to know.' it said. *'You need to know what is down that well? What is causing all of this? You owe that to yourself.'*

I should have ignored it, I should have just said no, told that voice that getting my family to safety was the most important thing. You have to understand, though, that voice had always been a friend. It had led me through my whole life to the point I was now. The irrational voice was the one that had usurped its power of late. The irrational voice was no friend of mine, what had it ever done for me? Nothing but frighten me. My decision was made.

I pulled up on our drive. Maggie and Mary walked across our front lawn to their own. I told them that Rachel and I would pop round later on just to see how they were doing.

Then I walked over to where Paul and the others still stood on their drive. It was time to listen to the inquisitive voice. It was time for answers.

CHAPTER THIRTY-THREE

I have to break my train of thought now briefly. These memories are painful. The events of that night were so horrendous and so inexplicable. I remember telling you at the start of this that you may find my story hard to believe. Some of you will have had trouble accepting the occurrences I have detailed already in this account, but I swear that I have been truthful with you. The series of events that were to follow on that awful night are way beyond anything I have yet described, but likewise they are the utter and terrible truth. Most of you will think I am mad. Certainly, that is what Dr Collins and his colleagues believe, that is why I am in this awful place.

When they made it back to the house Rachel and the girls changed out of their funeral clothes. I had done so already by that point. While the girls were busy, I asked Rachel to take them over to see her parents. I did not know what was going to happen, but if the well truly was the epicentre of all of these strange happenings, I did not want the girls in the house while we investigated it.

'I thought we were leaving?' Rachel said, her voice sounding tired.

'We are,' I said, kissing her gently on the forehead. 'I promise, ask your folks while you're there if we can stay a few days. If they say yes, come back here and we'll all pack up and go. If not, I'll book us into the Travelodge just out of town.'

'Why do you have to know what's down there?' she asked

'Because that's who I am,' I answered. 'I can't just run away without knowing what I'm running from. If I did that I wouldn't be me.'

She half smiled and rolled her eyes.

'No and then you wouldn't be the man I married,' she said, defeated. 'Please be careful though.'

'I will,' I said, holding her in my arms, 'No one's going to get hurt.'

How wrong I was.

I heard the side gate open and looked over and saw Thom enter the garden. He had with him two equally athletic looking young men. He saw me and waved. They walked over to where I stood. They were carrying what looked like bags of heavy equipment. Rick followed behind them. I learnt that Paul had opted instead to return to the university and continue research on the history of the site.

'Hey, Mr Martin,' Thom said as he approached. 'How are things?'

'Crazy,' I said.

'Why?' he said, looking confused.

'Oh it doesn't matter,' I said, shaking it off with a smile.

He pointed to the two young men with him.

'The tall guy here is Joe,' he said. I shook hands with him. He was very tall, at least six foot six. 'And this hippie is Mike.' I shook hands with the other man, who had hair halfway down his back.

'Pleased to meet you both,' I said,

'Me and these guys have explored about twenty-five caves together, so that well down there shouldn't be a real problem,' Thom said confidently.

'Well, I'm sure you all have plenty of experience,' I said, 'but promise me you'll be careful.'

'Worried we'll sue you?' Thom joked.

I shook my head.

'No, it's just...' I led him away from his friends slightly and spoke quietly. 'There's something strange about that well. You must have felt it when we were down there the other night?'

He looked at me for a few seconds, trying to read my face. Then he nodded.

'I thought it felt creepy down there,' he said. 'I felt a little dizzy at one point, and oh Christ, that smell!'

'Exactly,' I said.

'Don't worry, Dan,' he said. 'We'll be careful.'

It was true. They would be as careful as they had ever been, but it didn't stop what happened. Nothing apart from not going down there could have stopped what happened.

CHAPTER THIRTY-FOUR

Thom informed me that it would take them a little while to set everything up, so I went and made myself a coffee. I sat out in the garden, drinking the steaming coffee and smoking a couple of cigarettes. After about fifteen minutes, I decided to see how they were getting on. When I arrived down in the undercroft, not only was the winch and ropes set up but Thom was wearing a helmet with a lamp on top, knee and elbow pads and a harness. Over his shoulder he had a small bag.

'Ready for the show?' he asked with a grin.

The other undergraduates had left, leaving only myself, Rick, Thom and his two friends down in the crypt.

Joe, the tall friend, walked up to Thom and began tugging on different parts of the harness, making sure it was secure.

'Safety first,' Thom joked.

'We don't actually know how deep this well is, Thom,' he said. 'If your harness isn't on right and you slip out, you could fall into the centre of the earth for all we know.'

'We can hope,' said Mike, the hippie friend, with a wry smile. Thom walked over and playfully punched his arm.

'I know you don't mean it,' he said. 'Your life would be too boring without me.'

Rick and I stood a little away from the well as Joe hooked the rope to Thom's harness, attaching him to the winch. I stood back, partly out of not wanting to get in the way and put Thom at any risk, but also partly at my fear of the well and the memory of the feelings it had stirred in me the first time I encountered it. I looked to Rick; he was watching what the others were doing intently. I think he had felt it, too, that night, and thus he had no desire to get to close to the well.

Once Joe was satisfied that everything was correct and in safe, working order, Thom climbed up and sat on the lip of the well, his legs dangling into the seemingly endless blackness. Mike walked over and fitted a camera to a bracket mounted on his helmet.

'This is a night vision camera,' he explained, more for mine and Rick's benefit than Thom's, I thought. 'It records onto the card in the camera as well as wirelessly sending the feed straight to my laptop. We'll be able to see everything you see.'

Thom smiled.

'I know.' He turned to me. 'Mike loves his toys.'

Mike walked over to the fold up table that his laptop sat on. He picked up a walkie talkie and returned to Thom.

'This is so we can talk to you,' he said mockingly. 'The camera has no sound so you'll need to use this.'

'Or I could shout up to you,' Thom said.

Mike thought about it.

'Yeah, that'll work,' he said, taking the walkie talkie back off him. 'I'll keep hold of this then, you'd only lose it anyway.'

Joe flicked a switch on the motor and it whirred into life. I had been expecting a loud sputtering noise like a generator; instead, it was little more than a low hum. He walked over to Thom and tapped him on the helmet.

'You have any trouble down there, yell,' he said. 'I'll reverse the motor and pull you out as quick as I can.'

Thom nodded and the two shared a manly handclasp. Thom waved at me and Rick to come closer. We took a few steps forward. This was not close enough for Thom, who waved us over more emphatically. Rick and I exchanged a look, and in that instant I knew he felt the same apprehension at going over to the well. We smiled at each other nervously for support and then walked over to where Thom was sat. He was right about one thing. Although there was still a faint unpleasant odour coming up from the well, it was nothing in comparison to the night we had opened it up.

'Okay, it's about time to do this,' Thom said, then turned to Rick. 'If I die down there, you can have my room.' He smiled and then leapt off the lip of the well. I felt my heart rise into my throat as he did so. Of course, the rope stopped him and he just dangled there in the mouth of the well, He looked at me and Rick and laughed.

'Your faces are a picture,' he said. 'Okay, Joe, lower me down.'

'Aye aye,' Joe said and pushed a lever on the winch. The rope was smoothly released and Thom began to slowly descend into the well. Rick and I watched as he disappeared out of view, then we leant over the well and continued to watch his descent. It didn't take long for the blackness to engulf all but the light from the torch on his helmet.

'Are you seeing these walls, Mike?' Thom shouted up, his voice echoing through the darkness.

'Yeah,' Mike shouted back. 'They look great.'

Rick and I walked over to where Mike was monitoring the camera on his laptop. Like all night vision cameras, it gave everything a green hue. The walls looked solid and clean, perhaps a little too clean.

'Shouldn't there be some water damage on the stone?' I asked.

'Maybe,' Rick answered, 'but it depends how high the water got. He might still be above its highest point.'

'Six meters down,' Joe shouted down to Thom.

On the screen, we saw the movement as Thom looked down. There was nothing but blackness below him, even with the torch.

'No sign of the bottom yet,' he shouted up, his voice sounding more distant with every second.

The camera remained on the walls of the well. It seemed to be bricked a long way down. Still there was no sign of water damage.

'It's like it's never had any water in it,' I said.

'It's strange, I'll give you that,' Rick said. 'I've never seen a well that was this old that was bricked this far down. By now it should be just a rock or sediment wall.'

'Twelve meters down!' Joe shouted. 'Can you see the bottom yet?'

The image on the screen shifted again. Still we could see no end to the darkness on the night vision footage. Obviously Thom could make things out better than us.

'I think so,' he shouted up, sounding now like he was a world away, his words echoing increasingly. 'Looks like a solid surface about eight meters down.'

'Okay!' Joe shouted down.

'How long's the rope?' I asked him.

'About fifty meters,' Joe replied.

We watched on the screen as Thom continued his slow descent. The walls of the well remained and still showed no sign of water erosion. I began to think it wasn't a well at all, but something far worse. Suddenly as Thom looked down we saw the floor of the well. It was a smooth surface, like marble, and it was clean.

'What the fuck is this?' Thom shouted up. 'There's not a drop of water down here. It's dry as a bone.'

He looked back up and slowly turned around. Behind him was a door, a large wooden door, built to fit the contours of the well perfectly.

'Why is there a door down there?' I asked.

'It's not a well,' Rick said. 'It's an entrance.'

'To what?' I asked, fear in my voice. 'An entrance to what?'

CHAPTER THIRTY-FIVE

'There must be a subchamber,' Rick said. Suddenly he was an archaeologist again, his tone excited by the prospect of another level of this place to explore. He ran over to the well and shouted down to Thom. 'Can you open it?'

'I'll try,' Thom shouted up.

I could tell by the way my skin was crawling that this was a bad idea. I know I wanted answers, but perhaps I was better off without them. I wanted to tell Joe to pull him back up, I was paralysed with dread, I could not protest. On the screen I saw the door get larger as Thom approached it. His hand came into shot; he reached for the crude handle on the door and pulled. At first, it appeared that the door would not budge and I began to feel a little relief but then he tried again, pulling more forcefully. The door slowly opened. Thom examined the door. It was thick and heavy.

'It opens,' he shouted up.

Rick ran back to the monitor and looked as Thom examined the door.

'Amazing,' Rick said, with a glint in his eye. 'This is the find of the century.'

On the screen we began to see what lay behind the door as Thom peered inside. It looked like a cave tunnel, carved out by hand.

'I'm going to check it out,' Thom shouted up.

'The fuck you are?' Joe shouted down. 'You didn't take a walkie talkie with you, how are we going to know if you're okay?'

'If I get in trouble I'll tug hard on the line,' he shouted up. 'Three times. If you see that you pull me up.'

'If that door closes behind you I won't be able to pull you out,' Joe shouted, concern in his voice.

'If that happens you or Mike will have to come down on a second line and open it, but there's not a hint of a breeze down here and this door is really heavy. I don't think it's going anywhere, I have to check it out.'

Joe looked to Mike, who shrugged back at him. Joe sighed then shouted down the well.

'Okay, but be really fucking careful,' he shouted down.

'Aye aye,' came the response.

We watched the screen as Thom went through the door and began to walk down the tunnel. It quickly led into a cavernous chamber, stalactites and stalagmites adorned the floor and ceiling. How large the chamber was we could not tell for sure. As Thom walked further into it, there was only more blackness ahead. He stopped and looked around. It went on into darkness in all directions except the way he had come. We could still see the gaping mouth of the tunnel he had traversed. This cavern had been here since time immemorial. I began to suspect that this was where the entity 'resided,' as Jean had put it.

As he turned back round to continue walking, the picture on the camera began to break up. On a corner of the screen I suddenly spotted something move. The image was blurry and distorted. I could not make out exactly what I was seeing. All I could tell was that it was too big to be a rodent. It was easily as big as Thom, if not bigger.

Digital artifacts appeared, a few at first and then a few seconds later they had destroyed the whole picture.

'There's something down there with him!' I yelled like a mad man. 'Did you see it?'

Rick shook his head.

'I saw something at the corner of the screen,' Mike said, 'but I think it was just some distortion on the image.'

'It looked like a figure,' I said nervously.

'Faces in the fire,' Mike said. I knew what he was referring to. It was a well-known fact that the human brain looked for recognisable patterns, even in the most random of things it sees. I supposed he could be right, but I felt uneasy.

'Thom?' Joe yelled down the well. 'Can you hear me?' We listened for a response. None came, not even the faintest hint of a voice. I saw panic forming in Joe's eyes.

'He's in trouble,' he said.

'We don't know that,' Mike said, trying to reassure him. 'He hasn't pulled on the line has he?'

'No, but maybe he can't,' Joe said.

'Just give him a minute,' Mike said. 'He's a more experienced cave diver than any of us.'

Joe looked worried but nodded.

'Two minutes,' he said, 'then I try to winch him up.'

Mike nodded.

All of us stood there around the well in silence, watching the rope for any sign of movement. With each passing second, Joe's face expressed more concern. The rope hung still; it was now extended to its full length.

Thom should have run out of slack on it and begun his return. Yet still the rope did not so much as sway. I was becoming rapidly more convinced that I had seen a figure on the screen, and that whatever it was now had Thom.

'We have to try to pull him up,' Joe said again.

'What if the door's closed?' Mike asked.

'We'll throw another line down and you can go down and open it,' Joe answered.

Mike nodded in agreement.

Joe moved towards the controls on the winch. The lever was nearly in his hand when we heard it, the most pained and ghastly scream I have ever heard. It was made all the worse by its distance and the way it echoed up the well.

'Pull him up!' I screamed, fearing I was right.

Joe grabbed the lever and pulled it back hard. The rope began to wind back around the wheel on the winch, slowly. It seemed to be moving even slower than it had on the way down.

'Can't it go any quicker?' Rick yelled.

Joe shook his head.

'The motor's not powerful enough!' he said. 'But it's still quicker than if we had tried to pull him out by hand.'

The rope continued its slow return. I prayed with each inch that it would move faster, but it kept on at the same plodding pace. Rick, Mike and I were all leaning over the lip of the well, searching the darkness for any hint of Thom, to no avail.

'What if the line broke? Or the door did close?' I asked.

'Not possible,' Joe answered. 'If the line had broke and it wasn't holding Thom's weight it would be moving quicker and if the door had shut it wouldn't be moving at all now. Can you see him?'

I peered down the well. It was useless. Even with torches in our hands, we could only illuminate about twelve feet down.

'Not yet,' I said. Then something caught my eye in the dimness below. At first, I thought it was my eyes playing tricks on me. The way they sometimes do when you stare into utter blackness. Your eyes see flashes of light. As I saw it again, I realised its point of origin. I yelled pointing down.

'I can see his lamp!' I exclaimed.

Rick and Mike peered into the well. I saw from the relief on their faces they saw it, too.

'He's right,' Mike yelled. 'He's about eight metres down. Thom? Are you okay?'

There was no response from below. My heart sank and I feared the worst.

He was coming up so slowly that it seemed it would take forever for us to get him out.

'Oh fuck!' Mike exclaimed. 'Look!' He was pointing at the rope coming up into view of our torch beams. The rope had been white with blue stripes, the rope we saw now was deep red and glistening wet.

'He's hurt,' I shouted. Rick ran for the first aid kit, though I feared it would be worse than requiring a plaster and some antiseptic cream if the entity had attacked him.

'Uhn, nemma gurgh,' came a sound from below. It was Thom's voice, only different; he sounded incoherent and exhausted.

Finally, he started to come into view. At first, we could not see the source of the blood. He was dangling from the harness with his head down and the helmet obscuring our view of his face.

'Hold on, mate,' Mike said. 'We nearly got you.'

'Akk amna errm,' came Thom's voice again.

As he started to appear in the entrance to the well, Mike made a grab for him and with my help hauled him out. We set him on the floor. His face was covered in blood. We could not see the source in the dim light.

'Bring your torch over,' I called to Rick as Mike removed Thom's helmet.

When Rick shone the beam onto Thom's face, the true horror of the scene was shown to us. Rick collapsed to his knees. Mike gagged, almost vomiting on Thom. You see, we could see that Thom's hair had turned bright white, like the hair of a distinguished old man. The source of the blood was his eyes, more accurately his lack of eyes. As he opened his lids, we could see the red caverns of his eye sockets full to the brim with blood.

'Something tore out his fucking eyes!' Joe exclaimed.

I looked down at Thom's hands. They were also covered in blood and clenched in fists.

'No,' I said, prying open one of his hand and revealing the gelatinous orb of his eye.

'He tore them out himself.'

Whatever the thing was that I had seen on the screen, it was so horrendous and abhorrent that Thom had torn his own eyes from their sockets with his bare hands, rather than see it.

An air ambulance was dispatched and landed on the field behind the house. Thom was flown straight to Queens medical centre in Nottingham. We were told that they had the best eye specialists in the country and if anyone could save his eyes it would be them. Somehow, I doubted they would be able to. Even if they did, I didn't think they would be able to save his mind. He was just a gibbering wreck. He had seen something down there in the cavern, something that had terrified him beyond the point of sanity.

I didn't tell the paramedics anything about the haunting. I didn't want them carting me off as well, my family needed me. They agreed that the wounds appeared self-inflicted and that Thom must have suffered some sort of breakdown whilst down in the well. For safety's sake, they asked me not to permit anyone else to enter the well until a proper investigation could be done. I told them that this would be fine, as I had no intention of letting anyone down into the undercroft, let alone the well for some time.

CHAPTER THIRTY-SIX

'What's happened?' Rachel asked on her return. She could see from my face that something was very wrong. I'm not sure if I had ever seen her look as scared as she did at that moment. Even in the height of Anna's sleepwalking, the time she had left the house included, I had never seen my wife look so truly petrified as she did as she asked me that.

I explained about Thom's trip down the well and what he had done. She began to sob on my shoulder.

'What're we going to do?' Rachel sobbed.

'Get packed,' I said. 'Get packed and get the hell away from here.'

She nodded.

'Are your parents expecting us?' I asked.

Again, she nodded.

I led her into the house where the girls were waiting. Anna again looked nervous. I hugged her and kissed her forehead.

'It's going to be all right,' I said as soothingly as I could. 'We're going to stay at Granny's for a few days.'

Izzy, on the other hand, seemed perfectly content. The ignorance of youth, I supposed. She gave me a kiss.

'Right, go upstairs and pack a few bags,' I said. 'No need to take everything, we won't be staying there too long and I can always come back and collect a few things if need be.'

With that, the girls and Rachel headed upstairs to pack. I looked out of the kitchen window to the hole. I no longer wanted to know what was down there. It could keep its secrets. I just wanted my family away and safe.

The phone rang.

The phone call was from Paul, he was still at the university in Lincoln. Rick had called him and told him what had happened to Thom.

'I'm heading straight from here over to Nottingham. Rick's meeting me there. Thom doesn't have much family, it's the least we can do.' he said, his voice heavy with sadness. 'You have to get out of there, Dan.'

This scared me. Only a few hours ago Paul had been sceptical about the phenomena in the house. Now he was warning me to get out.

'What have you found out?' I asked.

'That place is bad,' he said. 'It always has been. I found earlier records of the monastery.'

He went on to explain that the reason the monastery was built on that site in the first place was the church felt the need to sanctify the ground here. The Monastery at Boston was overcrowded and this gave them the excuse they needed. The area already had a reputation; it had been used in pagan times as a religious site. Even then, stories told of its corruption and how the rituals became increasingly sadistic.

'Even before that, there were stories about the place,' Paul said. 'As far back as records go, that spot has been associated with evil.'

'Evil?' I was startled by this from such a rational young man. 'You mean like the Devil?'

'No,' Paul said. 'The Devil was created by man, as a way for the church to control people's behaviour.

I'm talking about something immeasurably older. The place has been gripped throughout history by a force of evil. It corrupts people, makes them do the most horrific things.'

'Like Dr Richards at the mental hospital,' I said.

'And like Mikkala poisoning Leo,' Paul said.

'Are you coming back?' I asked, already knowing the answer.

'No. I never want to see that street again,' Paul said.

I could understand that. It was easier for them as they were just renting their house. I was severely tempted just to let the house go, put it on the market and hope for the best.

'Good luck with everything,' I said. 'Tell Thom we're thinking of him.'

Paul said that he would and then we said our goodbyes. It was the last time I ever spoke to him.

I turned around and saw that Izzy was sat on the sofa. She had her Hello Kitty case next to her.

'You all packed honey?' I asked.

'Yep,' she said.

'Mummy and Anna ready yet?'

'Nope. They're taking ages,' she said, frowning.

'Yes they are,' I said. 'You put the telly on and watch something for a few minutes and I'll go and hurry them up.'

'Okay,' she said, using the remote to switch the TV on. I kissed the top of her head as she decided what to watch and then headed up the stairs. First, I came to our bedroom where Rachel was stood with two open cases on the bed and at least a month's worth of clothes on the bed.

'I said just pack the essentials.'

'I am,' she replied. 'I just have too many essentials.'

'Well come on, I want us out of here,' I said.

'I know. I know. I'll be done in two minutes.'

'Okay.'

I carried on walking down the corridor. I came to Anna's room; she was not in there. Her drawers and wardrobe were open and clothes were strewn across the floor. I carried on down the corridor and found her in Izzy's room stuffing clothes into a large sports bag. It was the one she used when she played hockey.

'What's taking so long?' I asked walking through the door and making her jump.

'Sorry, Dad,' she said. 'I just didn't want to stand in my room and pack. So I had to carry everything down here.'

'It's okay,' I said. 'Want a hand?'

She stuffed a few more things into the bag and zipped it up.

'Nope, I'm done,' she said with a smile.

'Good girl. Let's go,' I said

She put the bag over her shoulder and we headed down the corridor. As we reached the door to our room, Rachel stepped out struggling with the two cases she had packed. I grabbed one and carried it down the stairs. When we got to the living room, Izzy was no longer on the sofa. The TV was still on. I assumed that she had gone to get a drink or a biscuit.

'Come on, Izzy,' I called out. 'We're going now.'

There was no reply.

I set down the case and walked over to the kitchen.

'I said we're go...' I stopped talking. When I reached the kitchen, I saw that she was not in there. The door out to the garden was wide open.

Rachel appeared behind me as I peered out into the garden.

'Where is she?' she said, on the verge of panic.

'I don't know,' I said. 'You wait here with Anna and I'll go and look for her.'

I walked out into the garden. I checked the gate at the side of the house. The bolt was on at the top; there was no way that she could have reached it. I scanned the garden and the field beyond. There was no trace of her.

'Izzy?' I called out loudly. 'Come on, honey, we're leaving.'

There was no reply. I was getting angry with her. This was no time to be playing games with us.

'Issabella Martin. Get here now!' I shouted.

'Where is she?' It was Rachel stood at the kitchen door. She seemed more scared than angry. Then it hit me. What if something had happened to my baby girl?

'I don't know,' I said. 'Take Anna and go and see if she's gone next door to say goodbye to Mary. I'll check around here.'

'You don't think she's down there do you?' she said, pointing to the hole.

I shook my head, but I wasn't so sure.

Rachel nodded and headed back into the house. Through the window, I saw her and Anna leave the house. I turned around and looked around again, trying to see if I could see her in the field now. I could not.

'Izzy?' I called out. 'This isn't funny.' My voice sounded desperate.

Then I heard it—a giggle, the giggle of a small child. The giggle of my daughter. I knew instantly, from the reverb of the sound, where she was. The one place I did not want to go, the undercroft.

As I climbed down the rope ladder, I noticed that it was dark below. Rick and I had turned off the generator before we left. I would have to get it going before I searched for Izzy. I knew that it was near the bottom of the ladder. As I stepped off the last rung, I could not remember if it was too the left or the right. I bent over and stretched my arms out, fumbling blindly in the darkness. First, I checked the left of the ladder. After what seemed like forever just brushing the dusty floor of the crypt, I realised I must have picked the wrong side.

I turned around and did the same thing to the right of the ladder. In a few seconds, I found the generator. I examined it with my hands, trying to mentally picture what it looked like. I knew what I was looking for. After a few unsuccessful gropes, I found the ignition cord. I pulled hard. I heard the motor try to start and then sputter out.

'Shit!' I shouted, then jumped at the sound of my own voice echoing back at me.

I pulled the cord a second time. This time I used more force. It sputtered to life and the lamps suddenly spewed light into the room. I swept my eyes around the crypt. Within a few seconds I spotted her, she was stood in front of the well, her back to me. She looked as though she was looking up at something.

'Izzy? What the hell are you doing down here?' I said as I strode over towards her.

She didn't turn around, she kept her gaze above her as she spoke.

'Talking to my new friend,' she said. Her voice sounded wrong. Distant.

'Where is this friend, honey?' I said, becoming worried.

'Right here in front of me,' she said. There was a tone of mild annoyance in her voice, as though I had asked the most ridiculous question.

As I reached her, I noticed how fair her hair looked under these spotlights. It was usually blonde, but it looked almost white. I put my hands gently on her shoulders. I turned her round to face me. I collapsed back in horror when I saw her face. Her eyes. Her beautiful blue eyes were gone. There were only two bloody holes where they had been.

'What did you do?' I screamed, not knowing if I was asking Izzy or the evil thing in this place.

'It's okay, Daddy,' she said calmly, a smile on her face. Her smile had always melted my heart. Now without her eyes it looked so sinister. 'It doesn't hurt. My friend said if I looked at him without doing this first my brain would burst, he told me he'd stop the pain and he did.'

I grabbed her and picked her up, she began to growl and kick and scream at me.

'No, Daddy,' she yelled. 'He needs me.'

'Show yourself to me, you bastard!' I screamed.

At that moment, it appeared before me. It was floating just above the well. I do not have the words, I do not think they exist, to describe the horror of this creature. It was humanoid, but bulbous and gelatinous. Its skin was wet and oozing. I cannot describe its colour because I have never seen it before. It was something beyond our knowledge of the spectrum. It was a sickening colour that burnt my eyes. I had the urge to put my hands up and tear my eyeballs out of their socket just to make the pain stop. Its face was a mass of teeth and glowing eyes. It stared into me, not at me. I am convinced that this thing could see every inch of my being, as though each set of eyes was to see a different layer of existence. I felt my head start swimming. It felt as thought the floor was now made of rubber, moving in all directions at once. It opened its gargantuan mouth and began to speak in a tone words cannot describe. It was the voice I had heard in that awful dream I had the other night, the one where I was falling down the well. What it was saying I can't remember, but I knew what it meant. It wanted me to drop Izzy. With all of my being I tried to fight it, but, I was powerless and my daughter slipped from my grip.

As I looked at this thing, I could see the whole of space and time in its hideous countenance. I felt sharp pains in my head. I wanted to look at the girl, at that moment I forgot her name, but I could not take my eyes off this thing. I became aware that I did not know where I was, or even who I was. All I knew was this thing in front of me. The rest of my life no longer existed, there was nothing but the creature, there never had been. The pain inside my head became unbearable, it was pressure. My head was about to explode, or implode, or I was simply about to cease to exist. The lights became dimmer and dimmer until I was engulfed in the merciful darkness of unconsciousness

CHAPTER THIRTY-SEVEN

What happened next has haunted me every second of everyday since. I'm sitting here now in my cell. Dr Collins refers to it as my room, but it is a cell. They dress it up as a hospital, but this is a prison. A place to keep the most dangerous of the insane, which is what they think I am. Maybe they are right. I have seen things that would drive anyone mad, but I did not do the things they claim I did. They don't need to put me in a prison, for I am in one of my own construction. Inside my mind, I will never leave it, just as the images will never leave me. Every time I close my eyes, I replay some part of it. I try to avoid closing my eyes as much as possible. I do not sleep until I pass out from exhaustion, then maybe for a little while there is blissful peace. Then the dreams come, the dreams of the thing I saw in the crypt, the dreams of the horrors that came next.

The worst ones, though, are when my mind decides to tease me. I dream that things turned out different, I dream that we are all still together. I look at Rachel and my girls smiling at me. I dream of tucking the girls into bed and then making love to Rachel. Then it shatters and I wake up here, and I sob as I remember again what happened when I came around that night.

I woke up on the floor of the undercroft. It took me a few moments to realise where I was. A vision of the creature flashed before my eyes and panic gripped me. I looked around; there was no sign of it anymore, if it was ever really there in a physical sense. There was also no sign of Izzy. I suddenly saw the image of her face with her eyes missing. Her absence from the undercroft convinced me that it must have been a hallucination. The thing, that foul creature, had made me see her that way. Either that or she had not been down here at all and it had been a trap to lure me to the well.

I tried to sit up, but half way up my head began to swim again, and I fell back against the hard cold stone of the floor.

I tried again, and with great effort I managed to pull my self up into a seated position. There was a great pain in my head. I didn't think that it had been caused by it hitting the hard floor twice. The pain was centred behind my eyes. As I looked around again, I became aware that my vision was slightly blurred. Before that night, I had perfect vision. Since then, though, my eyesight has been getting gradually worse.

I looked at my watch and saw that it was 9 PM, I had been unconscious for well over an hour.

I was surprised that no one had come looking for me. I had gone to look for Izzy and I had not returned. I couldn't believe that Rachel wouldn't have thought to at least peek down into the hole. I would have been clearly visible, sprawled on the floor, even from up top. The fact that I had laid on this cold stone floor for so long, without being disturbed, filled me with dread.

I forced myself to fight throughout the pain and struggled to my feet. As well as the blurred vision, I felt a little off balance, like something was wrong with my inner ear. Another problem I did not have before, but that has got steadily worse since.

I staggered back to the rope ladder and began to pull myself back up to the surface. It was a strain. Every muscle in my body burned with pain. It felt as though I had just run a marathon. My joints were stiff.

After what seemed like forever, I pulled myself up into the night air. It was a mild night with a gentle breeze. I rolled onto my back on the grass and looked up at the stars; it was always something that had filled me with joy. As a boy I had been obsessed with astronomy, it was my first introduction to science. I had learned all the constellations. Their pattern had always been a comfort to me. They showed that on a universal scale there was order. Now as I looked at them I felt sick, they reminded me how small and insignificant I was, that behind all order was chaos. How else could that thing I saw down there exist?

I had no time to wallow in pity. I rolled onto my knees and then got up and staggered to the house. I entered through the open kitchen door. Something was wrong. The kitchen drawers had been ransacked. Cutlery and cooking tools lay scattered on the floor.

'Rachel?' I called out, my voice hoarse.

There was no reply.

'Rachel?' I shouted louder.

Still there was no sound. I dragged myself out of the kitchen and into the living room. I used the walls to help keep myself steady. There was no one in the room. The bags and cases that Rachel and the girls had packed earlie were still sat where they had left them. I pulled myself along the walls to the hall and then to the foot of the stairs. I looked up. I could see no evidence of there being any lights on. I couldn't hear any movement. Just to be sure, I called out again.

'Rachel?' Nothing. 'Anna? Izzy?'

If they were up there they must have been deliberately ignoring me.

.

CHAPTER THIRTY-EIGHT

I turned around and noticed that the front door was slightly ajar. Perhaps they were still next door with Mary and Maggie.

Then I heard it, a thunderous noise from above. I have never been to a war zone, but the sound that I heard upstairs at that moment is how I had always assumed that a building being hit with a missile would sound. It was a deafening rumble that shook the very foundations of the house. It felt like the sound had momentarily destroyed my inner ear. I lost not only my balance, but all sense of what was up and what was down. I fell to the floor, hard.

The sound only lasted a matter of seconds and then was gone. What followed was a deep guttural laughter from above. It was the laugh of the creature I had seen in the undercroft.

It had my family up there. It wanted me to know that it had won.

Not yet, it hadn't. Not while I still lived. I pushed myself upright and ran up the stairs.

I was expecting to find devastation. The sort of destruction you see on the news when there has been a major earthquake somewhere. Instead, everything was as it should be. There was no sign of what had caused the explosive sound.

I ran from room to room, searching for Rachel and the girls. They were not in our room, the bathroom, or either Anna's or Izzy's room. I ran up the second staircase, to the top floor of the house. There was no one in the office. I crossed the small landing and went into the guest bedroom. Rachel and the girls weren't in there, but someone was.

As I entered, I saw the figure stood with his back to me looking out of the window. He was tall and slim and dressed in a white coat, or should I say a 'should have been' white coat. As it was, the coat was stained all over. Patches of black, patches of brown and most notably patches of fresh, red blood.

I gasped. I knew at once that I was seeing a ghost. I knew, also, who it was. This was Dr Richards, the doctor who had tortured and murdered countless women at the insane asylum that used to stand behind our garden. A man who had committed unspeakable crimes, and then killed himself in custody

'Where are they?' I screamed.

The figure showed no sign of acknowledging me.

'Where is my family?' I screamed.

This time he slowly started to turn to face me. His face was ashen, and his cheeks and eye sockets were sunken.

'I never meant to do it,' he said, his voice full of pain and remorse.

'Where are they?' I yelled.

He smiled, the most menacing smile I had ever seen. It was as if he was becoming inhuman before my very eyes.

With no warning, he charged at me. I raised my arms to defend myself, but as he came crashing into me, I felt no jolt of impact. Instead, it was as if our bodies were merging into one. I felt the world growing dark.

I came to and I was no longer in the house. In

fact, there no longer was a house. I stood in front of the grand, gothic styled, red-bricked facade of the Darton Mental Hospital. A building that had been pulled down many years ago. There it stood though, right in front of me, as solid as any building I have ever seen.

I was suddenly aware that I was moving. Except I wasn't. I was making no conscious effort to move. I looked down and saw that I was wearing a doctor's white coat, all pristine and white.

I was not me. I was inside the body of someone else, Dr Richards to be precise. Somehow, the manifestation of him in the guest bedroom of my house had transported me back in his life.

I/He was walking away from the hospital. I could tell from the geography of the tree line and other landmarks that we were walking towards where my house would stand in a few short years.

I felt a jolt and then a sharp shooting pain in his leg. His foot had gone through a hole in the floor. He pulled his leg out of the hole and checked it over. It was bleeding, but only from a very minor cut. He soon turned his attention to the hole. It felt hard around the edges, as though there was a stone surface below, and he had just fallen through part of it. He picked up a large rock that lay at his side and began to batter the ground with it. The hole got wider and wider.

Dear God, Richards had found the undercroft. That is why he had started his killing spree. He wasn't a madman, he was a man possessed by an evil he could not have understood.

The same thing had happened to Mikkala so recently. She had no control over what she had done, and neither had Richards. The local boogeyman was not a monster, he was a victim.

He looked up and there walking towards us was a hooded figure, dressed in long black robes. The hood obscured most of its face, but what could be seen was the lower part of the face, cheeks sunken, skin so pale that it looked blue.

Richards/I stood up to face it; it looked as solid as anything else around.

'What are you doing here?' Richards asked.

With that, the hooded figure bolted towards us at great speed. Just as I had done earlier, Richards put his arms up to defend himself. Once again, there was no jolt, just that strangely liquid sensation of merging, and once more, the darkness came.

This time when I came round, the hospital had vanished. The sky was almost black with some of the heaviest rain clouds I had ever seen. It was falling from the sky in sheets. I could feel it soaking my skin, except, of course, it was not my skin. I looked down and saw the long black robes I/he was wearing. I saw the abbey looming ahead in the distance. It was bigger than I had imagined it to be. It was built of the same local sandstone as the undercroft. It was a large structure, with giant stained glass windows housed in gothic arches.

I looked beside me and saw eight others in similar soaking robes to the ones I/he wore. I knew now who we were, we were the nine blackfriars. The nine Dominican friars who were tortured, raped and, bar one, murdered by the evil Benedictine monks of the abbey.

I wanted to scream a warning to the others, tell them not to go on, that there would be more shelter a few miles down the road, that this place was cursed, and only evil would befall them here. Of course, this was not my body, not my mouth and not my time. There was nothing I could do but watch in horror as we approached the large wooden doors that led into the Abbey.

I felt things dimming, as though I was being forced somewhere else. I prayed that it would be far from here, and back home.

There was no such relief. As I came back to consciousness I realised that I was in the undercroft, but not the undercroft of my time. I was still in the time of the abbey. I was still in the body of the blackfriar.

Flaming torches lit the undercroft, casting it in an eerie, flickering, orange light. I became aware of the screaming, the sound of multiple men in agony all around me. I looked around as much as I could. I felt the body I was in struggling against the ropes that bound him.

Opposite me was one of my fellow blackfriars. Two of the abbey monks were inserting a white-hot poker into his eyes, not deep enough to kill him, but just enough to burn his eyes out. He howled with the excruciating pain.

Beside him, another monk was buggering one of the blackfriars, whilst choking him. It seemed that the friar had thankfully passed out from the ordeal.

I felt my/his pain also. He, too, had been raped. I am grateful that I was spared experiencing this with him.

From what I could see, the monks who were not indulging in rape and torture were watching the show, drinking ale and laughing at our plight. Then I saw the well.

A group of monks, in ceremonial robes and masks that crudely tried to depict the creature I had seen earlier, were stood at the well. They were chanting some kind of incantation. They poured wine down the well, and then ale. Another monk brought over a large bowl. As one of the masked men poured the contents into the well, I realised that it was the blood of one of the friars.

The monk holding the bowl handed it back to the one who brought it over. He leant over and said something. Then pointed directly at me, the unmasked monk nodded and began walking to wards me with a knife.

I felt the blackfriar, whose body I was a passenger in, struggle harder against his bonds. I heard his voice screaming for mercy, and for God to save him.

The monk with the knife cut the rope on my/his feet and start to drag me/him towards the well. He tried to fight. I felt him using all the strength he had to try to free himself from the monks grasp. However, the combination of the pain, from whatever they had done to him in my absence and whatever they had drugged him with, made him to weak to succeed.

Soon I/he stood in front of the well. One of the masked monks put a wreath of wildflowers around my/his neck. Another poured wine over my/his head. Finally, we were thrown into the well.

The fall seemed to happen in slow motion, I could hear the man whose body I was in screaming. At first, it was as though I was falling into eternal darkness. I could not perceive that the well had a base, I had been falling for so long. Then I saw it, faint and small at first, but becoming rapidly clearer as we approached it. There, at the bottom of the well, was the creature I had seen earlier, its arms outstretched upwards ready to catch me/him.

I braced for the pain that was sure to come when we either collided with the base of the well or were grabbed by the creature's massive, taloned hands.

Yet as I saw its hands reach for our body, I felt nothing but that same, liquid feeling. Dear God, I was merging with the creature itself.

This time when I came to, I felt unbelievably dizzy. My mind was trying to inhabit a body it had no reference point for. I could not interpret the things the creature was experiencing physically as I had no framework for understanding how its body worked.

I looked around and saw yellow and black sulphur coloured rocks. The air was thick with acrid, orange smoke. All around the were pools of boiling tar, bubbling like hot treacle. There were mountains all around, many of them spewing rivers of molten lava down. Balls of fire fell from the sky, crashing to the ground with deafening booms. If I had been a religious man, I would probably have believed myself to be in Hell. After all, what other explanation could there be for where a creature such as this had come from?

Of course, I was not a religious man. I was a scientist. I knew that I was still in Glenley, or at least what would one day become Glenley eons from now. I guessed that I was somewhere in the late Hadean eon, probably about 4.4 billion years ago. I was witnessing the creation of the earth. It was about a million years since the earth had formed and it was still in the process of cooling down. Rocks had formed, but there was still much lava being pumped out, shaping the continents.

I was horrified to be inside this creature, but I was in awe of what I was witnessing, something no human had ever seen, the majesty of creation itself. Then I saw them.

Across one of the larger tar pools stood a group of creatures just like the one I inhabited. There were more of them. They had been here all that time. I could not even begin to speculate what they were. Primordial life did not exist on earth until the Archean eon, around 3.8 billion years ago, and these creatures were far from primordial. They were in many ways superior to mankind. How could these things have existed here on Earth so long ago? My mind whirred with the possibilities of what they were and where they could have come from. Were they demons? Were they gods? Aliens? Or some form of life that had been completely eradicated from history, all trace of them lost until now?

My thoughts were interrupted by the way that the group of creatures across the tar pool were looking up above me. I did the same, and saw the blinding light of the burning meteorite heading directly towards me.

CHAPTER THIRTY-NINE

I woke up on the floor of the guest room. I was groggy; it felt like the worst kind of jet lag anyone had ever experienced. Then again, I had just travelled across eons of history in a few short minutes.

Rachel and the girls!

Suddenly I remembered that I had been looking for them. I needed to find them, whatever state that Izzy was in. There had to be something we could do to help her. I rushed down the stairs. They must have gone next door.

I looked in the mirror in the hallway. I was still covered in dust from rolling around on the floor of the undercroft, I brushed as much of the dust as I could from my hair and clothes. I wiped my face on one of my fleece jackets that was hanging up nearby. I wiped the cold sweat from my skin. When I was done, I passed for human, barely.

I left the house and walked across our front lawn and then Mary's to get to the house. The curtains were closed as I passed the living room window, but I could see that the lights were on and I could faintly hear people talking. I felt relief rise in me. They were safe.

When I got to the front door, I knocked loudly. At first, there was no answer. I knocked again and tried the door. It was open and I pushed it open a little. I stepped into the doorway.

'Hello?' I called. 'Anyone in?'

'Daddy!' I heard Izzy cry ecstatically before she came running into the hall. She had her arms outstretched to me. Her face was an image of perfection. There was no trace of the hideous wounds

313

and white hair I had seen down in the undercroft. I dropped to my knees and began to weep in joy as I engulfed her in my arms and kissed her.

'Oh, baby. You're okay,' I said.

'Of course I am, silly,' she said. 'I only came to say bye to Auntie Mary.'

I picked her up.

'You didn't go down the hole?' I asked.

'No,' she said, shaking her head. 'You told me it was bad.'

'Good girl,' I said, kissing her again. I set her down. Everything was going to be okay. The visions I had down there had been the entity's last attempt to scare me. It had worked, but it was over now. My family and I could escape this place now and put this horror behind us.

Izzy walked into the lounge and sat on the sofa. She was again watching *Peppa Pig*. I looked in the room and saw that no one else was in there. Izzy must have seen the look on my face. She turned to me and smiled.

'They're in the kitchen, Daddy,' she said

'Thanks, baby,' I said and wandered to the kitchen. The nightmare was nearly over. I would say goodbye to Mary and Maggie and then we would leave this damned street forever.

As I stepped into the kitchen, my whole world fell apart. Arranged around the dining table were Mary, Maggie, Rachel and Anna. All of them were dead, their throats slashed wide open. The blood covered the table and pooled on the floor. The knife that had been used was sat on the table. Despite how filthy with blood it was, I recognised that it was one of ours, taken from our ransacked kitchen. I dropped to my knees in the blood between my wife and daughter. I let out a primal cry of pain and despair. No words could come out. I was overwhelmed with grief and shock. It felt as though my life was over, Dan Martin no longer existed. I was now just a wraith, a revenant. The fleshy body that still breathed and moved was just a hollow shell, a husk of what had once been. Whatever it was that made me the man I was, my soul or whatever you choose to call it, was no more.

I saw that their heads had been tied to the backs of the chairs by the hair to keep their heads upright. All of their eyes were open and staring at me, looking at me with expressions of pain and fear.

I pulled Anna's cold body to mine and held her close. I prayed to the God I had never believed in to take this vision away. To make everything better. To bring them back to me, but as I felt the sticky blood soaking into my shirt, I knew that it was too late. They were gone forever. I had lost everything. No one should ever have to outlive their child; it is not the natural order of things. The pain is greater than any other you can imagine.

'I missed you, Daddy.' I heard Izzy's voice from the doorway. I turned to her. Again she looked as she had done down in the crypt. Her hair had turned as white as snow and her eyes were missing. She grinned at me. It was a hateful smile. It was the smile of the thing down the well. She had been dead all along. That evil thing had just been playing with me, giving me false hope. It must have got pleasure from torturing me.

'She begged for you to save her,' it said. Its voice was no longer Izzy's, it was the low rumble of the entity now speaking English. 'She screamed for you over and over. "Daddy, help!" But you didn't come, did you?'

I hugged Anna's body harder. I kissed her forehead and whispered to her.

'I'm so sorry, Anna.'

'Your wife cursed you as I made her watch me slit your daughter's throat,' it said and then laughed, a thick and callous sound.

I suddenly felt nothing but rage. It was as though every other extreme of emotion I was feeling transferred in that instant into pure hatred for this thing. It was not my daughter. I knew that Izzy was as dead as her mother and sister. This thing, this ancient and evil being that had corrupted so many people on this site over the centuries, was using her as little more than a marionette.

I stood quickly and grabbed the knife from the table. In one fluid movement, I lunged at the thing. I buried the knife to the hilt in its chest. It roared in pain and shock. It coughed up a thick black fluid. I removed the knife and plunged it into its chest again. Another roar and it began to flail, trying to escape me. I had it on the back foot. If it had been prepared for my attack it might have been able to use its psychic ability to make me slit my own throat with the knife, but it didn't have time. It was in pain, and despite everything, this was the body of a six-year-old girl. I could overpower it quite easily. I pulled the knife out again and this time I dragged the cutting edge against the thing's throat, splitting it wide. A spray of that foul black corruption shot out, covering me.

It dropped to the floor and rolled onto its front. It tried to crawl away from me. I grabbed at it, but it kicked me hard in the face. Warm blood ran down my face. Its kick had split the skin above my right eye. It stunned me enough for it to get out of my reach. It got to its feet and staggered away clutching its chest. Thick tar-like blood oozed between its fingers.

The thing shouted in a language I did not understand, but I could tell its words were full of hate and malice. I looked at it and wiped the stinging blood from my eye. I wondered why it didn't destroy me with its great powers, then I realised it couldn't. I had damaged its host body too badly. The thing didn't have the strength to use its powers.

I yelled again, a war cry. Then I charged at it again. It turned and tried to run away from me, but the wounded body of a little girl was not quick enough. I grabbed it and knocked it to the floor. Its face hit the ground hard. I brought the knife up high above my head.

'Daddy!' it cried out, again imitating the voice of Izzy.

I didn't falter. I brought the knife down and buried it in the back of its head. It felt like stabbing a pumpkin. All movement ceased. My family was dead. The thing was back in the well. It was over. It was all over.

Mojo came running from upstairs, where he had been hiding. He ran over and jumped into my lap. I sat there stroking the shaking dog, surrounded by the corpses of my family and friends. That was how I stayed until the next morning, when Alex came home and found the horrific scene. I didn't do anything. I didn't say anything. He saw what had happened and made the natural assumption that I was to blame. Perhaps he was right. I had not killed any of them, except for the creature that inhabited my little girl's body. However, if I had heeded all the warnings sooner, surely none of this would have happened.

'You fucking monster!' Alex howled at me as he began his attack. He kicked and punched me repeatedly. I made no attempt to defend myself. I suppose I was hoping that he wouldn't stop until I was dead, and with my beautiful family once more.

He did break six of my ribs; one of them punctured a lung. He broke my nose and my jaw, and fractured my skull in two places. Alas, though, he became exhausted before he managed to kill me.

He collapsed on the floor next to me. He pulled out his phone and made a call to the police.

He told them through his sobs that his neighbour had killed his family, and that he in turn had beaten me to a bloody pulp.

They came quick enough to save my life, but not my soul.

CHAPTER FORTY

I have told my story now. It is the one I told to the police. It is the one I told the courts. It also the one I have repeated time and time again to Dr Collins since it was determined that I was unfit to stand trial. Since then, I have been here in Broadmoor. My neighbours now are the worst of the country's insane, I was surrounded by serial killers and child molesters.

The police and the courts and I'm sure Dr Collins all believed that I had murdered my wife and children as well as my neighbours. They are wrong. Everything I have told you is true, as unbelievable as it sounds.

'What about the evidence? What about the witnesses?' I hear you ask. You're right, of course. If my story was true, there would be some evidence wouldn't there? The hole and the undercroft, for one. The well and the enormous cavern below, for another. Yes, the undercroft was still there. A full investigation of it revealed nothing untoward whatsoever. They told me that they found nothing in the cavern beneath that would help my story.

My friend DCI Parker led up the investigation. He wanted to believe that there was some grain of truth to what I was saying, but in the end he had to concede that all the evidence pointed to me. I was just another victim of the cluster effect he had talked to me about outside the church on the day of Bill's funeral.

The only people who could help me were Jean and Sarah. They were the only ones who had experienced anything supernatural in the house. However, in what I am convinced is no coincidence, they died that night on their way home. The police concluded it was a normal road accident. I don't believe it. I am sure that the thing was responsible.

Paul argued my case as much as he could, giving them the history of the location, and all the terrible things that had happened throughout history. When questioned if he had seen any of the supernatural occurrences with his own eyes, he had to say that he had not. Likewise, he had not discussed these incidents with anyone in my family except for myself. There was no way he could have known if they knew of what was happening or if I was planning my defence. So in his attempt to help me he actually had a hand in condemning me.

What happened to Thom down the well was glossed over by the police as mere coincidence. He died in the hospital two days later from his wounds.

My solicitor told me there was no conceivable way I could win on any other plea than insanity. The judge agreed that I was insane and unfit for trial.

So I have sat here night after night, trying to block out the horror of those events by writing them down. If I wrote for long enough exhaustion would carry me off into troubled sleep. At least it was sleep.

Sometimes, even when awake I am visited by visions. I see the thing in its true form, the one it showed me in the undercroft, all eyes and teeth. It sits in the corner of my room. It says nothing, but I know it is mocking me. It wants me to know that it is still there, and it always will be. It wants me to know that it has destroyed me completely, and that I have done nothing to harm it.

I see my daughters. Sometimes they come to me as they were in life. They are happy and want me to play with them. Other times they come to me as they were in death. They ask me over and over again why I did not save them.

Rachel comes, too. She curses me for letting our children die. She tells me she hates me and wishes me dead and rotting in Hell. I want this all to end.

With each day that has gone by my eyesight has deteriorated. I can barely see at all now. My vision is dim and blurred. The optician said that it was down to less than 10%. At first, Dr Collins had believed that I was faking my loss of vision. Now he believes it to be a psychosomatic symptom of my guilt over my horrendous crimes, my mind trying to break through the barrier of fantasy he thinks I have created to protect myself from the truth.

Likewise, the problem with my inner ear has gotten worse in the months since that night. Now I cannot walk without a frame to keep me up. If I stand for too long unaided, I will fall.

I do not know what the thing in the well was. Maybe it was a demon. Maybe it was a creature from beyond the stars. Maybe it was one of the old gods that the pagan faiths believed in. It does not matter, though, what it was. All that matters is that it existed. It lingered in that place. I am sure it lingers there still, waiting for its next chance to corrupt our world.

I hope that it is the only one of its kind in existence. I doubt that. There are more of them out there. After all, I had seen a group of them when it had taken me for a ride in its body. Maybe there is one somewhere near you now, its evil seeping into your life. Making things go wrong in your life. Making you do wrong. Evil is real. I know that now.

I cannot live with this knowledge any longer. I have to go now. I have to join my family.

The End

ABOUT THE AUTHOR

Kit Tinsley is an English horror author. He is a fan of all things horror.

He graduated from DMU Leicester in 2002 with a BA (hons) in Media Studies and English. Since then he has spent time teaching both subjects in secondary and further education.

He has also worked on several independent films, writing a film called *Red Route* in 2007. Unfortunately, the film, which Kit also acted in, has been lost in postproduction hell since completion.

Most recently he has worked on production of a film called *Shadows of a Stranger*, working with actors from the popular TV shows *Doctor Who*, *Rainbow* and *Torchwood*, as well as an actor who appeared in both *Batman Begins* and *The Dark Knight*. The film is being prepared for its release as we speak.

Kit is also a musician, He is lead vocalist/ guitarist for a punk/folk/rock band called Dog Goblins.

He was born in Shropshire in 1978, but has lived in Lincolnshire since 1985.

He lives with his wife and their young son.

For more info, visit kit-tinsley.com.

Keep reading for a bonus short story from the forthcoming collection *Dark County: Tales of Terror From Rural England.*

FEAR THY NEIGHBOUR
Kit Tinsley

Timmy looked out of his window and saw the old man, Mr Phelps, looking up at him. Timmy did not like Mr Phelps at all. He was scared of him. The old man lived in the house next door all on his own. Mummy said that Timmy was being silly, that Mr Phelps was just a lonely and nosy old man, but Timmy knew better. Mr Phelps would stand out there on his front porch staring up at Timmy's house, staring at Timmy, for hours on end.

Mummy had spoken to Mr Phelps a few times when they had first moved into the house, three months back. Mr Phelps had knocked on the door that first evening and introduced himself; Mummy had done the same. Timmy had hidden upstairs, peeking down and listening to them talk. The old man's voice was deep and rasping. It frightened Timmy; it reminded him of the way the bad man had spoken.

'So there's just you and yer boy?' Mr Phelps had asked.

'Yes, that's right,' Mummy had answered. 'His father left sometime ago.'

Daddy had left after the bad man had taken Timmy, after Timmy had gotten sick. Mummy said that Daddy was not a bad man, he just didn't know how to deal with what had happened, that he had been unable to protect his son.

Mummy was sick, too, Timmy had given her the disease. She didn't blame him, though, it was after the bad man had taken him and done the vile things to him. The bad man had the sickness and passed it onto Timmy when he did the bad thing to him. There was no way they could have known he was poorly when he got home, covered in blood and bruises. Mummy had cleaned his wounds up, but she had a cut on her hand, and that was how she had gotten sick, too. The sickness scared Timmy; he would often cry himself to sleep worrying about dying. Mummy would come in and comfort him, saying that they both had a long time before they had to worry about that. Timmy was not so sure, though. Who could know how long they would have?

They had lived in the city then and Timmy had gone to school, but that had all changed now. They now lived on the edge of a small village in the countryside. Their house and Mr Phelps' were the only two around for some distance. Timmy didn't like being so far away from other people, especially with the way that Mr Phelps looked at him like he wanted to hurt him, like the bad man.

Timmy didn't go to school anymore. Mummy taught him at home. She was afraid that if she sent him to school then the other children would learn about him being poorly, and they wouldn't understand. So they would sit in the living room and Mummy would teach him to do sums and read books and everything else he did at school anyway. Sometimes Mummy got frustrated with him, because he was a slow learner. He never used to be, before the bad man took him. Since then, though, he had found it increasingly hard to concentrate, things would not sink in the way they used to. Mummy would shout at him for getting things wrong, then she would cry and hug him tight and tell him she was sorry.

Tomorrow was Timmy's birthday. Mummy had promised him that she would take him out for dinner and they would go to the cinema. He loved going to the cinema more than anything. Mummy kissed him goodnight and he went up to his room. He was changing into his pyjamas when he saw Mr Phelps stood on his porch looking up at him. He just stood there smoking his stinky pipe and watching Timmy get changed. Timmy knew the look on his face; it was the same one the bad man had when he did the bad thing to him. Timmy pulled his thick, heavy curtains shut and ran downstairs.

'I thought you were going to sleep?' Mummy said. 'It's your big day tomorrow.'

'Mr Phelps was watching me,' he said.

'Oh don't be silly,' Mummy said.

'He wants to hurt me.'

'No, he doesn't,' Mummy said. 'He's just a lonely old man. No one is going to hurt you ever again. I won't let them.'

She held him close to her, then patted his bottom.

'Now go to sleep.'

Timmy went back to his room and laid down, he couldn't sleep. His mind kept racing with a thousand thoughts. He remembered his Daddy, happy times of them playing together in the park. He thought about what he and Mummy would do the next day, what they would have to eat, and what the film would be like. These were all happy thoughts. He knew that they would go somewhere quiet to eat; Mummy didn't like to eating in crowded places. Then they would drive the fourteen miles to Lincoln to go to the cinema.

The image of Mr Phelps staring up at him kept popping back into his head and filling him with fear. Then he would remember the bad man, the way he had looked at Timmy as he walked home that winter evening. He remembered how he had just grabbed him, so strong, and carried him away. Then there was his foul smell, the thought of it made Timmy feel sick, and of course the pain.

Eventually he fell asleep, only to be woken by a loud banging on the front door. It was a furious thumping that scared him. He heard Mummy moving around downstairs, heading for the door. He wanted to scream at her not to open it, to come and hide with him, but the words would not come. Instead, all he could do was silently creep to the top of the stairs and watch in horror as the scene unfolded before him.

The banging on the door continued, getting heavier and faster. Mummy stepped in the hallway.

'Just a minute,' she said cheerfully, as though the force of the knocking was nothing unusual. How could she not be afraid? It was as if whoever was outside was trying to hammer their way into the house. Of course Timmy knew who was outside, Mr Phelps.

Mummy opened the door, and sure enough there stood the old man from next door. He seemed bigger standing in the doorway than he ever had when Timmy had seen him through the window. He stood there with his hands behind his back. Mummy looked startled to see him, but acted friendly enough.

'Mr Phelps,' she said. 'Is everything all right?'

Mr Phelps didn't answer, he just stood there silently looking at Mummy, and then his eyes moved slowly up the staircase. He met Timmy's gaze. Timmy was so scared that he darted his head back into his room.

'Mr Phelps,' he heard Mummy say. 'Is there something I can help you with?'

There was no reply. Timmy looked back through the door carefully, just peeking out enough to see. Mr Phelps was still just standing motionless in the doorway, his hands behind his back. Mummy was starting to look annoyed.

'Mr Phelps, I don't mean to be rude, but if there's nothing I can do for you, then I'm sorry but I'm a little busy at the moment.'

A strange smile crossed the old man's face. Timmy didn't like it. It seemed full of hate and evil, like the bad man.

Mummy began to shut the door, but Mr Phelps shot out one of his arms and held it open, that sinister smile still on his face.

'Mr Phelps, let me shut my door please,' Mummy said. She was starting to sound cross.

'No,' the old man said in a rumbling tone that filled Timmy with dread. 'It's time.'

'Time for wha...' Mummy began to say, but before she could finish Mr Phelps lifted his other arm from behind his back. He was holding a long knife, Timmy thought it was called a machete, but he wasn't sure.

Mr Phelps lunged at Mummy with the knife raised high, the blade hurtling through the air towards her. She was more agile, though, and managed to sidestep the attack. Mr Phelps fell through the door, crashing to the floor. Mummy looked up the stairs and met Timmy's terrified gaze.

'Timmy, hide!' she shouted up.

He wanted to, really he did, he wanted to find somewhere safe to curl up and make all of this go away, but he couldn't. He was frozen to the spot in fear, unable to stop watching the terrible things happening before him.

Mummy tried to step over the lump on the floor that was Mr Phelps and get to the stairs. Mr Phelps, though, had other ideas. His hand shot out and pulled on Mummy's ankle. She screamed as she fell to the floor. They struggled on the floor; Mummy was hitting the old man, clawing at his face and even trying to bite him, something she'd told Timmy he must never do.

Mr Phelps was too strong, though, he pinned her down and then brought the blade down hard into Mummy's chest. She looked up at Timmy, blood seeping from her mouth, her eyes full of pain and fear.

'Run,' she managed to rasp.

Mr Phelps looked up directly at Timmy; his face was covered in Mummy's blood. He smiled up at Timmy. The paralysis of fear was broken and Timmy was up on his feet. He wanted to run out of the house, but knew there was no way that he could get past Mr Phelps without the murderous old man catching him. Instead, he ran to Mummy's room. He knew there was a built-in wardrobe that had a shelved area at the back that he would be able to fit in. Mr Phelps would be able to find him easily, but Timmy hoped that the old man would not be able to reach him back there. As he began to run towards Mummy's room, he heard the thunderous footfalls of the old man running up the stairs. Timmy had never felt so scared in his life, not even when the bad man had taken him. At least the bad man had told him that if Timmy let him do what he wanted without fighting, then he would not kill him. Timmy knew that was exactly what Mr Phelps wanted to do. He wanted to kill him just like he had killed Mummy.

He flew into Mummy's room, not even bothering to shut the door behind him; it would take more time than he had. Mr Phelps was quick for his age and was almost right behind him. Timmy ran to the wardrobe and pulled open the door. Turning back, he saw Mr Phelps entering the room. Timmy crouched down and went to climb into the space under the shelves. To his horror, he saw that the space was full of boxes wrapped in colourful paper. His birthday presents.

Mr Phelps grabbed him by the ankles and pulled him out of the wardrobe. He looked down at Timmy with that same dark smile.

'It's time,' he said.

Timmy saw the blade coming down towards his chest and screamed.

Then darkness.

He was aware of the sound of his own screaming in the darkness.

Then the sound of Mummy's voice.

'Timmy, what's wrong?' she said as she came into the room. Even under his cover he could see the light come to life. Mummy pulled his cover off him and pulled him to her.

'Mr Phelps!' Timmy said through hysterical tears. 'He killed you and tried to kill me.'

Mummy stroked his hair.

'I'm right here, baby, no one has killed me, no one's going to,' she said soothingly. 'It was just a bad dream.'

'It seemed so real,' Timmy sobbed.

'No one is ever going to hurt you, or me. As long as we're careful,' she said.

She sat there holding him for some time, until his sobs had near enough subsided, then she gently lowered him back down.

'I love you, Mummy,' Timmy said, feeling himself getting sleepy again.

'I love you, too,' she said, planting a little kiss on his forehead with her cool lips. 'Now sleep tight, it's your 130th birthday tomorrow.'

Timmy smiled.

Mummy smiled, her perfect white fangs glinting as she did, nothing like the horrible, yellow and stained things the bad man had.

Mummy gently closed the lid of his coffin as Timmy drifted off into a peaceful sleep.

23524634R00183

Printed in Great Britain
by Amazon